TRUTH

THE ALEX CONNER CHRONICLES
BOOK TWO

TRUTH

THE ALEX CONNER CHRONICLES
BOOK TWO

BY

PARKER SINCLAIR

RAWLINGS BOOKS, LLC

Rawlings Books, LLC
Visit our Web site at
www.Parker.Sinclair.net/RawlingsBooks

Printed in the United States of America

Cover Art by Mike Dine
Edited by Meredith Tennant
Book Design by Maureen Cutajar

The characters and events portrayed in this book are fictitious. Any similarity to
real persons, livings or dead, is coincidental and not intended by the author.

Hardcover Edition ISBN 978-0-9908565-6-6
Paperback Edition ISBN 978-0-9908565-3-5
EPub Edition ISBN 978-0-9908565-4-2
Mobi Edition ISBN 978-0-9908565-5-9

For Lyla, Ella, and my husband. You are all so precious to me.
Thank you for supporting and sacrificing for me as I chase my dream.

Acknowledgements

To my friends and early readers, thank you for all the support, cheerleading, and for keeping me positive.

To my editor, you've taken my writing to a whole new level. Thank you.

To Mike Dine, your talent impresses me each and every step we take.

To Kim, you have ridden this wave with me all year and I can't thank you enough.

To Amy, my friend for life and one of the strongest, sassiest, and savviest professionals I know.

To The Weekend for the sexy tones that drove me through the end of *Truth*, Ed Sheeran for helping me start book two, and to Mumford and Sons for stepping into new territory and taking me with you.

To Club X for pushing me, supporting me, and helping me find the much-needed laughs every step of the way.

To my family and friends, I couldn't have done this without you.

To Stuart, your talent inspires me and I hope to bring you further into the light.

And to my husband and amazing daughters, I can do this—we can do this—together.

Contents

Men plan, God laughs for Choices we must bear
For time does a man make, decisions wear and tear.
Stand tall and straight and face the wind,
You're built with more than blood and sin,
You're built with more than bone and skin,
Your lessons learned are built within
And I will stand with you and face the wind,
Two men made by time and more.

– Son, S. A. Chamovitz, 2015

CHAPTER 1

Warrior

Journal Entry:

There is always that one recurring dream. One that feels so real when I wake, and I can tell I've had the dream before as I am dreaming it again. The darkness of night, moss under my feet, and a glowing blue gown chasing after me as I follow sparks of fairy wings, dandelion seeds, and forest creatures down a winding path. I have never felt so free, so unafraid, and so protected. I laugh with the critters as the fairies bid me to follow them. Sparkling dandelion seeds tickle my skin and touch lightly on my nose, causing it to twitch. I am free. There are no worries or fear. It is as if I am one with the earth, Gaia's own child living in nature, within her world, one of magic and beauty, not of pain and man. I wish I could stay in these moments.

It has been years since I last had this dream, but this time it seems to mean something more than it used to. The tumbling down the trail and the skipping and singing slow to a stop as I come upon the soft glow of a greenhouse in the middle of the woods. I tiptoe on bare feet, feeling the warmth radiating off the glass, seeing the blurring of colors as the steam and age of the building hide the true treasures within. I can never find the door in my dream, no matter how many times I try. It feels like eternity as I move around the four sides, gliding my hand along the glass and metal bindings, searching for a way in, a secret door perhaps. Maybe if I push a pane just right, or hum the right tune or give the secret knock, the secret greenhouse—more like a giant treasure box—will open

1

for me. But it never does, not for me anyway. It does always open for him, the boy, as young as I am, twelve, but taller, and with hair as dark as night.

He makes his presence known as a small squirrel runs toward him and up the length of him as if he were a tree. The darn thing squeals, squeaks, and swoons over him in each and every dream. Her fellow four-legged creatures and the flocks of various birds nearly roll their eyes at me and shake their heads, embarrassed by her obvious infatuation with the boy. All the while, these animals hover around my feet and take turns cuddling in the crook of my arm or finding a perch upon my shoulder to give me small nudges and pecks on my cheeks.

His laugh is comforting, free and innocent; not a man's laugh, but not nearly as childish as I know some may seem at our age. No, he is just perfect and steady. So steady it seems as though an earthquake wouldn't move him, and not even a raging bear would make him flinch. His eyes gaze into mine and I have to shake myself from getting lost in them as I realize he is asking me something.

"What? I'm sorry. Did you say something?" He gives me a laugh and a small shake of his head, not in a condescending way, but rather as though he is in awe—in awe of me?

"I've seen you before, here at this moment, in this time. We have been here before, haven't we?" As he talks, he moves toward the greenhouse, laying a single hand upon it as a door becomes visible and opens for the boy instantly. I nearly stomp my feet in annoyance at the ease at which he has penetrated the secret treasure box. I quickly forget my jealousy as my eyes gaze upon the glorious array of flowers and water features inside.

"Well, are you going to come with me? You want to see what's inside, right? Come on in; I'll show you." As he says the words, he turns to me with his hand open. I see the etchings of a tree limb tattooed from his wrist up his arm and into the sleeve toward his shoulder. I have seen that exact tree limb before and in an instant I am stumbling backwards as I realize that although I thought I had known someone else over the last year and a half, I may have known him for much longer. I reach out my hand and touch the markings on his arm, Justin's arm. The tree tattoo responds to my touch, giving the impression of limbs waving in the breeze, leaves floating in the air, and I swear I see a speckling of dandelion seeds floating among the beauty. The boy smiles at me

and grabs my hand. We are two children together, running into Gaia's greenhouse surrounded by magic, colors, and smells.

The first time I had this dream was when I was twelve. I woke up sweating in my bed in my grandmother's home, wondering what had just happened, my feet still tingling with dew from the moss on the trails, my face still warm from the greenhouse lamps, and the kiss I received on my cheek. A sweet kiss the mystery boy gave me while we gazed upon the orchids.

This time when I wake up, I am much older; I know Justin. Did I just put him into my recurring dream or has he been there all along? And if he has, then what does that mean? And what is he?

The constant banging against my chest is my own damn fault. I should really try to get rid of this blasted thing again, but for some reason I can't seem to make such an absolute decision. Desert sand flows around me as I exert more force, arcing and sending the staff into a spin, smacking balls of light out of the air. At first, Dana sends them to me all nice and sweet-like, spinning them around me lightly, giving me a chance to whack a few. In essence, I think she is trying to get me dizzy and off my game. I take the staff up then down to the left, sending a red ball sparking off into the distance. I then balance on the staff, kicking upward with my right leg and shattering another into sparks of purple and blue. The ring whips around on its chain, losing its place inside my shirt and spinning around to crack me on the cheek. Damn ring. Damn Ryan. The beautiful sterling silver ring with the endlessly chasing sun, moon, and stars constantly remind me of Ryan's deceit. The anger gives me enough motivation to spin kick into the air and take out three more balls as I realize Dana is now dive-bombing me with them instead of playing solar system.

We've been in this desert outside of Dana's RV park on and off for nearly three weeks now. And let me tell ya, using cell phones as a hot zone for doing my work remotely has been giving Carmen fits. As my best friend and business partner, she is in a constant state of worry about the state of things with our party-planning company, Feelyne Productions. What she worries about the most though, is what she perceives as my deteriorating mental health. Good thing my college buddy Shane is there to help her with Feelyne. With his new San Diego Gaslamp club Rapture opened, there have been plenty of people to cross over and help for both businesses. Shane gave me a set of keys to Rapture on opening night. We had spent countless hours creating the ultimate club in our heads, and Rapture is the result. I still have the keys in my bag, but I doubt I'll ever be able to dedicate myself to being the business partner he needs, not since my whole world was flipped upside down. And now, instead of playing in the Gaslamp, I'm stuck out here playing ninja, busting vicious earthen balls of pain in the desert.

I told Carmen that I needed a little break from San Diego after having a successful hypnotherapy treatment from Dr. McAdams. Ya, that's what happened, at least that's what Carmen and my other friends Shane, Justin, and Nic need to think. Only my grandmother's most trusted, and dare I say a tad bit crazy friend Dana, my Seer friend Sandra, my mom, and Ryan know the truth about what really happened that night. This is how it has to be in my world, my world of danger, magic, and hiding the truth. But back to being out here...in the middle of nowhere, waiting for word from my mother so we know where she is, where my dad is, and what in the hell we are going to do next.

Sometimes I wonder if Dana and my mom did all of this on purpose to get me worked up and out the door and away from my life in San Diego. I thought my life was finally going to start getting back to normal after Steven met his demise and my nightmares came to an end. Oh, but no! Wishful thinking! My life will never get back to normalcy. After all, there is still my wicked-ass foster brother Greg to catch, and let's not forget I have to find my father, who is goddess knows where. I've never known my father. Honestly, I had always been told he was dead, but apparently I'm not the only one who keeps secrets. And of course, let's not forget the cat is out of the bag about Ryan and I being forbidden to ever be together because of some stupid Council 'rule.' A rule that requires Earthen Protectors, like Ryan and me, to help spread our abilities through the generations by finding partners outside of our secret world. The Council, bah, some group of Earthen Protector leaders I have never met nor do I ever care to meet.

Yep, I thought things would be all hunky dory after Ryan and I caught up with Greg and saved my mom...ugh, who am I kidding? It was all a ruse. Greg never had my mom in captivity. His sniveling ass is in the wind, and my life is in shambles. Being in the desert right now may be the best thing for me and Dana and my mom knew it. Oh, and big shocker! Apparently I am not battle ready yet. I guess yoga, running on the beach, occasional kickboxing, and club dancing doesn't cut it when one decides to join this little good-versus-evil war instead of staying out of the game.

My 'being captured by Greg' stunt didn't really impress the seasoned Earthen Protectors, aka Mom and Dana. Being a descendant of powerful Earthen Protectors and Healers, I have the ability to harness power from the earth and bend it to my will. However, that isn't enough when it comes to protecting others, or in the case of what occurred three weeks ago, even keeping myself safe. As a result of my capture, Dana said it was Mom's orders to get me ready for what was to come, and to keep me from getting into that heap of a hot mess again.

In my defense, I was under duress from lack of sleep, migraines, and mind-assaulting nightmares, not to mention they had a Demon on their side. Who has a Demon on their side, anyhow? Don't get me started on that, or him for that matter. I'm still cringing from the idea of Valant coming to 'visit.' I left that topic out of my discussions with Dana, although I am fairly sure she smelled him on me. Yep, I said smelled. She is the Master, Mistress, High Priestess of Potions and Weaponry. I don't think much gets past her, which is probably why she told me my staffs were badass enough to kick even a Demon's ass.

So, little Miss Weapons and Potions has been kicking my booty day in and day out with her little toys-of-fun while my body screams in agony over newly torn and reformed muscles and burns from various colorful earthen power balls of light. My blisters are finally forming into calluses, accumulated by using my favorite weapon: Dana's hairpin staffs. Yep, they are exactly as they sound. Dana forged and ornately carved hairpins filled with tough-ass titanium metal. With the tiniest command from my power, these beautiful hairpins transform into fight-ready staffs. They are twins. I call them Serenity and Chaos; the latter defines my life and the former I can only wish for.

Once I take the hairpins into my hands and call their names, they change from elegant pieces of wood into wicked fighting weapons. Their lengths, covered in intricate vine carvings reflecting the nature of my power, are intermingled with dandelion seeds to symbolize my grandma. Cresting waves encircle both ends of each staff, and a fox hiding in the foliage represents my beloved fox friend Vex. I haven't seen Vex in nearly two years. He has helped me more than I would have ever thought possible, bringing me back from the brink of insanity more than once. I wonder where he was during all the stresses of this past year. He always told me I wouldn't be alone, and to accept the help sent to me, but apparently that didn't mean from him.

Aside from being aesthetically beautiful, my staffs are tremendously powerful. They have the extraordinary ability to be shaped into various fighter-friendly lengths. My favorite options are to either use them as a couple of two-and-a-half-foot pieces, or meld them together to form a single five-foot ass-kicking staff. Their sickly trick, one that I rarely use, is accomplished by willing the titanium metal running within their center to protrude to a sharp point at either end. Honestly, it scares me a bit, but it's nice to know that if I ever need to up my game a notch, I can.

Dana gets a kick out of all of it. My obvious lack of ability to balance the large staff from the very beginning doesn't discourage her from sending those earthen balls of light at me at all times of the day and night, searching for ways to make me fall on my ass. If I ever put my weapons away and tried to use my kickboxing skills to take on the barrage of lights with feet and fists, she made the lights dense and painful, like rocks hitting my flesh and bones. This technique basically forced me to add the weapons to my repertoire, lest I find myself bloody and broken. She did tend to my injuries in the best ways possible, with natural remedies in the form of cooling and warming salves, teas, and delicious feel-good foods.

A silver ball of light grazes my hip, spinning me to the right and causing a slight growl to escape my lips. She has taken advantage of my reverie, and I'm paying for it dearly. The bitch about these balls is their target-reaching addiction, like little torpedoes locked on to me. Their weight not only knocks me in all different directions, but they shock or burn me as well. It really depends on how sadistic she's feeling. I eye her silhouette on the hill above me; it reminds me of Rafiki, that crazy baboon from the Lion King, except I am the one with the staff.

That's it. She and her little round weapons are going down tonight. I hold the five-foot staff with both hands parallel to the earth and call upon Gaia's energy. I command it to change into the two short staffs. I spin the staffs gently in my hands and take my stance, eyeballing the silver ball as it arcs back my way, while at the same time watching a bright pink ball form in Dana's hand before that too makes its way toward me. Trying to keep them both in sight becomes difficult as they adjust until one aims at my front and the other directly at my back. I need a distraction to allow me to face off with one at a time.

Holding the staffs tightly, I point my fingers to the ground, pulling energy into my being, willing it to grab brush and dead cactus from the ground. I fling the brush and cactus at the silver ball heading directly toward me before wheeling around and running to meet the pink ball of torture head on. I swerve and smack at it with my right staff before spinning left to give the pink glowing nightmare a crack with my left staff as it tries to redirect itself. After taking its licking, the ball hits the ground and sputters out of existence. A slight buzzing hits my awareness. I swiftly drop to the ground in a lunge before bringing both arms above my head, moving them in a figure eight as the silver ball attempts to whiz past me before meeting its demise. Sparks rain down around me, lighting up my eyes before vanishing, leaving me in nearly complete darkness with the only light coming from the moon and a soft glow of green from the visual show of power blazing in my eyes. I stay in my lunge, muscles taut, awaiting another onslaught before I sense the force of rocks being kicked up by tires not more than five miles away.

"Your boy toy is here!" Shit! Dana is so damn quick and quiet she causes me to jump into a crouch and aim my staffs in her direction. She is right, of course. My heart flutters in my chest as I send my awareness outwards, picking up on flickers of Justin's presence.

CHAPTER 2

Diffusion and Magnetism

Journal Entry:

"Think of it as ions flowing in and out of your cells, your neurons firing and sending transmitters from synapse to synapse." I look at Grandma, confused of course, since I am only nine and have not even begun to get into that level of biology or psychology. She stops, realizing her error, and looks down at me.

"Of course, of course. I forget sometimes how young you are," she scolds herself, shaking her head and digging around in that powerful mind of hers for a better method of explaining. Explaining to her granddaughter how the Earthen power works, and how we are able to pull it from the earth and water to have it do what can only be described as our bidding. It's quite fantastical I must say, the amount of control I have over the world as a child really, but no, I was never much of a child with Stacy Conner as my mom. I had to grow up fast in her world.

"Okay, let's try this." She takes one of my play buckets and fills it with water as she tells me to fetch food coloring from inside the house. "I'll show you how you are able to take up the power, but it's harder to explain where it comes from since you cannot see the history. So I will lay it out for you. No, dear, our history is not what you learn in school."

I return with the coloring and Grandma places a single blue drop into the bucket. We watch as the blue droplet moves as a globule, dancing through the water until it turns the crystal-clear liquid blue.

9

"You see, my dear, the high concentration...hum, let's see, what's a better word? How about deepness? Yes, the deepness of the blue coloring in the droplet moves to balance itself in the water. The amount of blue dye from that one drop wants to, or rather has to, make its color evenly distributed...ah, diffused is the word I want to use, in the water. Now it is all blue, not as blue or as vivid as the original source of course, but it has now spread to make all the water in the bucket blue. It's as if the blue droplet is attracted to the clear water like a magnet. With Earthen power, or magic as some may call it, the levels of Earthen energy deep in the soil and our bodies of water is in such high concentration that Mother Earth would truly explode without us balancing it out. You see, without moving her deep blue droplets from her body into ours, the very nature of the negative and positive charges in our world would spin the earth out of control." I think I understood where she is going with this...sort of.

"So, I'm a magnet?" She stops looking at the swirling blue liquid and smiles brightly.

"Alexis dear, you may truly be destined to be the strongest of us with that quick wit, ability to pull on the power, and your knack for healing. Really, I knew you were a keen observer from the day you were born, eyes wide open and alert as your mom held you." Her eyes well up with tears just thinking about it. I know she misses my mom as much as I do. It has been a year since we last saw her. She was supposed to be in rehab, but she checked herself out and disappeared. I can only hope she isn't falling back into industrial drugs and horrible men as a way to keep her fear of her own powers at bay, but I know I am only fooling myself.

Grandma always said observation has a lot to do with my ability. I always thought I was just a kid who couldn't relax for a minute, always seeing every movement, every change in a room, in the wind, in a smell drifting in the breeze. But how do those abilities help me with my powers? I need to ask her. I have to find out more about what makes me so different as an Earthen Protector.

"Grandma, you always say being observant has something to do with being able to use the Earthen power so well at such a young age, but how does that make me a stronger magnet?" And then it clicks in my brain and I instantly know the answer. I can sense the changes everywhere. I can find my opposite, the negative to my positive. The words tumble out of my mouth.

"Being observant makes me a better magnet, doesn't it? I can find the power even in the deepest and most hidden places, can't I?" I know I am right, but I want to hear it from her. She kneels down and takes my face into her hands, brushing a small brunette curl from my eyes.

"Yes, darling, you are an exceptionally strong magnet, pulling the power from the ancient gods and goddesses from the very body they have left us to live in. You, my dear, can adapt to the changes you observe. You don't get trapped in them by concern, worry, or doubt. You go with the flow of the changes and break free from the constraint others may feel from the path they are on. You move to survive and carry on. It's an ability that will keep you safe, one that your mom sadly never fully developed. She got stuck in worry and doubt too often."

I try to let the feelings these words about my mother conjure up inside me slide over me, the way they should if I really am the person my grandmom is describing, but my mom is my weakness. I miss her; I always do. Grandma's explanation about Earthen Protectors moving high concentrations of Earthen power in the earth to lower concentrations in ourselves makes me wonder how the evil wielders of our power, those who call themselves Absolute Protectors, can take power from others. Something Grandma told me they do quite often. Despite my sadness, my curiosity gets the better of me, and I move on to other questions, primarily focusing on those evildoers.

"But how do the Absolute Protectors get power from others if they have the highest concentration and steal power from those with lesser power? It goes against the explanation you just gave me, doesn't it?" I am dead serious, but she stands and chuckles.

"You never cease to amaze me, dear. Yes, you're right. It does go against the rule, if you will. That is why they are some of the most powerful beings because it takes an enormous amount of energy to take from a lower level to a higher level. It goes against the natural flow of the power. That is why many suffer bouts of insanity, sickness, and even death from trying. But to others it comes easily since they possess such large amounts of power. Levels close to what I feel you may have, but none of them nearly as pure or as strong. They are our enemies, Alexis dear. They are who we may need to face one day."

A chill runs through me at hearing these words. One day I will have to fight, won't I? I am only nine, but I can picture it clearly in my mind. I will *face danger. I will face evil. My face curves into a Cheshire grin, and I look up at her before speaking.*

"I'm not scared, Grandma, because I know we will win."

Dana is always right, or if she isn't, I swear it's either because she lies on purpose to test me or out of pure boredom. Must suck to always be right. Yet, I know that even if she weren't one of my grandmom's oldest and dearest friends, I would still love and respect her as much as I do. However, right now, I don't have time to get into it with her about how I'm not focused enough to have picked up on Justin's presence before she did. Nope, I don't need another tongue lashing about how I am supposed to be the young whippersnapper with all these special abilities. The first of my kind in generations and yet I am constantly getting upstaged by her "old ass." Her words, not mine! It has been a recurring conversation since we got here, part of the training I suppose.

The bit of Arizona desert that Dana calls home, in the town of Why to be exact, is just desolate enough to find pockets of privacy where we can train without being noticed. Being an Earthen Protector and a Healer, I am apparently a unique mixture that only comes about every other generation, if that. Apparently even those two labels don't account for everything I am capable of doing. Dana thinks I must have inherited the most powerful parts of the ancient gods and goddesses that created our world. The power that very few can harness, let alone learn how to use. The life forces of the gods and goddesses never left the earth they created. They integrated into the body of our planet, allowing those of the Earthen power heritage to manipulate their powers and impact the world around them.

Not knowing my father, being taken away from my addicted yet powerful mother, and then at the age of thirteen losing my guardian and guide in the form of my grandmother, didn't leave me with anyone to help navigate my capabilities but my own damn self. I had done okay but now, with Dana's help, I am becoming the warrior worthy of my heritage.

The terrifying experiences with my foster brother Greg and his father Steven's attempt to return to his fierce glory have awoken the fighter within me. Realizing my father is alive, and finally working with my mom to find him, blazed that spark to a full-on raging fire.

Then there is Ryan; well, there was Ryan. He was the first person who was like me that I had been around since I banished Steven to some alternate hell dimension fourteen years ago. Ryan was my guardian, the man who saved me from Steven, who killed him for me. It was only three weeks ago, but it feels like an eternity since that dreadful day in the basement where Steven perished. Unfortunately, I created another monster in the form of Greg. I'll never forget the night I finally found the person who was responsible for my year in hell, of monstrous nightmares and psychological torment.

I was truly astonished that Greg, aka Dr. McAdams, was the catalyst and the person who trapped me in his cellar, forcing me to help him free the evil Absolute Protector, Steven. Greg's whole plan was to free his father from the bind that I banished him to. But of course, in order to do so, I needed to be sacrificed. I tried to talk some sense into him about why Steven needed to stay banished, but he was too far gone with Steven's brainwashing, so he had to learn the hard way. Steven turned on Greg, hating him even. Their demon friend Valant took way too much pride and joy in telling Greg that Steven was not his real father. Yep, Mrs. Nestrour hated her husband enough to bump uglies with his brother. Yet even that little wake-up call didn't help temper Greg's anger toward me. He blamed me for his misery because I was the easiest, and really the only, target.

If Ryan hadn't found me when he did, if his ring that I continue to wear around my neck hadn't led him to me...who knows what would have happened. The thought makes me shudder. The knowledge that Steven is gone for good doesn't really faze me. There was no other way but to kill Steven. If we had shown mercy, Steven would have never left me alone. No, he wouldn't have given up until I was in perpetual torture at the hands of my own Demon, or dead myself.

Valant has kept his word for the most part, after releasing Greg from his control. Valant promised to never pop in on me as long as I keep my end of the bargain and invite him to observe my disaster of a life from time to time. I think it is how Demons are able to survive. Apparently, they feed and get nourishment from the hurt and pain felt by others. Gross! I guess it's better than having to feed a vampire. Wait: are vampires real, too? Ah crap, I don't want to know. Greg is enough of a real vampire to me. That weasel collaborated with Steven and Valant to torture me with vicious REM-stealing nightmares and migraines. Greg was still MIA after we realized, too late, that he didn't have my mom locked up somewhere in a deep, dark dungeon. No, he's probably sucking down Mai Tais on an island in the Pacific. That asshole is at the top of my who-needs-an-ass-kicking list, but right now it is time to focus on learning how to fight harder, faster, and stronger to help find my father.

I did digress from the point, didn't I? Ryan. I haven't called him back or answered a single text despite his multiple attempts to contact me. I'm sure he was stunned when he returned to my house expecting us to take off after Greg together. Instead, Ryan found it empty with only a note telling him to pretty much piss off. Instead of taking Ryan's calls, I answered Justin's calls instead. Safe, truthful, reliable Justin, who is nearly at Dana's campground entrance and I'm still up here in the Pozo Redonido Mountains with a massive staff in my hands and a crazy lady dancing around snatching up fiery balls of death like they are squishy marshmallows.

I have to focus and get back to her trailer before Justin gets there. I place my ear buds in as the Red Hot Chili Peppers' lead vocalist Anthony Kiedus transports me over the bridge downtown; the lyrics take over my mind and I start to move. I tug on the Earthen power and use it to force the staff in two before shrinking them into my unassuming little wooden hairpins. I place them delicately in my hair, turning my ponytail into an intricate braid in the process. I look down at my nearly destroyed and smoking clothes, wondering if they can stay intact enough for me to run at top speed back to the trailer. I see no point in changing now, so I hope for the best and take off at a jog.

The sterling silver chain clinks around my neck as I swing my backpack on and start moving toward the trailer. I have a good two miles ahead of me so I transition into a run, feeling the ring swing around and tap my chest in rhythm with my stride. I take one more pull on the earth to help catapult me faster through the desert terrain while also working on changing Ryan's ring into the pendant Justin knows, a glorious arching dolphin with the ring's sun, moon, and stars etched in its body.

For some reason, I cannot get rid of the ring. What else can I do? I tried to leave the ring in San Diego the night I left with Dana instead of following the plan to find Greg with Ryan. I placed the ring in an envelope and left it on my coffee table with a note, knowing Sandra or Ryan would find it, but I woke in Dana's car to find it snugly attached to my right ring finger again.

Ryan's ring, the one with a life of its own that attached to me the night we spent together in Scottsdale, Arizona, when I thought he would be by my side always. But Dana has made it perfectly clear that Ryan can never be with me. The Council would never allow it.

What a bunch of bullshit! Bullshit that Ryan kept from me. So I left without warning and haven't communicated with him since. I am sure Dana could find a way to permanently rid me of the ring, but I haven't pulled the trigger and asked her for help. Obviously, the ring is a comfort as well as an annoyance. After all, the ring saved my life that night in San Diego by summoning Ryan.

Enough about Ryan; I need to focus on Justin. Justin has been doing work in Puerto Penasco, Mexico, only about two hours from here. I met up with him a couple of times after our kiss on that fateful night I was taken by Greg. I had ignored his texts for a while, just as I have Ryan's, but my feelings for him never fully faded. The desert seems to revive and enhance my feelings for Justin. We quickly started up our relationship again, but something is different this time around. Something I didn't notice before. Maybe because of all of Steven's shit being in the mix pretty much from the very beginning of our relationship a little over a year ago. Whatever the case, there exists what I can only describe as an undeniable flow of energy between us. Something similar to what I feel when I pull on the Earthen power, like Justin and I are being pulled together like magnets. When we touch now, I feel something similar to what I felt with Ryan, but still somehow different.

Ryan is a strong Earthen Protector so I could feel that connection even though Steven, Greg, and Valant were jerking me around. That powerful trio nearly drove me insane and almost ruined my relationship with my best friend Carmen, and with Justin. Although I did have a hand in that as well by almost falling for Ryan, a man I hardly know. Stupid, stupid, Alex. It is a mistake Dana doesn't let me forget as she tests my body, mind, and spirit daily. Maybe that is why I sense Justin differently now. More than ever, I am poised to find out everything and anything about a person. I have always been a deeply intense observer, but now I must be able to feel the Earthen energy in him, what some may call an aura or spirit. Boy, does he feel good, pure, and loving. Yep, that has to be it...right?

As for Ryan, I am over him, or will be sooner rather than later, I hope. My anger at his massive omission and the distance and time away from him has been helping me. I hope when I do see him again, as I am sure I will, those feelings will be gone for good. Though there's no denying that Ryan will always hold a special place in my heart. How could he not? After all, he saved me and even killed for me. That's something I will never forget and will be forever grateful.

CHAPTER 3

A Desert Wind

Journal Entry:

Even with the thin layer of my eyelids closed the twinkling light catches my eyes, and I can still see and, in turn, feel the sparkling light flashing in and out of my vision. The click of metal turns my dull attention to a more alert awakening as I fall away from my dream and into the growing brightness of my room. Bear stands on my bed nearby, the silver circle of his tag catching the light rays as they pierce through the cracks of existence between the drapes and the windowpane. His large Labrador eyes smile at me urgently as he lets out a whine and jumps off the bed.

"Bear, you know it's too early for a pee run. Remember, full daylight please, daylight." He spins in a circle, yips, and heads out of my bedroom before standing in the hall and giving a low bark.

"Okay, okay! Don't wake Grandma! I'm coming." Grandma was up at four a.m. like she is every morning. Unable to sleep, she sits in her reading chair and cuddles up to a book or does a crossword puzzle before turning in again for what I call her morning nap from five to seven.

Since it is a school day, Bear wakes me up at six a.m., an hour before my bus comes to take me to the hell that is 7th grade. I'm an early riser, partially to have enough time to mentally prep for the onslaught of teasing by my peers about everything from my brace face to my skinny legs. I try to hide behind textbooks, waiting for the bell to ring to signal the end of my torment. The glorious final tone means I can run far away from it all for miles and miles at track practice. My early wake-up call is also to spend time with Bear on our morning walk. Spring has been mild in Western Colorado, so it is merely brisk and not freezing.

Bear practically drags me down our long, rocky driveway; my sneakers trudge on the red sand and rock mix as we head toward the road. I hear the mewing before we make it to a large sage bush along the left side of the road. A rock goes skidding off into the brush when I nick it with my toe, the commotion setting four quick-footed quails off in a scurried line to the opposite side of the road, their plumes comically bouncing around the tops of their heads. The mewing brings my attention back to the bush as Bear circles around it and whines in time with his laps.

As I get closer, I notice portions of the bush ripped and torn about; a predator has been here, and whatever was its prey may or may not have gotten away with their lives. At least one is trapped in there still, most likely traumatized, hurt, and scared. I crouch down to look and catch sight of a white ball of fur trembling under a large root where the animal is trapped. I use the weight of my hiking boots to carefully stretch the bush to one side, trying to make a small amount of room to pull the critter out. The light gloves I'm wearing won't protect me from a bite, so I try to get a good eyeball on the location of the nape of its neck. Having already experienced my ability to heal my first fox and other small animals, birds, and plants, I know I need to send soft tendrils of Earthen energy into the little body, willing it to be calm. Hopefully, whatever it is won't remove a chunk of my fingertip in the process.

I gently take hold of soft fur and safely maneuver the small body out from under the ensnaring root, and turn the creature so I can look into its dark blue eyes. The kitten is tiny, shivering, and bloodied. I continue to reach out with my healing power, sweeping over the little body as Bear sits, tilting his head at the subtle change in the charge of the air as the powerful Earthen energy shifts into my being, allowing me to work my magic on this baby creature. As my senses pick up on her gender and her injuries simultaneously, I know two legs and some impossibly small ribs are broken, and her heart is fluttering out of control. I continue to calm her and hold her close to me as Bear and I make our way back home. My power flows around her as I hum softly, letting the tones of my voice mimic the musical flow of my energy as I heal her. As I continue on my path home, I make a list in my head of what Grandma should get at the pet store to help us raise this kitten, in case I can't track down her mom, if she is even still alive. Grandma will love this little girl; she loves her cats, half wild though they are, as they prefer to live in our backyard and in 'their' sunroom. They are definitely smart enough not to run off into the desert and become victims like this little one.

As I approach the front door I see it creak open, and my lips part into a smile at the billowing glow that breaks through the barrier of our closed door. Grandma's eyes lock with mine before she falls to the ground. Bear dashes off ahead of me as I try to keep up, only managing to see dust kick up from his heels. I simultaneously pull the gloves from my hands, creating a nest for the kitten and cozying her in them before placing her tiny body in my pocket. All the while, I push my healing power into my grandma as I close in on her location. Before I can reach her, an immense wave of power strikes through me in my panic, and I stumble to the ground, bracing my body so as to not harm the little life in my pocket.

Strong hands turn me over gently, and I look into my grandmom's eyes, searching them for an answer as to what happened, if she was okay.

"My dear Alexis, you are the strongest of us, aren't you? Truly amazing, my dear. Thank you for your help, my sweet child. Now come inside and let's take a look at that sweet little girl you've found." I look at her, shaking my head, tears in my eyes.

"But what...are you okay, Grandma? You just fell to the ground. What happened? We need to take you to a doctor." I take her hand and stand up. She brushes my curls away from my eyes and holds my head in her hands, speaking to me with such love and emotion.

"No, dear, I'm just fine now. All thanks to you." She turns, taking the little kitten and cradling her in her weathered hands. She glances once over her shoulder into the distance and then heads into the house. I begin to follow her when I hear a faint rumble and then a whine from Bear's chest, so low even Grandma doesn't hear it. I turn and follow his eyes in the direction he is fixating on and feel something, like someone is there, watching us. We are in a remote piece of land, no neighbors nearby, and this is not a presence I have ever sensed before, yet it feels familiar all the same. I step toward the source but Bear steps in front of me, raising his hackles and huffing. Just like that, whatever or whoever is gone. A chill runs through me and I reach down to pet Bear's large Labrador head, letting him lead me back to the house.

I round the corner of Dana's metal-working hut, aka weaponry, potions, and mischief making, and tear past her trailer toward a smaller one she got on loan from a friend. I suppose it is smart to have a pretty convincing cover when one is creating some seriously dangerous stuff in the Arizona desert. Although she has been known to give the retirees more than just the occasional iron art piece, I swear a love potion of hers is going around this place.

The trailer I am staying in is on loan, so I have my own space, or as Dana calls it, my "boom-chicka-bow-wow" space for Justin and me. I kick my boots off onto the faux grass mat and slam the metal door behind me as I quickly undress and toss my filthy clothes into the hamper. I might as well torch them at this point, but there is no time for that now. My awareness makes Justin's tires crunching the rocks underneath seem like they are right outside, but I probably have a good five minutes before he arrives.

I try washing my face by looking in the tiny mirror in my cabinet and hoping I don't miss anything major. My hair is another story as my brush snags in it in all places, and I find myself carefully picking a sharp cactus needle out of my ponytail. Hazards of the job, I guess. Boy, do I miss the full time work and stressful days of party planning! At least I wasn't in physical danger most of the time.

I really need to check in with Shane and Carmen today. It's been about a week since we verbally talked. Emails and texts don't really do the job, especially when we are best friends as well. Actually talking to each other gives us the much needed support and understanding that can't be done through typing of any sort. Hearing someone's voice and being able to judge what he or she is feeling makes it much easier on everyone. I know that is the reason things continue to go so well. We all know we have to make time for each other.

With my ponytail redone and face somewhat clean, I am only left with what clothes to find and a pointless longing for a shower. I really need to hit up the laundromat down the road. There isn't much of a selection in the tiny closet to choose from.

As I start to put on some hardly-can-be-called-clean yoga pants, I see bruises forming, scratches, and even some oh-so-stingy burn marks all over my legs. The effort required to pull on my pants has me cursing up a storm, and I swear I can hear Dana hooting and hollering outside. I'm sure my little camper is rocking as I hop on one foot to shimmy into the other pant leg. I throw on a bra and cami that are really for sleeping, but I don't have much choice. After grabbing a sweater, I haul ass out of there to meet Justin with a smile. I rethink my process and run back in to grab gum and some lip-gloss. Hey, I can still look purdy while roughing it, right? I only hope the dancing of the firelight from Dana's sparking fire will make me look less disgusting than I feel.

Justin's white truck comes into view and tingles shoot up into my happy places as I swear I can smell his earthiness even from this distance. Being a child of Gaia, I am probably more in tune with the smells of his botanical projects than the normal person, and I am not complaining. His dedication to making the world a better place by understanding the way our ecosystems work together in the oceans, estuaries, and other waterways will truly protect us in the long run. I guess we are sort of similar in that respect. We are both protectors of Mother Earth.

His hat sits low over his brow, giving him an air of mystery and sexiness that fits nicely with how kind, intelligent, and strong he is. The days he spends outside give him a natural rugged glow and, despite all his labors, his hands are soft, even in my most delicate of places. I have to get it together, or I am going to drag him into the camper right now and there is no way Dana would ever let me live that down. I can tell she is in her camper and out of sight, but I know she is watching; she always is in one way or another. Justin exits the truck and grabs his bag behind his seat, which is my sign that he's staying here tonight. I figured he would because of the lateness of the hour, but when we last spoke he wasn't sure since he has to be back in Mexico so early tomorrow.

"I thought for sure you weren't coming when I didn't hear from you. You may have been greeted by a whole different me, at least a clean me." I embrace him, dirt, burns, and all. I know he doesn't care. We are both used to being in the muck. Hell, our first date was trudging through an estuary, for goodness sake!

21

He holds onto me, weary I can tell. Some of his interns didn't turn out to be what he had hoped, and he is picking up some of their serious slack. He has too many of his employees tied up with dissertations to come help him with fieldwork this far out, especially the low-pay kind. I need to remind him to let me work on his website and program advertising to get him more eager students. He says he doesn't need the help but I can tell he does, and I want to do this for him. After all, I need an energetic Justin in my tiny, I-can't-believe-you-can-call-that-a-queen bed. Classy lady right here!

"Sorry about that, Alex. My phone got wrecked trying to tie up the boats, and I just felt I needed to get on the road and just drive. It's been a long day. You know I'm happy to see any version of you. Besides, sweaty, dirt-caked Alex is my favorite." He rubs some remnants of my tango in the desert off my neck and follows it with a kiss. My jelly legs wobble a bit and not only from my physical exertion.

When I tell you something is different between us this time around, I am not making that up. He taps into parts of me that never used to stand to attention before. Don't get me wrong, sex with Justin has always been amazing, but I never got the chance to connect with him as much as we have now. No, he doesn't, and may never know my secrets, but it doesn't bother me as much now because I'm clear headed. I know how much he loves me, and I trust him completely. Trust has always been a huge issue for me, and now, with Justin it isn't even a question. Someday I may finally be able to say I love him too. Not yet, of course, but I have teased it around in my head. Having not loved many men, I think it is pretty obvious that I may and probably always have loved Justin. I'm just not ready to tell him yet.

"Eh-hem." Ah, Dana, right on cue to ruin my moment. "Sorry to interrupt your thoughts, but I'm sure Justin wants a shower and some food, am I right? I have some steaks and peppers on the grill; should be ready in about fifteen minutes. Justin, you are more than welcome to use my shower, Alexis always does. Well, not tonight apparently." Smart-ass. Regardless of how I feel about snarky-ass Dana, she is right. Justin looks like he is daydreaming wistfully about hot water and delicious grilled meat. So I help him along in case he is lingering on my account.

"Go ahead, Professor, you deserve it. I'll be here when you're done." I place a kiss full of promises on his cheek, and let Dana lead him to her camper door. Once Justin is inside and the water running, Dana returns to interrupt my reverie as I stare into the pyro-kinetic light show.

"Okay, Alexis dear, we need to talk. All was fine and dandy when I was under the delusion that maybe I could count on Justin to just be an occasional booty call to keep you from going stir crazy, but now I'm picking up on some overly obvious love vibes from you, and it has to stop." I turn from the fire to stare at her, shocked more by someone calling me out on the 'L' word than a sixty-some-year-old using the term "booty call."

"I thought you liked Justin, Dana. Why does it matter how serious our relationship is? He isn't interfering with anything we're trying to do here. Here in this desert alone, with no word from Mom in how long? If we're going to start airing our issues with the current state of things, let's start with waiting with no word from a woman who claims to know where my previously believed to be dead father is. Is this just some charade? A hot pile of steaming crap? If you and Mom wanted to train me, I would have come willingly you know. Hell, you could have trained me in San Diego where I could still run my company and the new club!" I take a breath, watching her closely for any indication that I've hit the nail on the head. So far it looks like I haven't even come close, so I continue.

"I'm a grown woman and I can see who I like and love who I want to love. Oh, except for Ryan, of course, that was made perfectly clear, but now Justin too? Am I not on my game? Am I not giving my all to you, to this desert, to this supposed mission prep? I'm in a hundred percent, but you can't take everything from me." I am shaking a bit, feeling the adrenaline from our training session still pumping through my blood.

"It's simply this, Alexis. I need...we need you focused and on the balls of your feet in more ways than one. We need you to be ready to hightail it out of here at a moment's notice to wherever your mother tells us to go, whether that be the Amazon, Antarctica, or China. We will need to go, and love makes that extremely difficult for most people, even people like us with all our power and talents. Your mom is well aware, all too familiar with the tangles of love, and the mistakes, treachery, and pain it can cause. You may want to consider dialing things back a bit. We don't need Dr. Jones following us on our mission when we get out of Dodge, which can be any day now." Ha, any day now! She's been saying that every day since I got here. I sense the water turning off in the camper, so I decide to bring this little dance to an end.

"Okay, Dana, I hear you. I completely understand the delicate game we're playing. I won't let my relationship with Justin cloud my judgment. I'm smart enough to make sure I have an exit strategy that's clean and without question. Now, I'd like to take a shower as well, if that's okay with you, eat some delicious food and then maybe, just maybe, use that trailer for the very thing you so lovingly named it. But what I will not do is blindly turn my back on another man I care about when there are ways to have both of my worlds without letting them collide. I'm not my mother, I've never been my mother, and I don't have her fear or addictions. So please, don't worry. I've got this." I place my hand on her shoulder and squeeze it enough to let her know I respect and care for her, but also that I am capable of not totally fucking up my life like Mom. Before I completely move past her, I step back to whisper in her ear now that I know Justin is on his way to the door handle.

"I know now is not the time, but I hope tomorrow, when Justin is gone, we'll talk further about my mother and her mistakes. I think it's time I know what really happened to her and my father. It is him you are speaking of, isn't it?" She smiles at me and nods as I slip past her, hoping to grab a quick shower myself while he dresses in my dinky trailer.

After dinner and some wine, Justin and I say goodnight to Dana and make our way to my RV. I barely hear the last echoes of the door click beneath my hands as I push the old door shut when I feel Justin's arm around my waist as his right hand grabs the back of my thigh. His warm, strong touch sends a throbbing urge clinching inside my body. I feel myself moisten instantly under the sway of his touch and the memories of how he feels inside me. The expectation is palpable as I feel his breath on my neck, alternating back and forth between wanting to turn around and taste his lips on mine, or working on removing my pants and having him take me right here and now. With my face inches from the door, I have to steady my weakening knees by holding on tightly to the wall with both hands. I allow my right arm to ease off the wall and snake behind me to grip the back of his neck as I arc back slightly, moaning upwards as his hand feels boiling hot against the sensitive area nestled between my thighs. Nope, I'm not leaving this spot until I have him right here, hard and held tightly against him and the cold aluminum door, the chilled metal making my nipples hard and sensitive.

My hair, still wet from the shower, begins untangling from its haphazard ponytail, the wet strands sending additional chills along my neck. Yet, before I can grab a hold of it to free the fleeing hair completely, Justin takes it gently, delicately putting it back in its spot, before tugging rougher than required to keep it in place. I don't mind it a bit as his aggressive touch turns me on even more than I already am. My legs rub together in his hands' absence, the friction releasing a moan of need as his hands shove my legs apart before one finds my spot again. Justin's other hand works to remove my yoga pants, the urgency I feel making my body annoyed that I'm not getting out of them quickly enough.

I attempt to move my right hand backward to touch him, but he grabs it, forcing it back to its spot on the wall. I feel his fingers lifting the soft cotton of my underwear, allowing others to find their way in, diving into my flesh, pulling out and rubbing all in perfect timing and succession. The wetness is overwhelming. I move against him, causing his fingers to go in deeper and harder. His left hand reaches up, grasping my breast and lightly circling my already aroused nipples in such a way that I have to beg.

"Please let me touch you, I want to feel you." I try to reach back again, but am taken off track by the sound of his zipper followed by his jeans hitting the floor. He takes my hand in his again, this time pressing it lightly to the door before trailing his fingers from my hand

25

to my elbow, then my waist, and lastly to grip my thigh. He lifts my leg slightly to allow him some leverage as he angles inside me. My body floods with warmth, beautiful pressure, and a teasing throbbing. I clench against his hard smoothness as I work against him just as he moves slowly against me, his breath quickening until his lips trail kisses along my neck, silencing it.

"I love the way your skin tastes, the temperature of it under my lips, your smell. Alex, you're perfect." His words only send my body further into a frenzy, pushing and arcing against him in a rhythm, our rhythm. He lets my right thigh go, and I fold over while pressing my face further away from the wall allowing him easier access to the deepest parts of me.

"I love the way you feel inside me," I gasp. His hands continue to excite me as they move over my back, lowering until his hands hold firmly to both cheeks, pulling and pushing them against him causing even more excitement to shoot through me.

Justin continues to hold me close with his left hand while his right finds its way to the front of me, teasing the sensitive skin of my clitoris, driving me nearly mad with intense pleasure that teeters on the edge of pain. My body heats up even more from an intense flame to a raging hot fire, building to the inevitable climax. I know he is right with me as he fills me even more, moaning with desire.

I grit my teeth, careful not to cry out; such a sound would echo throughout this entire RV park. Trust me, I've heard it before. Justin's soft lips press hard into my back as his groans of satisfaction are smothered by my skin, before planting kisses along my back. I lift and turn to him, my body shaking and sated. He holds my face in his hands, searching my eyes before kissing me. He draws back, looking at me again with an expression as if he thought he saw something. For a minute, I worry my power had trickled out, and he could see my eyes change to an emerald glow, but my worry eases as he smiles and then speaks.

"Your eyes never seem to be the same color, yet I always see you in them. You're amazing. Your body feels unreal at times. I don't ever want to lose you again. Seeing you healthy and happy is all I ever wanted, and now you're just that." I smile back at him and wrap my arms tighter around him.

"You have a lot to do with my happiness, you know. You didn't have to come back to me after how bad things got. I know how lucky I am. How lucky we both are for being able to come back to each other after all the craziness." I can't help but feel my heart pound inside from both the excitement of having a second chance with Justin, and from the tingle of fear that trickles up my spine knowing that the craziness has just begun.

What he doesn't fully know won't hurt him, right? I can only hope so. Maybe once things die down with my father and Greg, I can seriously look at our future. I mean, I am supposed to 'mate' with a non-magic wielder, right? Well, the most amazing one is right in front of me, and he isn't going anywhere.

I nestle my head in the crook of Justin's neck as the feelings of warmth and pleasure send my satisfied self into a peaceful sleep. The last thing I hear is the relaxed ebb and flow of Justin's breathing, its ease sending me off to my dreams.

I suddenly feel cold and reach for the covers I share with Justin, only to have my fingers grab onto cold, smooth pebbles. I instantly lift myself up in a panic. Fur nestles alongside me as Vex, my mysterious fox friend and possible animal spirit guide, puts his head under my hand and pushes into me. It is an odd feeling, not only due to the fact that I should be cuddling with a hunk of a man instead of with a fox, but also because Vex usually mock nips my fingers when I try to pet him. When he speaks, I hear worry in his voice, which is far from his usual smart-ass self.

"Not good, Alex. Not good at all. Do you feel that? Something is wrong. I can't place it, but something is happening, and I don't think this is the beginning. I hope we aren't too late." As I am about to ask Vex what he is rambling about, where in the hell we are, and what he is feeling, I am struck by an intense level of pain. It feels like my very soul is being pulled from my body.

"Alex, Alex, oh shit! Alex, what's wrong? What's happening?" The tugging is so intense I crumble back to the rocky bed and my muscles fire, spasming to the point of having me completely paralyzed in a fetal position. I concentrate on anything but the pain, and get my head right enough to start pulling energy into my being, demanding it to tether my soul down, to keep me with my body. It starts to work, and my eyes open as feather-like fern fronds in a kaleidoscope of dark greens float around bright emerald vines. Vex's power is shining through as he works with me to fight off whatever is happening.

In the next moment a scream blasts through the sky, and we look across the darkness to see a dark form outstretched in the distance, floating two feet above the ground, head thrown back—the obvious source of the tortured sound. At first I think the person to be my assailant, but then I notice bright balls of light being pulled from her like orange water droplets, arcing away into the distance before vanishing. It is obvious now that it is a woman. I swear she turns in our direction before her last living sound is uttered, and her body given back to the goddess. Bones, muscle, all of it is transferred instantly into the cold, rocky ground. The shaking that ensues after the ghastly sight is like an uncontrollable chill that has taken over my muscles, the fear keeping me from taking a hold of myself. Vex's eyes come into focus, and I try to concentrate on his bronze irises as his mouth moves, my ears not hearing him at first.

"Alex, Alex! Snap out of it! We need to get out of here. Something is coming." I slow my breathing and concentrate again on pulling energy carefully and slowly into me, calming my reaction and forcing me up from the ground. I stand shakily and place my hand on Vex's head before looking down at him.

"Did you hear what she said, Vex? 'Help us.' What in the world just happened and where are we?" I kneel down to look into his eyes, both hands caressing his face to show my gratitude for him being here and for my own selfishness as his soft fur continues to calm my nerves.

"We're on a Dreamwalk. We just witnessed a woman's power being ripped from her. You're obviously an Empath on this journey, actually feeling what was happening to her as well. Even though we're only visitors to this vision, this isn't some ordinary power play. That woman was one of the strongest Healers we have, and she wasn't even able to fight back, let alone survive the attack. We need to get out of here before whoever did this senses that they have company." His eyes skirt around, and I move to have my back to him so we can both make a good scan of the area.

"Do you sense it?" Vex's question pops into my head at the same time as another power source becomes very apparent. I try to calm myself of the worry that Steven is somehow still alive. He was one of the most powerful Absolute Protectors I knew, and even though I saw him die, this was his MO for sure. The power signature comes back different from Steven's, although the feeling of desperation, need, and desire is the same. Whoever did this isn't done. They want more and Vex and I need to get the hell out of this place now!

"Yes, I feel it, Vex. We need to move, but how do we get out of here?" I kneel beside him again, holding him to me and shivering from the cold.

"Close your eyes; concentrate on where you were before we met here. Keep your hand touching me, and we'll work on this together." A cold wind pierces my skin. I am in the same barely-there clothes from the RV, which don't lend much protection. I'm just thankful I put something on instead of my usual nothing bedtime attire! Another blast of cold hits me, and I feel Vex shiver.

"We need to move now, Alex! Concentrate! Where were you? What did it feel, sound, and smell like?" I use the same observant and empathic abilities that allowed me to feel the Healer's pain to recall Justin. The recollection of what he feels like, smells like, sounds like. I draw a picture in my head of him lying next to me, of hearing his breath coming in and out of his lungs. The icy wind picks up and almost feels like frosty fingertips caressing my arms and legs.

"Almost there, Alex. Okay, this might feel a little strange," Vex said. A loud pop in my ears is followed by the howling of a pack of coyotes as I sit up abruptly. I can feel the covers on top of me, my shivering subsiding as the warmth of Justin's skin sends the chills away. I look around for Vex, only seeing a trail of fern fronds floating off toward the RV door. I slowly lay back down, shaken by my experience, my mind reeling. I thought I would never fall back asleep, but the sounds of the coyotes in the distance lull my eyes shut.

"Do you hear that?" Justin's voice startles me, and my mouth won't move as I speak the answer in my mind instead.

"They sound close by, but the echoes out here make them only appear so." Geez, like he can hear me. Speak, dummy.

"Ya, I'm sure we could mathematically figure out their distance, but I'm too tired now. Good night, Alex. I love you." Justin's words connect with my brain instead of my ears. Is this really happening? Is this a dream? How is he able to speak to me? And seriously, could this night get any weirder?

"Good night..." is all I manage to mumble. I don't think I can handle much more weirdness tonight. I'll deal with this new development, hallucination, or whatever it is, tomorrow. It must be some sort of dream; my mind must be beyond traumatized. I feel stunned, tired, and scared—not of Justin, but of what I witnessed in that rocky, cold, vast mystery land. The last thing I remember is the woman's plea filling my head before I fall into a thankfully dreamless sleep.

"Help us!"

CHAPTER 4

A Mother's Curse

Journal Entry:

"Will you stop panting in my ear, you big oaf?" I lovingly nudge Bear away as I try to listen in on my grandmother's phone conversation. I can hear her muffled voice through the floor vent. It's two a.m. so there is no way this is some normal chat. Her voice, hardly ever heard with this stern a tone, is an attempted whisper, but I have already crept close enough to hear her clearly. I can only hope she is too agitated to sense me out. Plus, this massive Labrador is leering all over me like camouflage.

"Don't change the subject on me, young lady. I am not calling you so you can pretend to worry about me. I need to know if there is a chance." There's a deafening pause as my own teeth grind in anticipation. "Because, as I have said, the amount of power I felt could not have only come from her, that's why. Someone else was here, and if it's one of your friends or lackeys checking up on her, then I need to know, because if not...she may be in danger." Her nails click against the phone receiver, and I hear her pacing back and forth in her room. A small "mew" makes me feel some sort of relief that the cat is in there with her. She always seems to calm Grandma down.

"Stacy, I'm not asking you to do anything. I know you can't leave wherever or whatever you're doing, not even for Alex, but if you can, please double check. Maybe there's something or someone we overlooked. I can only hope that since this person appeared to be helping us, they mean no harm, but even

knowing where she is makes that person a threat to her." It's my mom. Little girl flutters take control of my stomach and I feel longing and anger simultaneously. Either Grandma knew how to reach her all along, or she found a way to make my mom call her.

"Oh, we should move?! Okay, that wasn't what I was asking. I'm not going to pick up and run. I'm hoping my daughter, who in some way seems connected to anything and everything, could do some digging and find out if anyone knows about her daughter." She lets out an exasperated sigh as my mom apparently makes some comment that drains her patience.

"No, we have been careful; we never practice around anyone. If someone found her, they were looking for her." Another pause and another drop of drool on my shoulder from Bear.

"Thank you. Yes, you can use this phone again. No one else knows about it. Before you go, are you okay...clean?" I can almost hear the fuming, venom-filled vocalizations from the other side of the call.

"Well, I'm still your mother, so I have a right to ask!" Ugh, if only I could hear the other side of this terse conversation. My eyes start to well up with tears before I can freeze them in their previously closed, nesting ducts. Bear nudges me supportively, leaning his warm head against my cheek knowingly. I slowly begin to rise; pins and needles trickle through me after being in a frozen crouch for so long.

"Well, that's good to hear. Yes, she's fine, very powerful and learning fast. Be careful, Stacy. I love you...we love you." I sneak backward, easing down the hallway until I hit my bedroom doorway and dive quietly into my bed. A few minutes pass before I hear the light touch of her toes on my carpet. The familiar scent of her vanilla shampoo tickle my olfactory receptors, and I close my eyes tighter, taking in the comfort of having her near me.

My grandmother kisses the top of my head and presses her cheek to mine. The wetness is warm and her tears cling to my skin, chilling instantly as she pulls away. It takes everything I have within me not to give myself away. All I want to do is hold her, cry with her, and let her know that not only is she the best grandmom in the world, but a great mom as well. My thirteen-year-old heart aches for her, empathizes with her because I miss Mom as well, but what is it like to lose a child versus losing a mother? I mean, that's what this is: loss, grief. She's not here now, and will never be. But I stay silent; I let her have her own moment and privacy. Someday I will let my mom know exactly what she has done to our family, and it won't be pretty.

After a nice morning breakfast, coffee for the two of them from the percolator and tea for me from fresh leaves, Justin is on his way back to Mexico. I plan on joining him at some point during this round of fieldwork. I truly enjoy the Sea of Cortez towns in Mexico. He only has five days left there, so I hope to head down soon. Dana is willing to drive me halfway to Mexico, once I make the commitment to go.

I love having Justin here, but getting him back to work is the only way I am going to be able to dig around in Dana's brain about the tragedy shadowing my mother's past, and to let her know about the Dreamwalk with Vex. Both are tragedies, yet the former is one that not only turned my mother's life upside down but also, ultimately, mine as well. I will never abandon my mother's quest to find my father, no matter how many issues with my own abandonment at her hands I have, but I sure as hell will use that threat as some leverage if I have to. I am hoping Dana will just come out with the details, but I have a feeling it is going to come at a cost to my muscles and yesterday's new scrapes and burns. They respond to this knowledge by sending a fiery protest through my body, in a way wincing at the thought of another onslaught. She is a big proponent of working hard before, well, before pretty much anything, so I have no doubt my mother's story will come at a price.

I take my time cleaning up after breakfast; this way I won't seem so eager to get information from her, and maybe, just maybe, curb her retaliation in the form of brutal training. It is late summer in the desert, so I can dress in shorts and a t-shirt during the day even though the nights are cool. I slip on my boots, tuck my hairpins inconspicuously into an intricate twist, and step outside my camper, immediately dropping into a slight crouch and scanning the area. Dana sits at the picnic table, whistling and...what the hell...is she knitting? I inch my hand toward my head, ready to defend myself from what appears to be a new stealthy way of hiding some of her super-dangerous weaponry. Nothing to see here folks, just a little old lady knitting a bonnet and then bam, a limb goes flying off into the distance.

Her voice stops my hand on its rise to defend myself, which instead tucks a stray curl behind my ear.

"Come and sit down, Alexis. I think it's time somebody told—or rather showed you—the truth about what happened to your parents. The only reason you never knew before was for your own protection, but I think you've found plenty of danger on your own, so what's a little more red on your ledger? Might even make you stronger, in my opinion. Holding that resentment and anger toward your mother deep down inside will only weigh you down. Let's bring a little understanding and enlightenment to your life, shall we? I don't think there is any harm at this point. I'm sure my dear friend JoAnna, your grandmother, would agree if she were here."

With a clink and a shush of fabric, Dana drops her knitting into her bag next to her fold-up camping chair. In its place, she pulls out a silver object, nearly as big as a shoe, solid looking, menacing, and charming all at once in the shape of a stunning fox.

"Is that Vex?" I ask Dana. Dang, that little imp gets around, doesn't he?! "Did he pose for you or something? It looks just like him." She waves her hand at the air, shushing me.

"Don't get sidetracked dear; we have work to do. Now, what better way to tell you what happened than to show you and this little spitfire." She points at silver Vex and strokes his head with her finger. I shit you not, I swear he sneers! Yep, it is Vex all right.

"Vex owed me a favor, so he allowed me to forge an idol after him to help us on our Dreamwalks. We're going to watch something that happened in the past. We'll be able to see first hand the source of your mother's strife, and judge for ourselves what happened. Your mother could never really recount every detail of that day your father was lost to her. Post-traumatic shock I think the Healers called it, but perhaps she just didn't want to tell the entire story to anyone. Remember: judge not lest you be judged, my dear, for she was merely a child, the youngest in the group at nineteen. She and your father were newly married, and in love. We do crazy things for love, and even crazier things when it is lost."

I shudder at the amount of energy I pull from the earth in my eagerness to dive into this Dreamwalk, to finally have the answers about my mom's past. I can't help feeling annoyed about how much of my life has gone by without knowing, and whether knowing would have helped me? Or her? What was the 'big bad' anyhow? I mean, it couldn't be that terrible, could it? I shiver again and this time it isn't from excitement, but from a sense of warning that pulls my attention to the Vex statue. I swear he is staring right at me. Dana snaps me out of my paralyzed moment of dread with her 'let's have at it' stare.

"Well, Miss Thing, are you ready? Or are you going to come over and start talking to this hunk of metal like you do that real finicky fox friend of yours?" She is right: time to get prepared for this. It is what I want, right?

"Okay, let's do this. Do I stand? Sit? Are we staying here out in the open?" She motions me to pull a chair up next to hers and to sit down. I am pretty sure a "shut up" was unspoken in the directions.

"Oh, we won't be exposed, dear; we'll just watch." She flicks back the head of the Vex figure like she was opening a Zippo. A cloud of white mist escapes from the opening and shimmers over us in a protective dome.

"That's better. I wasn't sure if it would work. This is the first time since Vex gave up the goods that I've tried it." Oh great, another guinea-pig moment for me. What's new? I have lots of tested-on spots all over my body by now. I should be getting paid or at least getting health insurance seeing as how I am working my good lovings off for this woman. I train day in and day out, trying to become the Earthen Protector everyone wants me to be; that incudes myself, right? All I can do is sit patiently on the edge of my seat, not knowing what to expect. Thankfully, she begins to speak again.

"All right, now the real fun begins!"

Before I can get a "wait" or "I should have peed" out, I feel a tug on my temples, like a light suction, a subtle touch of pressure and then a yank. Yep, I am going to be sick. We whoosh in a circle within the dome; I grip my chair with white knuckles as we spin around like Disney Tea Cups. I seriously think we are going to take flight, but instead, the world around us begins to fade, and a new one drops in as though brought to us. I can see the familiar surroundings of the Colorado National Monument, near Grandmom's land in Colorado. Towers of rock loom over us; the sun is getting close to beginning its true display of color in fantastic desert sunset fashion. I'm just getting my bearings when I hear voices and instinctively take a defensive tackle's crouch behind my chair. Ya, like its vinyl measiliness is going to protect me.

"Ease up there, Bruce Lee, no one can see or hear us. We're merely observers on this ride." She cackles at me and places Silver-Vex in her bag before taking out a canteen and taking a swig, of what I do not know. She offers it to me, but I shake my head emphatically. This is already trippy enough. I don't need any of Dana's special anything at the moment. Besides, I have a few words for her chuckling ass.

"Well, maybe a little heads up on how this is going to work would have been nice!" I snap. "It's not like we just did this yesterday. Or ever, for that matter." I know it's the anticipation making me tense. Dana's method wasn't really a surprise and even though I may get bruised and battered from time to time, I know I am always safe with her. I think...

The voices come from over a small rise, so Dana and I begin to walk toward the ebb and flow of the excitedly happy tones. I am pretty sure that we are far into the trail of the Monument, so there is no mistaking what lies ahead.

This is the Devil's Kitchen Trail, the rock formations unique and powerful. I tingle from the unique and familiar feelings of Gaia's Earthen energy, not only in the desert floor, but also from the four figures huddled together on the massive rock centerpiece. Towering over the boulder that is big enough to easily fit the four young adults are natural pillars forming the desert's version of skyscrapers. It is both awe-inspiring and, at this moment, unsettling as some of the power signatures on that boulder are wired so hot that it is obvious that they are capable of great and terrible things.

My mother's blond hair drifts above her head, forming a stunning vision of twinkling blond stars in sunlight-tickled strands. A strong, tanned hand smoothes down the strands before resting on her side and pulling her close to a man's body. She eases in comfortably, and my breath catches. This is my father; I know it in an instant. I can't help myself, and apparently my feet can't help me either as the bumbling idiot that I am nearly bites it into solid rock as I make my way down the trail to get a closer look. I mean, can you blame me? I have never seen this man in the flesh, this man of my flesh. His long dark hair tumbles around his eyes, thick locks of brown. I touch my own hair knowing that I am his child; I have his hair, his lips and his...I gasp at the sight of his green eyes. Those familiar orbs are intensely staring at my mother and the feeling of love he is giving off toward her is enough to take my breath away and to understand what this man means to her, and why she fell apart when he was gone.

"Okay, lovebirds, do you think you two can focus on something other than each other for a second? Are we going to do this or not?" The source of the voice grates on my nerves, not only for its interruption, but also for the obvious fact that the bad and powerful mojo I am picking up is primarily radiating from him, the other guy. Why is my mother here with this creep? Can't she tell he is bad news?

"Why is my mother here with that creep? Can't she tell he is bad news?" I speak out loud this time, shaking my head and berating my mom with my eyes. A hand lands softly on my shoulder. I jump at Dana's touch even though I know she is here.

"The redhead next to your mom is her best friend Gillian, and that boy whose intentions you are rightfully questioning is Gillian's boyfriend Bryan. Your grandmother was never a fan of your mother's friends, aside from Alexander that is; perhaps she sensed something in Bryan as well. These four were inseparable since they were kids; all very bright, but like most young adults they could be reckless and stuck in their own worlds and desires." Part of me feels she is also talking about me.

"You have to remember that you're a very strong, observant Earthen Protector, and a Healer. You can sense things that others, who may have been the strongest of us at the time, couldn't even pick up on. I agree that Bryan appears to be more than just an annoying twit, but regardless of what we think now, they were close friends and they obviously trusted each other. Plus, your mother has a lot of mixed wiring going on at this moment." Dana glances down at my mother. I follow her gaze and see my mother carefully hold and at times, caress her stomach. She is glowing and smiling, I mean really fucking smiling like I have never seen her smile before.

"Are you shitting me? Am I in there? I'm here? Well, I guess kind of here right now? Aren't two worlds going to collide into cosmic destruction or something?" Dana places her hand on my arm before responding.

"Easy there. You've seen way too many movies. You're like a little zygote in there, so there's no chance of you meeting yourself; not today at least." Ha, ha, isn't she funny? I, on the other hand, can't stop staring at my mother, at her hand touching where I would continue to grow, and my stunned realization that whatever happens right here, right now, I was a part of it on some level.

"Does he know? My dad, I mean. Do any of them know?"

"Alexander doesn't know. I think if he had known there'd be no way they'd have been out here. And your mom—there was no test. She's barely even five weeks along, but she knows all the same and is waiting for the right time to tell him. He wanted to come out here. The four of them have been waiting all year for this exact time, with the full moon and the setting sun, to do their test. This has to take place today, and she seems to be the strongest of them all, so if they're going to practice, to experiment, she has to be there." I take a breath with her pause, and then Dana continues.

"Your father always wanted to sway power our way, to help tip the scales in our favor. Loving your mother makes him want to ensure her safety. Alexander struggles with his identity as a Healer. He so wants to take a more active role in the fight as a Protector. When he found two strong Earthen Protectors in your mom and Bryan, they became his inspiration to bring forth a weapon that generations of Earthen Protectors had always viewed as being off limits. Your father was the brain behind the movement of the then-young Earthen power-wielders. They pushed to allow the use of stealing the Earthen powers from others, as a weapon against the Absolute Protectors."

I take this information in and reel at the thought of taking away someone's power. Steven took mine and I have never felt so powerless, scared, and empty. My grandmother had explained this weapon of choice by the Absolute Protectors and that they aren't afraid to use it on even their own kin.

Dana continues her tale to prelude what I am watching play out.

"Your father hit a lot of resistance from the elders in the Council all around the world who felt that type of ability was only for the Absolute Protectors and was what kept us apart from the power-hungry dark side. They didn't trust that it wouldn't instantly turn the user evil or insane. Bryan was the ideal person to latch on to because his family comes from a very strong, powerful lineage, and he was always open to trying new things. He and your father thought they could find a way to cripple the Absolute Protectors' power this way if they could only prove that it wasn't as evil a use of our Earthen magic as the elders feared."

Dana's explanation sends a shiver up my spine at the thought of these four naïve, barely out of their teens, adults tangoing and experimenting with this level of power, in a place that is always spiked with high levels of Earthen energy. I should know because I used to visit here as a child, and I always felt that an unusually high concentration existed here. It was what kept drawing me back to the place. Drifting back to my childhood reminds me that I am/was growing inside one of the women on that rock, who is about to do something foolish, and most of all, dangerous.

I don't even know for sure what is about to happen. I start to get mad at the Stacy Conner just sitting there as if there isn't a care in the world. Frustration builds within me with the knowledge that I was growing inside her, and that I know something terrible is about to happen that I can't prevent; something so terrible that my mom won't be able to stand ever being truly herself again. I know we had different teenage years. She didn't go through what I went through. She didn't have that innate mistrust and fear. No, my mom was living life, loving life, and being the teenager I could only read about in my psychology books. No worries, no regrets, and an undeveloped brain!

"Okay! Okay, Bryan! Hold on a second." It is my dad's voice, and he turns to my mom.

"Are you sure you want to try this, Stace? You said you weren't feeling very well earlier. We can always wait."

"No, we can't." Bryan's rude, overly eager ass chimes in. "What's happening with the planets and the earth's core right now only happens once a year. We would have to wait a whole year, right Gill?" Gillian, who looks to be busying herself picking at her nails, is in la la land, and needs a jolt to pay attention. Bryan gives her a pinch on her side, causing her to laugh out loud and smack at him. She must think he is horsing around. All I see is a horse's ass, if you ask me.

"Ya, ya, Bryan, that's right. I've researched it over and over. Tonight is the night, or we wait another year maybe even longer." Well, at least Gillian seems to be book smart. I'm not so sure about the rest of her. I have no idea what this planet and earth core thing is they are all talking about, but it seems to end my dad's protest as the group proceeds with their plan.

Alexander, my father, stands up and stretches. He is over six feet tall, muscular, and handsome. I feel a sharp pain pull at my heart, of loss, of something missing. I don't know if I can watch the rest of this. I start to breathe fast and suddenly feel dizzy. I sit down and watch, horrified, knowing something is about to start, as the other three stand around. Bryan speaks up, and it takes everything in me not to attack the shit out of him in a pointless and wasteful manner. Hell, attacking Bryan would make me feel better.

"Okay, Stacy, you first. You can pull a little power out of all three of us to see if it works. We should be able to do this safely, just to practice in case we ever need to defend ourselves against the Absolute Protectors and prove to the elders once and for all that knowing how to use it won't turn us evil. Stacy is the strongest, as of now, so she'll pull a little from me before I take it back from her. If that all goes well she'll try it on the rest of you. Alexander can heal himself and then the rest of us, so no harm done. If we can do this, we can prove to the others that this is a fighting skill worth using and not something to be afraid of. Why should we fear what the Absolute Protectors can do to us? Shouldn't they be afraid of us doing it to them? I mean, bind them away? How permanent is that really?" Humph, I can answer that one for good ole Bryan...surprise: it's not permanent at all.

Gillian, Bryan, and my father stand on one side of the massive boulder and my mother on the other. She speaks, looking mainly at my dad.

"Let me know if it hurts too much, and I'll stop." They all nod in agreement and my mother concentrates, hands flexing toward the earth as red sand lifts off the ground and Bryan's hair begins to float from his taut body. I am watching my mother siphon energy out of Bryan. It is just as horrifying to see as when Vex and I watched the woman Healer on the rocky beach during last night's Dreamwalk. Here, Bryan's eyes are bulging, as are his muscles, but he speaks to my mother.

"Don't stop, Stacy, keep going; I'm fine." But my mom is hesitating like she knows something is wrong.

"Something feels weird...what is that, Bryan? Do you feel it?" Before she can continue, a massive, bright white light bursts from Bryan's chest, there is screaming, and his hand reaches out for Stacy. My mother backs away, and Alexander makes a move toward her. In that agonizing second, the white light lacing from Bryan connects with tissue, but not my mother's, my dad's, and he too is instantly set afire with the light. It begins burning through his chest, tearing out of his eyes in a lancing hot intensity. I can see him trying to fight it with a yellow, glowing light, but as a Healer he can only mend but so fast as the blaze consumes him.

"Stacy, stop!" Bryan wails. "What are you doing, Stacy? Stop!" But my dad only turns to look at Bryan, his hands reaching for him, reaching to try and grip around his neck. Gillian is screaming, but my mother, she is just trembling and falling like a slow motion drop of water to the earth. There is no power coming off her any longer, but still the fire burns. It burns until Bryan and my father are no more.

There isn't a single trace of them, no ash, no smoke. No. This was the work of some terrifying magic that leaves no trace. Someone meant this scene to look like a use of power gone wrong, but I tingle with knowing awareness. Now that I know Dad isn't dead, this was clearly an excellently manufactured falsity.

Gillian's screams fade to a muffled sobbing before she turns to my mother. She is raging with power. As she makes her way to Stacy's crumpled body, she unleashes a tirade of unforgivable tongue lashes at my mom.

"Stacy! What the fuck have you done? You killed them, Stacy! Why? You said you could control it! You said you and Alex have done this before! They're gone! They're gone because of you!" My mother looks up at Gillian, tears spilling down her face in a blue glow as her power lingers in the droplets. Gillian slaps her hard across the face and runs away.

I want to run to Stacy, to my mom, to hold her and tell her dad is alive, that she didn't do this. It had to be Bryan. I could sense treachery in him. He planned this all along, and I won't rest until I find out if he is still alive. If he isn't a corpse, I'm going to make him pay.

Truthfully, all that matters at this moment is that I can't help my mother. I can't save my mother from her past.

As I witness my mom move her hands to her belly, she touches me and tears begin to fall again down her face. Watching that snapshot of time, I know that my mother not only blames herself for what happened this day—she blames me, too.

CHAPTER 5

The Brightest Sun

Journal Entry:

The sun is mercilessly bright in the summer sky of the Western Colorado Desert. Most wouldn't dare venture out mid-day on a hike in the Monument, but I am not most people, and I am banking on having my special place all to myself.

The air around my skin is so dry I swear I can feel the moisture being forcefully removed from each and every one of my pores. Bear's paws are touching the ground lightly as he alternates them as quickly as he can to evenly distribute the blistering heat radiating from the red dirt. He worries me as I notice how he also skirts around the small amount of shade close to rocks and low-lying brush. I had asked him to stay home, but he wasn't having it, howling and jumping on the door to come along. To be even more self-destructive, Bear keeps refusing water, so I speed up alongside him, pouring water into my hand and rubbing it along his head, ears, and neck. He doesn't stop for even a second though, his eyes on the awe-inspiring rock formation ahead. I, too, am eager to reach the large boulder set in the center of massive, redstone pillars, standing formative and tall; intimidating protectors circling the gigantic stone at Devil's Kitchen. The stone can hold six adults easily, but today, it is going to be little ole thirteen-year-old me.

This place always seems to ooze Earthen energy. It is easy to cast my power into the desert land and pull the Goddesses' energy into my being. I feel stronger

43

here, more alive, and for some reason, a little ashamed at how much I enjoy the extra power boost. Aren't the Absolute Protectors the power-hungry, evil ones? I shake the thought away, knowing this place is a pure source of Gaia's energy, and where better to practice than at a source this potent?

My hair feels incredibly sweaty even in the long ponytail and baseball cap that keep my curls at bay, the hat becoming more of a hindering sauna than protection. I remove the little cotton furnace and my glasses now that I am in the shade of the natural skyscraper-like structure. I give Bear some water before climbing up on the cool, stone boulder.

Bear and I are alone, as I had hoped; the business of tourism dies off in the afternoon's intense desert heat. I take my time climbing on the boulder, looking for subtle differences and proof of erosion. The pillars wrap around me stoically, giving the area a cave-like feel. I lie down on my back, making sizzling noises with my mouth as my hot skin touches the cool roughness of the rock. For a few minutes, I take in slow, deep breaths, enjoying the quiet silence of the summer desert. The last six months have been rough. At first Grandmom seemed to have fully recovered from her dizzy spell, but then the cancer diagnosis came and her health started to worsen quickly. I hadn't known she had been given a liver transplant before I arrived, over four years ago. I should have known, what with all the pills she took, that the cancer might be in remission, but she had to maintain the new organ in her body, which required anti-rejection medication. All those prescriptions lowered her immune system and limited some of our travel. She is home resting now, and for me, this is the kind of therapy I need to take my mind off my fear of the inevitable—losing someone else I love and being left alone.

I send my awareness outward again and easily find the pool of energy seeping through the stone, dirt, and sand. Bear's panting can be heard below me as he eagerly drinks the water I provided him in his canvas bowl. He stops mid-lap when the pull of my power causes a small cyclone of wind to pick up, blowing gritty particles of red dirt and sand into my eyes. I am glad no one is here because even though I drop my secretiveness when I am alone, I didn't mean to do that!

I can feel the tiniest hints of Earthen energy in the living organisms around me, from the prickly cactus to the snakes and lizards sunning and milling about. My senses pick up on a small body moving toward me, and I chuckle as his squat form propels him into view. The horny toad makes his way closer to me, the horns above his eyes and down his back shaking back and forth as he skitters to a stop, checking me out before hustling to me again. I have an affinity for these little reptiles, so I call him to me and place my hand palm up for him to crawl upon. I raise him to my face to take a closer look at his dragon-like appearance. His gray body is accented with pastels in blues and yellows. What a formidable creature he would be at a larger size. Scarier than the cartoon dragon Maleficent transforms into as her last-ditch attempt to keep Sleeping Beauty in her nightmarish state.

He looks back at me, eyelids clicking as they move upward to close and then reopen. He is certainly getting mighty comfortable where he is, so I start to talk to him about his day as if he can hear me, his head tilting from side to side in a questioning manner. Bear huffs, and what I think is puppy jealousy suddenly turns worrisome as I pick up on a shift in the Earthen power, right before I hear the voice.

"Wow, it looks like you've got him trained. Is he a friend of yours?" The suddenness of the masculine voice nearly has me tossing Mr. Toad into his own version of a wild ride. I compose myself after a stern look from my tiny dragon and lower my head, telling him silently to scurry along. He stares back at me for a second, puffs his body a bit to show off his horns, and then he is gone. My startled state quickly turns to annoyance, not only at this stranger spoiling my private time, but also the fact that I obviously did not pick up on his presence. I take a moment to assess this guy. There is no doubt he is tall and his blond hair is shocking, especially against his bright blue handkerchief that is serving as a sweatband. The wind picks up a bit, by itself this time, but Bear gives me a disapproving look anyhow. I give him one in return before looking back at the man. The wind does its damage as the man turns to shield his eyes, mumbling something about damn contacts and fidgeting with his sunglasses before placing them back on his face. He turns back to me and lifts his hands in a placating manner.

"I didn't mean to interrupt you. I'm usually lucky enough to have this space to myself when given the free time. I guess I should have figured out that at some point I'd be caught off guard by a dragon-taming little girl." Oh, so he has jokes? Great. Does this mean Mr. Intrusive is going to try to stay and chat? Even though I am tall and strong and Grandmom has me training in self-defense, I'm not going to linger around with anyone, even with my skills and Bear. After overhearing Grandmom and Mom's conversation, I know I need to keep my power hidden even more now. He must be picking up on my concern, as he moves further away from me before taking his pack off.

"You don't mind if I take a bit of shade and water, do you? I promise I'm of no danger to you; if that even matters coming from a stranger." I shake my head before answering, hoping after his drink he will go away.

"That's fine. Bear and I could take you anyhow, or at least outrun you." Why was I joking with this guy? He already has my spidey senses tingling, wondering if there is a possibility that this isn't a coincidence, but after overhearing that phone call I am always on edge.

He laughs out loud at my proclamation, but also shakes his head knowingly.

"Undoubtedly, young lady, I am not the young man I used to be." His smile shows a hint of relief. Part of me wonders if that is due to worrying he had frightened me, or because I am interacting with him. He is a large man, but I am not intimidated. Bear eases closer to the boulder, staring at the man who turns to take a sip from his canteen before doing some stretching.

I hate myself for staring when his right pant leg lifts and I notice his prosthetic leg. Instantly, I feel ashamed for taunting this man. Shit, he is probably a war hero or something. Bear doesn't seem the least bit on edge. In fact, he keeps stealing glances at the man and sniffing the air, wagging his tail, and then staring up at me. I incline my head toward the man, giving Bear the signal to go ahead and check him out.

"I hope you are cool with dogs since one is headed your way." The echo-enhancing surroundings cause my voice to come out as more of a roar than my intended shout-out. I wince at the volume for an instant and then straighten up, not wanting to appear waifish. He smiles in my direction as Bear heads over at a trot, easily closing the twenty feet of distance between the center boulder and the framing pillar against which the man is leaning. The blond stranger intrigues me. I don't interact with many people, unless it's required at school and during sports, but when I do, it's typically with adults. I don't seem to relate well to kids my own age. Of course, what teenager thinks they are understood, let alone relatable?

The man looks at me first, and then down at Bear, allowing him to sniff his hand before stroking his large, soft, black head. In response, the man is greeted by a propeller-like tail wag that shakes Bear's entire body, and of course, a sloppy Labrador grin topped off with a lick of the hand. My so-called protector and brother is turning to mush! What a traitor! Instead of showing my displeasure at Bear, I turn away, jump off the boulder, grab my bag, and walk off in the opposite direction, toward the sun. I keep my power on alert, hovering over Bear, and keeping a read on his emotions. One can never be too paranoid, right?

After fitting my hat to my head and my sunglasses over my eyes, I call over my shoulder.

"It's all yours! Let's go, Bear."

I don't hear the soft drift and downfalls of his large paws following, so I turn around to assess the situation. Bear's big brown eyes can be seen clearly despite the distance between us of some thirty feet. He looks from me to the stranger, wagging his tail. When I call to him again, his crazed puppy nonsense kicks in as he dances between the man and me, trying to play with us. I have never seen this behavior from Bear with anyone he doesn't know, and even with someone he does know, it is few and far between. Guess I am to blame for that, being not very social myself. Maybe this display by Bear is due to his annoyance with our solitude. Just in case, I send a stronger tendril of power out toward the man, searching him out again, testing to see if I can sense whether he is an evildoer, or maybe even an Earthen Protector like me.

As soon as my power reaches the boulder that is splitting the distance between us, confusing sounds and indistinct voices invade my mind, seemingly coming from the boulder. It is almost if they are creating a wall, not allowing me to get past and reach the man. I have tested this boulder with my powers plenty of times, pulling from it, even casting away objects into different dimensions while sitting upon it, and not once have I ever experienced something like this. I stare at the man, wondering if he is the wild card here and if so, is he a friend or foe? My mind triggers my body onto the precipice of fight or flight. Bear and the stranger could care less about what I am experiencing. They are engrossed with each other, the man crouching down to Bear, smoothing his large head and talking to him about being a 'good boy' and asking where his ball is. While these two engage in their little bromance in the shade, my mind is reeling as the noises swarm around in my head like devilishly loud mosquitos. The sounds become louder and the voices clearer. I can make out screams, a slap, and the agonizing tones of a heart breaking, drowning in gasps of air and fits of crying. At the crescendo, an intense wail breaks through all the other maddening vibrations, breaking them into nonexistent pieces. My connection to Gaia also breaks and immediately my muscles clinch tight, causing my body to shake as I reach slowly for my water, trying to calm myself.

Bear moves away from the man and toward the sounds of my water splashing around in the canteen. I can't be certain whether he was put into motion by his own thirst, or if he realizes the state I am in as water misses my mouth and splashes onto my face, my arms, and my hands, which are shaking uncontrollably as the memory of the screams and sadness become physical entities, pulsating through my very core. I feel like I have heard all that madness before, somewhere, somehow, but my thirteen-year-old brain knows I would have remembered something that disturbing, had I been a witness. That tortured pain was someone's, and it had all happened here. Maybe it happened since the last time I was here, but something inside me has a feeling this was an old occurrence, and one that somehow seemed to include me.

I return to the shade, moving toward the boulder, hesitant to touch it at first, but it is apparent that whatever had seeped from its immoveable body has now gone. Though there is no way I am tapping into Gaia's Earthen energy around it again anytime soon, if ever. Bear follows me and I give him some water, and then place my hand on the boulder, feeling its coolness. My shaking finally subsides to a small tremor. Bear gazes up at me with curious and worried eyes, nudging my hand and continuing his back and forth eye movements between the man and me. The stranger must have finally noticed something was off with me and he calls out, moving slightly toward me as he speaks.

"Are you okay? Do you need some help?" I remove my hat and sunglasses; their sheer weight are making the fierceness of the experience worse, and my head is as hot as the coals in Grandmom's grill.

"No, I'll be okay, just a hot day." My hair is falling loose from my ponytail; dark curls dance around my face in the breeze as I turn toward him to give him a hard smile. There is no way a stranger is going to come near me, let alone have a pity party for me. When I meet his eyes I see a fleeting look of surprise, followed by relief. It was so quick I doubt many others would have even noticed. He instantly turns from me, and I feel exposed, like I have given him something he wanted and needed, without my consent.

Looking down at my hands, I am greeted by my reflection in the lens of my sunglasses. I nearly drop them when I see the small blaze of green flaring in my eyes. I quickly put them back on before looking again at the stranger with his missing leg and bright blond hair. Did he see? Was that the reason for the emotions that dashed across his face?

He mimics my action, hiding behind the mask of his glasses. Standing still as stone, I can tell he is assessing me. Sweat drips down his temples and one solitary drop moves down his cheek. The quiet between us is tight with tension, not of fear, but of wondering.

"Best be off then. I don't get much time to linger. Maybe we will cross paths again one day. So long Bear; take care of your friend now." He turns his back to us and moves from the cool shadows into the bright sun. What a weird day this is turning out to be. My trembling eases off completely while the echoes of the furor and sorrow strengthen. I nearly feel myself start to cry, but I won't allow it with Blondie still in hearing range.

The man spins back toward me one last time before he disappears from sight.

"Oh, and Alex, you should be more careful. No one should be able to sneak up on you as I did. Even if they are of your own blood."

The wind picks up before my mind and body can fully register what he just said. I make a move to chase after him, but small stones and dirt blast through the protective circle of tall stone and I kneel to the ground, covering my face for a moment. I don't know what I am thinking as I run from the enclosed space and haul ass after him. Bear is right behind me and Gaia's power rushes into my being as I prepare to confront this man, this man who is obviously not as much of a stranger as I thought. I break through the shade and into the brutal heat of the sun. Even though I knew it was coming, the blast of light from the sun catches me off guard. The world feels as if it is tilting and I stumble, letting go of my hold on the Earthen energy in order to focus on staying upright, while looking in the direction the man seemed to be headed when he spoke those words. When he said my name.

I catch a glimpse of his blond hair in the distance. Damn, he is fast. He looks back at me one last time, removes his glasses, and I glimpse the sun's *yellow fire ablaze in his eyes. My mouth begins to open, but abruptly closes as the light grows incredibly fierce and I have to shield myself by turning away and crouching protectively next to Bear. The last thing I hear is his voice over the roar of the fiery light.*

"I don't have much time to linger, young one. Watch your back, Alexis."
When the intensity subsides I rise and turn back, only to find that the blazing light and the mystery man have disappeared without a trace.

Bear and I book it to get back to the trail; we both run faster than I ever thought possible for our small bodies to manage. I call my Grandmom's friend, Wendy, for a ride home. She drove us here but seems surprised I am ready to go home already. When we finally make it home, Grandmom is in her window seat, her head resting against the warm window pane, a smile spread across her face as the sun's heat makes her cheeks and hair glow like an angel. What is she going to say or do when I tell her about the man at Devil's Kitchen? A man who obviously knows who and what I am? I haven't thought this all the way through. I only focused on running as fast as we could to get home. Now that I am here, I freeze. What if she makes us move? What if we have to leave, and I lose another home? Where would we go? Would we be even further off the grid? Maybe to Arizona where her best friend lives, or to Montana where there isn't even any cell service? Am I ready for my life to be turned and tossed upside-down again? I mean, if the man meant to do me harm, why didn't he drop the hammer on me right then and there? Maybe he is watching over us, like a guardian angel. Grandmom breaks into my reverie, changing the course of my future forever.

"Well, dear, I think it is time to go. Please call Wendy back before she gets too far down the Monument." She squeezes my hand, and I see the pain and exhaustion in her eyes. I know the fight is over for her, for us. I look blankly at my phone and make my way to her room while I dial Wendy. After grabbing her hospital bag, my legs move on their own accord as I zombie march to my room where I absent-mindedly pack some items, knowing I won't be leaving her side while she has her final moments in hospice.

"What the fuck was that?" The vinyl and metal camping chair sails off behind me after I leap from it as the vision of my mother and her happy band of crazy-ass misfits subsides. The trip back in time to the origin of my mother's self-created turmoil and subsequent nomadic and drug-addicted nature has royally screwed with my heart and mind.

"She blames both of us. Her own reckless and stupid decision and the growing baby inside of her which, wait for it...was me!" I toss out the last two words like a rocket, pointing at my chest and struggling to hold back tears. Did my mother secretly hate me? Well, when I look back, maybe I am the only dimwit who didn't realize Mom's true feelings for me. I mean, she did abandon me, and that was after years of neglect and exposure to innumerable depraved situations no young child should witness. All along I thought she loved me and cared for me the best she could. That we leaned on each other, that we needed each other. I defended her against my grandmother, social services, and rude foster parents. Now, I am stunned by the possibility that she lost the love of her life, my father, because of me. Dana breaks through my torturous mind race, walking toward me as if she was approaching a feral cat.

"Okay, now let's calm down a bit and take a few breaths. There you go. We don't know that you had anything to do with what happened. You were barely a zygote, hardly developing a brain at that time. I think perhaps something else was amiss. There were a lot of players in that scene we just saw, and the fact that we know your father is alive makes me wonder even more where he has been this whole time, and how he could have let you and your mother think he was dead." She is making some good points, and some I have been thinking about every day since I heard he was alive. How could he have left us grieving, and in my case, never having known him? The only way to find out is to find him, and somehow also look for the one I feel was really to blame: Bryan, my dad's faux BFF.

"Dana, are you going to call Mom today? I know this isn't something I can talk to her about over the phone, so we need to see her. I need to know if, when this happened, they ever even considered that he wasn't dead. Maybe Dad has been in another dimension? Oh, goddess, maybe in a hell dimension, like Steven? Maybe that's why he could never come to us. But even Steven had hall passes. I mean, for crying out loud, he was able to communicate with Greg all the time and we hear nothing from my Dad until now? Over twenty-six years later?" Of course, I have a feeling Valant is a rare Demon, one who seems to enjoy being in our world instead of his, so maybe he is looser on the reins.

"I don't know, Alex, but whatever the case, and wherever he has been, he's here now for some reason, and we need to help your mom find him. I'll call her today and tell her we need a pow-wow in person and soon. We won't drop the bomb about today's Dreamwalk until she's here, or she may never come. I'm sure she's been reliving that day over and over again in her mind since she found out your dad is alive, so Bryan may be on her list already, especially now that she's cleaner and thinking clearer than ever."

Dana hasn't mentioned my mom's lack of consistent sobriety much, but I am sure she is as nervous as I am that Mom might fall off said wagon again at any time. Stress can do that to the strongest of us. Dana smiles at me as if she knows exactly what I am thinking, and places her hand on my shoulder, moving closer for a side hug. She is always verbally affectionate, but physically, she is normally beating the shit out of me in our training sessions. Needless to say, I am uneasy at first, but then fall against her.

"I know this must all be a blow to you. How about some training to get your mind off it?" So much for a good cuddle and a cry. I nod my head in agreement and start to excuse myself.

"Oh, Alex, I'll tell her about the Healer's death you and Vex witnessed, so she senses our urgency to see her. She'll want to know more about that, I'm sure."

"Yes, I agree, that should help get her here."

Once in Dana's camper bathroom, I splash water on my face and look in the mirror. My eyes are vivid green right now, reflecting my father's eyes and not my mother's blue eyes. I place my sunglasses on my face and freeze, reaching back in my mind to the memory of the last time I was ever in Devil's Kitchen with Bear, of the stranger who knew me, who warned me, but didn't have much time to stay. I recall the blaze of yellow fire from his eyes before he disappeared; yellow and blue makes green, does it not? My mom's blue and my father's yellow visual manifestation of their power intertwined, forming my green vines with their union. Pictures, words, and feelings from that memory wash into me, along with the Dreamwalk Dana created, back in time at the exact same spot, and I know now without a doubt that the mystery man in the desert was my father. He was obviously injured, changed into someone unidentifiable, and perhaps until sometime before I saw him had been trapped in a hell he could not permanently escape. My father had tried to help me, warn me even, but I was too afraid of worrying my grandmother.

That day with Bear, the rock did something it had never done before and it was due to the presence of my father. Maybe he had been trying to tell me something the whole time, yet couldn't come right out with it. He was there on borrowed time; he even mentioned not being able to stick around. If I had not been told my whole life that he had died in an accident, maybe I would have picked up on this coincidence before. Now, knowing he is alive and seeing him in the Dreamwalk in all his glory before he was taken from us, I am sure he was the blond man in the desert.

A feeling blossoms in my heart, one I had never known, since I was born without ever knowing him, but I recognize it and it is love. Love for my father mixed with hope for our future together.

CHAPTER 6

A Rocky Point

Journal Entry:

How does an abuser face the abused day in and day out? Well, my abuser, the monster named Steven Nestrour, puts on his best suit and tie, and kisses his wife and daughter goodbye before touching my back with his disgustingly poisonous hand. His flesh sears into me, reminding me to keep my mouth shut with a promise of more pain and violation than I have already experienced. The power Steven has over my body and over me terrifies me every day. I have been invaded body, mind, and soul. Not only do I fear for myself, but I also fear for my foster sister Cheyenne. He has threatened that she will be his next target if I do not continue to submit to him. Even when I tried to fight him off, he paralyzed me with his powers and forced himself on me.

I am disgusted with myself, with my lack of ability to fight him off, with the fear I feel day in and out, and with my longing to leave this place forever. Not only does he hurt me, but I have also begun to hurt myself, cutting my body in places that are easily hidden. The self-inflicted violence covers the emotional pain I cannot live with. Yes, I have tried to leave with Bear. We even made it to the edge of the Nestrour's property once, but Steven always destroyed all hopes of escape. His powers as an Absolute Protector seem to have no bounds, and he preaches about soon leading the evil ones and getting rid of the Earthen Protectors for good, ridding this place of them and the humans who are lower beings, in his eyes. I shudder at his predictions, losing little bits of hope each day. I still do not know what I am to him, why he needed to seek me out in particular. Whatever his reasoning is, he isn't letting on, and only tells me repeatedly that I will know in time.

Just when I think I will never survive this, Bear shows me the way. I come home from school one day, Bear comes to the door, and I know Steven is home as well. Cheyenne runs inside and Bear comes out the door as she goes in. As Bear reaches my side, a growl begins to rumble in his body and I send the smallest trickle of power into him to calm his anger. I may be lost, but I'll be damned if I lose my dog as well. I flinch as Steven strolls toward me, but he seems unaware of the power I just used. If he had been, I would have either been punished on the spot, or at the very least threatened with future hell to pay once no one else was around.

However, Steven seems clueless, and I realize I have found a way to either mask my power, or do it at such a low level that he can't sense me. It was something he did to me the first time he revealed his true nature. I remember being so happy to find a foster family that could take Bear and me in, with acres of land in which to roam free. At least that was what I thought at first. Steven shattered all of those dreams by turning out to be a psychotic Absolute Protector.

If I can shield my power maybe I can use it against him somehow; maybe I can use it to sneak away. I've camouflaged myself in the past to appear like my surroundings when I practiced my powers while living with my grandmother. She was both furious and delighted at that trick, but what about Cheyenne? If he can do this to me, I know he will eventually do it to her. She is just a little girl. I can't let that happen to her. I couldn't live with myself if her innocence is taken from her, too. No, this isn't about running and hiding; it is time to turn this into vengeance and protection—the latter being what generations of my family were meant to provide. I am an Earthen Protector, after all, stronger than he thinks I am, and that will be my abuser's undoing.

After hours of training with Dana, the afternoon starts to peak and the desert becomes hotter; I feel spring may be leading into summer quicker than anticipated. I want to head down to Mexico to meet up with Justin after all this craziness, but I feel like heading down alone. Dana is cool with me taking the Jeep. Her four-wheeler is still intact, for emergencies, and I have a feeling she has some desert mirage batmobile hidden somewhere under a hillside if need be. I manage to shower fairly well despite the massive welts from hitting the ground a couple of times in the last half mile of a long run that was apparently Dana's preferred time to start sparring with me. She sent her inconspicuous daytime items flying at me: anything from rocks to metal flying balls and sticks.

The air feels amazing, tossing my untethered hair as I drive through the desert to the Sea of Cortez. The open Jeep and blaring beats from the radio set my heart afire with songs from Kaskade, Ed Sheeran, and Bob Marley, an eclectic mix without boundaries. I sent Justin a text before I left, stating I was on my way and heard back from him instantly. I'm sure by now he is knee deep in the waters or off in the middle of the sea on a tiny dinghy, registering various depths, saline content, and species. He won't be back by the time I arrive, but I know my way around by now, and I am looking forward to hitting up one of my favorite bars.

As I drive I wonder how different my life might be if I had let my grandmom know about the stranger in the desert who turned out to be my father. If I had only told her maybe I would have been safer, safe from Steven and Greg. Perhaps Dana would have been able to adopt me—not many places are safer than with the Weapon's Master and Grandmom would have been moved into action had she thought I was in even more danger. I wonder why Dana wasn't there to take me to begin with. Perhaps living with such a powerful Mistress of Earthen arts wasn't my grandmom's idea of a safe place for a child. I know Dana's life is very nomadic at times and a thirteen year old wouldn't have been able to tag along, not nearly as much I can now.

Instead, I was rendered powerless, my body and mind invaded by a man who had been stalking me down for years. If only I had made a different choice...and who would I be now if I had?

My reflection is turning my mood dark so I shake my head, trying to physically clear it as Puerto Penasco comes into view. I turn up the music and the tones and lyrics keep my mind from continuing to perseverate on the past. Anger is kept at bay, worry as well. I need to get into town first, and with a few shots of tequila and some beers, I plan to dig into my thoughts like a tick, teasing out my life and my past. I head right to Rosa's Cantina along the Sea of Cortez and instantly feel better as the saltwater air curls around my body and caresses my senses.

"Hola, Gomez. Patron and a shredded beef burrito smothered in Carla's salsa verde, por favor. How are the girls?" Gomez shoots me his bright white, winning smile, all teeth and twinkling eyes. He is about five foot four, round, and I swear happier than a pig in shit every time I see him. I envy his life sometimes, the owner of a small family restaurant located right on the beach. He knows how delicious his food is, and I swear he puts sprinkling fairy fun dust in his drinks. Liquor doesn't faze me, but this whole place revives and clears my mind. I have a plan this time around. A few too many and a joint Gomez passes to me in my bill is enough to get me ready to spend a few hours in my hotel room getting Vex's little ass here for a while. If anyone knows anything about everything, he does.

I've never truly summoned him before, but I think there is a way I can call him since each time I have seen him has been when I have been in some sort of altered state, whether from my own doing or by the numerous psychological states my crazy life has forced me into. There is too much going on right now for me to wait for him to help me. I may already be in too deep. What damage is he waiting for?

Bob Marley is cranked up as the sun begins its slow descent into twilight. What a beautiful night, hanging out on the balcony with the door open so the musical tones can drift in and out with the sea breeze. Long, shimmering curtains make rustling noises around me as they ride the waves of the air, seeming to dance with Bob's voice as he sings of love, solace, and three little birds of hope. I wonder if Bob might have been an Earthen Protector; he knew how to unite through his songs, to heal and fight away anger and fear. Maybe he was a mixture like I am, a Healer and a Protector. I move inside my room and light my little joint and get to work on getting Vex's bushy little ass into this dimension. I am not sure how this is going to work, but I am sure as hell going to try my best.

I take the bottle of tequila from the mini fridge and shake it up with cut limes and ice before pouring the drink into a glass. I take a few sips and then small pulls off the lit joint. I allow the smoke to play around my body before exhaling and returning to my balcony with the ice cubes clinking in rhythm with the lyrics of "Waiting in Vain." I lean against the balcony wall and close my eyes, letting my mind drift to Vex, soft fur, wild eyes, and pointed teeth. The pull on my energy is quicker than I thought it would be. I usually feel a small suction and then he pops into view. I smile, willing him closer when suddenly the warm breeze turns cold and the suction becomes stronger. There is no way he is coming to me; for some reason I am going to him, or going somewhere. Maybe it is the joint, but I become seriously paranoid. What if I am going back to the dream spot where the Healer was destroyed in front of my eyes? What if I am next?

The feeling of the cool Mexican tile disappears underneath my feet and is replaced with a feeling of warm, spongy moss. I crouch down as familiarity with my surroundings clicks around in my brain. A massive tree comes into view and mystical fairy light dances around me. It is black everywhere else I look, so I move around the tree, coming to an immediate stop when I find Vex lying still, slightly above the ground, cradled amongst the branches by the Tree Goddess herself. Terra isn't surprised to see me, but her eyes aren't exactly welcoming as her stress over Vex's situation shines through them in an intense glow of green, not unlike my own. Her gorgeous face is carved into the tree bark while the knots and crevices of the tree trunk define her hair. Terra's body ebbs and flows throughout the trunk and massive roots springing from the ground.

"Well, Elia, I guess your little trick brought you here at an opportune time. Now stop standing there staring and get over here and help Vex, or would you rather stand there while my moss and roots grow over your body?" I haven't been called Eila in a long time. It is my mother's real name for me, only truly coming from Terra and Vex's lips, or from the boy I know in my dreams. At her use of my name I move quickly into motion, crouching next to Terra and reaching for Vex.

"What happened to him, Terra? Will he be okay?" She allows me to touch him. His soft fur is wild with magic sparking off him and shocking my fingers.

"Vex found a way to track the Healers that were being attacked, early enough to attempt an intervention, the silly little mammal. I told him it was a fool's errand. I even told him to bring you, but he said there wasn't time and went on unaided." Vex, all alone against whatever the big bad is that is viciously taking down Healers. What was he thinking? I look at Terra before asking her more.

"You couldn't go with him? Help him somehow?" Terra laughs out loud, a sinister, yet somehow beautiful and even slightly erotic sound.

"I may be powerful, my dear, but I am trapped here, in this place of my own creation. I was however able to tell he was about to be destroyed and so I brought him back. He tried to shield that Healer boy and took a major beating, nearly beyond repair. But now that you are here, we can heal him together." I dread the question before it escapes my lips.

"And the Healer boy? Did he live?" Her face turns to the left and a low hanging branch becomes her arm; I follow it to the end of her finger where a body lies in the distance.

"I have stabilized them both; it seems their fates are intertwined for the moment—both must be saved or both shall die." I shiver at her matter-of-fact tone. Although I know she cares for Vex, something tells me getting him back to her wasn't easy. Terra seems slower than I remember, and she hasn't flitted to any other place along the massive tree that is her body.

I concentrate on seeking out Vex's injuries to determine if I need to repair or remove his injuries. The shallow breathing barely moves his body in any sort of rhythm, and his heartbeat is faint. His mouth moves slightly and his nose twitches; it is obviously all he can manage right now. As I seek out the source of his condition, I can see his fern-like powers try to rise from his fur, sizzling bright red and burning away before barely reaching the end of a single follicle. Something is burning him from within and the closer I get, the hotter I feel myself become. Darkness combined with fire greets me when I get near his injuries, deep in his mind. The red burn sizzles at his synapses and boils the chemical reactions; he is stuck in a state of lunacy, unable to break out. I pull on the fertile earth beneath me while Terra's wooden fingers entangle in my arms and hair.

"Now, my dear, we save him together." I am not prepared for the rush that comes through me. Pure, raw, Earthen energy sings through my body, feeling as if rocks, grit, and sand are pummeling me. It is as if I am being blasted away and tortured from the inside. I push the pain away, trying to trick my brain into thinking it doesn't exist, and concentrate instead on eradicating the flame within Vex's riddled brain. There is no way he is dying on me. I had somehow deluded myself that he couldn't ever die. That childish idealism works for me now as I refuse to let go of the power as it painfully races through me, taking out the flames that are attacking Vex.

I ease up slightly once I feel we have the upper hand, and pay for my mistake dearly as a searing, red-hot slap courses across my awareness, setting my mind afire for a moment. Terra's wooden fingers yank back on my hair and whisper viciously into my ear.

"Do not let your guard down again, Eila. The fire will find your weakness and take you next. Then what will you leave me with? A charred feral Chihuahua? Bones and ash of a Healer boy, and what of you? A drooling and worthless heroine who will never recover from her guilt and failure? Now, concentrate even if it tears your muscles and breaks your bones...I can always stitch you back up."

Terra's voice, frightening as it is, slides smoothly along my eardrums and motivates me to fight against the torturing flames and cease their damage once and for all. The power from Gaia and Terra herself sings into me at full throttle, and I allow it to take parts of me with it. I feel my shoulder pop, my back stinging as if a bullet hit my spine, but I keep my hands on Vex, refusing to let go. Seconds pass like hours, and Vex's breathing and heartbeat slowly begin to return to normal. His spitted curses don't shock me as much as his eyes, filling with tears that seem to hold gratitude and fear. He is my rock, and here I am saving him, something I hoped I would never have to do for real, but all the same, I feel honored to have been able to.

Vex allows me to gather him in my lap; even Terra leans in to give her version of a hug with the softest, mossy parts of her bark, touching Vex's face and soothing my shoulder and back where I have been injured.

"What happened, Vex?" Terra asks, still touching him as her fingers trail along his front legs to his paws. I had nearly forgotten the Healer boy when I hear a moan. We look toward him, watching him slowly rise to a seated position. He is definitely disorientated, but okay. Vex looks from the boy to us, somehow communicating to Terra without saying a word. She moves away from Vex and allows her roots to take an interest in the boy, making a bed of sorts in the moss as small flowers let off puffs of purple dust that instantly put him to sleep.

Vex looks back at me. "I had a theory that something or someone was targeting Healers, so Terra and I have been looking for a pattern. I made contact with the Healers' leader after another Healer was taken, and she and I agreed to meet at a designated spot. When I showed up, this boy was there instead of the leader. I guess with all the worry and anxiety going around, the boy was assigned to greet me with plans to take me to another location where the Leader and I would meet."

Vex tries to sit up a bit more, but falls back into my lap before continuing. "The Leader's paranoia was dead on, and we were attacked before we were even able to greet each other." He coughs a bit, triggering leaves from Terra's body to drift down toward his mouth, dripping hydrating fluid into his recovering body before he was able to continue.

"We need to contact their Leader immediately! There is no doubt now that they are being hunted down. This must be a plan by the Absolute Protectors to weaken us—it has to be." Terra shifts away from us, instead allowing her body to move into the middle of the tree, the bark swelling and shrinking as if she is breathing. I notice some of the leaves on her lower branches begin to shrivel and drop off. Apparently the amount of healing she bestowed on Vex has taken its toll. It is her throaty voice I hear next, agitated and sleepy sounding, the latter extremely unbecoming of the Tree Goddess.

"The Healers do more than impact us physically; they hit us mentally as well. If word gets out that they are being picked off one by one, the panic may keep the Healers in hiding, and in that case, everyone will suffer." Before I can get a word in, Terra seizes up, her green eyes rolling toward the back of her head. Small knots of her curled hair untangle and wildly fly all around her while the branches of her arms begin to fold against her chest, but the most frightening of all is the voice that echoes in my mind.

"Crushing metal and pain leads to chaos in dark waters, crashing waves and the screams. Alex, help, help! Alex, help!" Terra drops into herself for a split second before her body transfers into a higher hanging branch above my head. She hangs upside down, looking at me in that famous Tobey McGuire Spiderman pose; I only hope she doesn't try to smooch me. Her green eyes are hypnotizing, and the small branches that outline her hands and fingers began to twine through my hair and caress my cheek.

"Ah, my Elia, it's time for you to go. Two pesky men, or shall I say beings closely resembling real men will soon cause great damage for you in the Pacific Ocean of Baja, Mexico, while a man you love suffers in their wake. You must go now; gather your soldier, and be gone. Vex and I will work on this puzzle, and then we'll come to you once we have some answers." I blink at her, the closeness of her face making me cross-eyed and dizzy.

I shake my head, releasing myself from Terra's spell. In one quick motion, I turn and crouch next to Vex, my eyes searching his, while my power reaches out one last time to assess his well-being. Vex's foxy nose twitches as he looks away from me and then that annoyed-as-hell voice speaks up.

"Did you not hear the Tree Goddess, you silly girl? Stop doting over me like I'm some kit needing to suckle. Get out of here now! I'll come to you soon." The boy stirs in his nest. I have to admit, the child intrigues me, so I really want to stick around to ask him some questions myself, but obviously something is up. Whatever it is, I need to get my ass back to my world right now.

"Okay, Terra. Vex, I'll get back and check things out." I don't let Vex off that easy though. I hug him close and kiss his nose before rising and nodding to each of them respectfully. With my eyes closed, I concentrate on the feel of my hotel room, the sounds and touch of the linen curtains floating, and the sense of the chair underneath me as Bob's voice drifts in and out with the sea's wind. Soon I am back on the balcony of my hotel room, instantly shaken out of my fogginess by Justin's voice calling out to me as he enters the room.

"Alex? Wow, what a day! I know I need a shower big time, but after that, it's tacos and tequila with my girl." The Dreamwalk with Vex and Terra has left me feeling tense and a little scared. Justin's voice is comforting and instantly arousing, causing me to stand robotically and follow his voice as it trails into the shower.

My quiet steps into the bathroom and light touch of my fingers on Justin's naked back make his muscles jump in response, startling him. He turns and takes me into his arms, nuzzling my ear. I move deliciously against his body as it presses against me. He smells of the sea, dirt, and sand. I can't help but feel safe as stress and worry melt away in his arms. My hands wrap around his neck while his arms wrap around my waist. We look into each other's eyes for a moment.

"I had hoped to be a little cleaner before you saw me, but this is a much better plan. I've missed you." I nod in agreement into his neck, and allow my hands to travel down his back and take a better position on his muscular backside. I use my palms to pull him toward me even closer, positioning myself so his growing hardness pushes against my clitoris and peaks my need for him even further. There is something about my power practices, training, and now this Dreamwalk that leaves me feeling like I have a constant itch to scratch, and Justin has all the right ways to relieve me.

"Oh, Alex, you turn me on so quickly; I want you so badly." Moving my face from his neck, I find his lips and kiss him softly, parting mine slightly and letting his tongue explore me. I pull away abruptly and lightly slip the straps of my sundress off my shoulders, allowing it to fall to the floor. My lace bra is next and when he moves to help me, I back away from him with a wicked smile and slowly remove it. Justin watches me with a hunger in his eyes as I hook my finger around the side of my underwear and slip them to the floor. I mesmerize him, feeling powerful and sexy under his gaze.

"Turn the water on, and let's get you cleaned up, shall we?" My voice is a sultry whisper. I look him up and down, smiling at his cock's hardness, wanting to take him now, but also needing to let the fun we are having play out. As he puts his back to me to turn on the shower, I slide behind him and reach around to get my hand wet in the stream before taking him fully. He moans, and so do I as he grows harder under my touch and I imagine how he will feel inside me. I stroke against him while kissing his back and then release him to step around him and into the shower.

The shower is glass on all sides but one, with flattened rocks on the remaining side. The floor is smooth under my feet. I turn around and Justin is standing there watching me, needing me. I motion for him to come to me. As soon as he steps toward me, I kiss him hard on the mouth and then trail my kisses down his neck, chest, and stomach, coming to my knees before him in a sort of reverie to his deliciousness as I take him into my mouth.

"Shit, oh, Alex, ah, that feels so good. Oh, god." I pull back and smile at his pleasure, stroking him and running my tongue along his shaft, caressing him gently one moment and then tightening my grip slightly the next. The water's slipperiness makes the action even sexier as the wetness gives my movements ease. I take him into my mouth again, giving some pressure on the way down his shaft, twisting a little and allowing my tongue to play around him. Before I can go any further, he pulls me up under my arms and kisses me hungrily on the mouth and neck before taking hold of my breasts and teasing at my nipples with his tongue and teeth. The feeling is both pain and arousal at the same time. Justin's hand holds me closely, greedily, gripping my ass and pushing me against him. In response, I rub against him, my breath quickening as his hand winds around my backside and spreads me open slightly to slip his fingers into my warmth.

"Oh, Alex, you're so wet. I want to taste you and feel inside you all at once." I lift my leg slightly to give his hand easier access and hold myself up with my hands against the wall. He moves in front of me, diving his fingers in one second and playing with my clitoris the next. His other hand continues its tug and pinch on my nipples as his mouth moves from one to the other. I moan with pleasure as I feel pressure building in me, a reaction to his conquest. He allows one finger to explore other areas, something we haven't done before, but right now I am excited for his touch pretty much anywhere. He takes my lack of rejection as a go-ahead, and his fingers enter me in both places, making it hard for me not to come right there and then. It is a sweet pressure, and I aggressively move against him, pushing him further into me. He growls into my mouth and pulls my head back by my hair, forcing me to look into his eyes. His carnal need makes me pant, and I can't help myself as my hand reaches for him and strokes him hard as he continues fingering me deeply.

"Fuck me, Justin! Oh, please, I want you." He growls again, and as his fingers slip from me I turn my back to him and rise on my toes, tipping forward slightly to give his hard cock easy access. The tip of him eases into me and I shudder with excitement. He is slow at first, only barely inside before grabbing my hips and diving fully into me. I yell out in pleasure, pushing toward and away from the wall with my hands in time with his movement. My hips make circles, increasing the excitement in both of us as I clench inside, enjoying his sharp intake of breath. We both moan and stimulate each other continually until the build-up reaches its pinnacle and we both shudder and cry out at the sweet release. It soothes and sends tingles through my body and mind, washing away my worries and fears.

Justin falls slowly against me and I rise to hold myself fully pressed against the wall, shuddering in pleasure and enjoying his warm breath as he nuzzles into my neck and gives me sweet kisses. I turn around, looking into his eyes, and kiss him slowly and softly. I know he is going to say he loves me; it is right there in his eyes and on his lips. Once again, my fear of it spikes and I grab the soap and hand it to him with my most innocent and endearing smile to break the moment.

"Sorry for the interruption. I'm sure you still want to wash up." I kiss him quickly and open the door to the shower, then close it and his unspoken words behind me. What am I so afraid of? Haven't I been feeling closer to him as well? Seeing him in my dreams has me wondering if maybe my mind is making him the boy from my childhood, letting me know I can open my world to him, that maybe he would understand and accept my unique abilities. But then the dread creeps in and with it Terra's words about someone I love being in trouble, which allows reality to smack me right in the face. Maybe I can't allow myself to hear that he loves me because I don't want someone to love me who will inevitably be hurt by me, and the chaos surrounding me. My fear of loving him had lessened until this Dreamwalk and now I am on high alert again. Justin would get hurt and I don't know if I could ever fully ensure his safety. My world is all about war, power struggles, lost loves and lives.

As if on cue, my phone starts to ring, and with its tones I can hear the nightmarish march of what is to come—my senses fill me with dread. As soon as the ringing stops, it immediately starts up again. I know my fear of its urgency is warranted. My heart drops into my stomach as Terra's warning swarms in my head like wasps on a course to destruction. My own emotions had momentarily blocked out the dire warning from Terra, but now that I have shaken off the intensity of the Dreamwalk by throwing all my concern into sexually ravaging Justin, I feel selfish and dumb for not checking in with everyone sooner.

I rush out of the bathroom in just my towel and nearly bite it as my wet feet slip on the tile floor. Before I even hold my phone, I can see Carmen's name flashing across the screen and my stomach hits the floor. Awareness vibrates in my skull and a chill runs through my core as I realize that Shane is the one in trouble. Carmen and Shane are in Rosarito Mexico, on a romantic getaway, right on the Pacific Ocean. He is my friend for life and someone I dearly love. My throat tightens, but I manage to speak up when the phone line comes to life.

"Carmen, what's wrong? What's going on?" Her voice is nearly hysterical as it hits my eardrum and my eyes begin to well up as my heart thumps harder in my chest.

"Oh, God, it's bad! It's really bad, Alex. Shane is in the hospital. He's hurt really bad, Alex. I don't even know what really happened, but his car is totaled. Please Alex, come back. I need you; Shane needs you."

"I'm on my way, Carmen. I'm leaving right now. I promise he'll be okay." As long as I can get there in time, that is. Shane will be okay—he has to be.

CHAPTER 7

Going Back to Cali

Journal Entry:

The bright orange glow wakes me gently. The feel of my sleeping bag and the small pad under it are the only things between me and the thin layer of the tent that rests on the ground. Droplets have formed upon the tent wall, the ceiling, and along the sides. Some of them stay where they are, warmed by the sun, evaporating slowly into the air while others lose their fight to gravity and trickle down the tent to the ground. I smile as I eye the snails that have joined the droplets on the sides of the tent, clinging to the waterproof fabric, enjoying the sunrise and the quiet in the crisp mountain air.

This has to be a dream; I haven't been in this tent since before my grandmother fell ill again. I sit up slowly and look around; everything seems the same, down to the very detail of my tattered old sleeping bag, duffle bag, and even my grandmom. She isn't in here with me, but it feels like she has been—everything feels so real.

Suddenly the water droplets begin to combine like mercury on the top of the tent. The tent's orange glow intensifies to the point of being unbearable, causing me to flush and scramble out from the heat of the sleeping bag with the speed of a rabbit escaping her hiding place while under attack. I use my power to pull energy from the ground and into my being; I feel it fill my fingertips, arms, and core of my body. I reach for the zipper of my tent and slowly pull it up, wincing at the sound as I prepare to catapult out, ready for an attack. But the bright yellow glow that greets me feels familiar, so I stand and turn to face the source.

A man with bright platinum hair stands before the lake near my tent, favoring a leg and holding his hands stiffly by his sides. He appears to be shaking and my senses pick up on a high level of anger that is causing him to tremble like an earthquake.

"As I said before, Alexis, you need to watch your back. I can't do what I would like to do at the moment, which is to snap Steven's neck like the piece of shit twig he is, but at least I can give you this." Within the time it takes for me to take my next breath, I begin to fill with fiery pain. The intensity is too much and I scream in pain, but now the heat is subsiding to a pleasant warmth that fills me from head to toe. Well, it would be agreeable if I weren't scared to death of what awaits me. Yet before I can take another breath, the sensation completely disappears, along with the mystery man.

I look around, viewing the mountain range in the distance and hearing the soft lake waves lap against the shore. My eyes travel down to my hands, and I watch my green vines as they twine within my fingers and along my arms. I see a change as a yellow spark joins my vines, and I know I am more powerful than I have ever been before. I smile into the sunlight and close my eyes to take in the feeling.

All of a sudden the world spins, and I bolt upright in my room at the Nestrour's house. The feeling of power radiates through me again, along with a hope that maybe, just maybe, the time would be soon, and I would escape Steven for good. However, a new thought forms, one full of an alien anger and vengeance beyond my own. No, I think, escape isn't the one true plan any longer. No, he will pay for what he has done to me, and I will succeed.

I wake on the plane, a dream playing in my mind still. One of power, anger, orange glows, and a man I now know as my father, with his bright platinum hair not true of the young man who disappeared from my mother's side in Colorado years ago. Where is he now? Did he give me the power and the plan to finally escape Steven when I was fourteen? I had thought all that occurred that night in the Nestrour's house had been entirely within me, but now I think I know better. Now I know my father has helped me three times in my life. Once to heal my grandmom, once to warn me, and the third to give me power and a plan to escape the man who had manipulated, abused, and nearly destroyed me.

So here I am, heading back to San Diego. I still hope I will make it in time to heal Shane, but now I wonder if my self-confidence has ever been warranted. I mean, some of the most powerful things I have done have been with my father's help, my grandmother's help...Ryan's help. At the thought of him the ring around my neck becomes colder, heavier even. I know I am going to reach out to him when I arrive in San Diego. Something is at play with the Shane situation and I need his help, no matter how much I wish I didn't.

I have already contacted Sandra as well, asking her to use her Seer skills to find out what happened to Shane. She told me when I was leaving Phoenix that she was heading to the hospital, that she needs something of his to really make a connection. Dear goddess, I hope it doesn't turn out to be a body part or something else of equal creepiness. I still barely understand her powers, and being forced to leave in the midst of just finding out about her being a Seer isn't helping. It isn't truly a topic for a nice Facetime chat or text.

I feel guilty for not being in San Diego with all my friends. Maybe if I hadn't left, Shane would be okay. Although I have a feeling that no matter where I was, this would have happened, and it may have everything to do with me. Mom's lifestyle as a lone gypsy is that way for a reason. What I am—what we are—is dangerous, and having people we care about only puts them at risk.

Since Carmen and Sandra are finishing up at the hospital, I opt for a cab to take me home. Nothing like the smell of BO, drunk patrons, and I don't even want to think of what else that lingers in those cabs to get me going. By the time I got to the airport my only option today was to fly out at ten and now it is pushing midnight. In a fog I grab my bags off the carousel, yet when I turn to walk toward the curb to find a cab I feel a buzzing excitement that crawls from my toes to my thighs, waking me instantly. I know that feeling, I mean how could I forget? I look back and forth, not seeing him at first but then his fit form slides out of a black SUV and heads toward me.

"Hey, Lex, need a ride?" How in the hell can he ask something so simple and sound so fucking sexy about it? Yes of course I need a ride, but wait, what kind of ride is he referring to? Damn it, I need to put my mental shields up around this man. I'm out of practice, having not been around this mental eavesdropper for so long.

I swear this man must be using some extra-sensual Ryan powers on me because not three hours ago I was naked with Justin in the hotel. Stress relief, I call it. Oh, and then there was the make-out session to end all make-out sessions in the car outside the airport and now here I am getting my panties all tangled at the thought of Ryan's mouth on mine. Okay, that settles it. Where is the cab pick-up?

"No thank you, Ryan. I have a perfectly reliable"—and not to mention very un-sexy—"ride right over there. Shouldn't you be at the club? I thought you were maintaining Rapture while Shane is in the hospital?" I know I need to get to the club as well. I hope to help heal Shane and then get over there to check things out before they get out of hand and his business becomes as big a mess as he is.

"Come on, hop in Lex, I'll get you there in no time. Plus, I think if we work together we may have a better chance helping him out, don't you? We've worked so well as a team in the past?" I can't deny that he is right about that, but he continues before I can concede. "I'm willing to forget your weeks of silence, oh and your disappearing act, to help out a friend, aren't you?" He looks me straight in the eye, not in a sexy way this time but more matter-of-fact and with a sprinkle of anger. His rage has never been aimed at me, but instead of cowering like everyone else on the planet seems to, I hold my ground and stare right into his storm. True, I never told him why I left. The note I left him only had a few words.

Going to help my mom. Don't try to contact me.

I feel he should know why I left; he must have felt guilty with all the intimate times we had together and him knowing all along we don't have a future. I mean, I am a pretty smart cookie, and with some powerful friends; he had to have known that I would find out. Yet, he still chose to hide it from me. Coward.

"Look, Ryan, I don't have time to play your games. I'll hop in with you but no small talk. I need to concentrate, and maybe you can help a girl out and stop by the coast for a moment. I need to recharge." He turns on his heel without a sound and I follow him to his car. The door is held open by a strong right hand, and I slide in as he takes my bag and places it in the back. I am surrounded by his scent; the feel of the leather underneath my thighs is so soft it reminds me of his hands on me. I shake my head. Get a grip, Alex, your friend is fighting for his life and you're thinking of Ryan's man hands on you, for goddess' sake. Get it together!

The driver's side door opens and Ryan slides into the driver's seat, smooth as a jaguar, and puts the SUV into drive. I know we need to talk; the information I have from Sandra is patchy, to say the least. She hasn't seen Shane or talked to the doctors, so I hope Ryan has more information for me.

"So, what do you know about what happened to Shane? Have you seen him yet?" I keep my voice even though I swear it cracks a bit while I try to focus on the matter at hand.

"Yes, I saw him through the ICU window. He's pretty banged-up, multiple broken bones, and a concussion. The internal bleeding in his head is what I worry about most. It's so frustrating to sense it happening and not have the skill to stop it, but you do. The doctors have tried, but it's tricky and they think he may have some pre-existing condition or something that's making it worse; somehow it makes the bleeding relentless and clotting impossible. His car is completely totaled, but I still managed to sweep through it and get rid of a few things." What things would he have to remove? A pit forms in my stomach as I contemplate what Ryan may have found in the car.

"Shane was pretty high, Lex. I know we all thought that that part of his life was far behind him, but I found a couple of eight balls of cocaine in the car. I know the club scene, especially owning a club, keeps you from escaping that lifestyle completely, but I also think the nerves about his upcoming proposal might have set him off." My head jerks toward him, eyes wide.

"Shane was going to propose to Carmen? This weekend in Rosarito? Why didn't he tell me? Hey, why did he tell you?" The level of shock and accusation in my voice must be quite amusing to him as the sides of his mouth twitch and he finally looks at me for a millisecond before focusing his eyes back on the road, which is all it takes for me to really take him in; my nipples tingle a bit. His dark skin and eyes are so familiar, warm, inviting, and dangerous. The muscles of his arm flex as he drives, causing my fingers to twitch a bit when my mind sends off tendrils of wanting to touchy for just a moment. I give myself a mental slap across the face and proceed to my normal line of questions, even though I am totally irritated and, yes, maybe a little aroused, damn it. Justin, Justin, think of Justin. His body, his touch, oh, but Ryan is a part of my world and he can take care of himself. Stop it, he is also a liar, dummy, remember Justin, his smell his...oh ya, there we go, much better.

"I'm waiting for an answer, Mr. Enigmatic. Now spill it." I cross my arms over my chest like a ticked-off child and begin to tap my foot impatiently.

"Well, Miss Conner, I think that was my first indication that Shane was using again. He didn't trust telling you. He gave me some rationale about you trying to talk him out of it because they hadn't been dating that long. He swears she is the one though, and who am I to stand in the way of true love." Ha, true love. I doubt Ryan even believes in it. The thought seems to jump out of my mind, and I instantly realize Ryan is in there. I had dropped my guard at the thought of Shane not trusting me enough to tell me his intentions. It was very unlike him, well, more like the Shane I knew in college who would keep me at arm's length and away from the realization of his drug use. Ryan's hands tighten around the steering wheel at my unintentional proclamation, but his eyes never leave the road.

I know my history with my ex, Carson, has a lot to do with why Shane kept me in the dark. No matter how many times I tried to tell Shane that I wasn't judging him, that he wasn't Carson, he still hid things from me. But he is also a stronger, more wickedly businesslike smart than Carson is, so Shane knew he had to get himself out if he wanted to achieve his goals. Hearing now that he has slipped back in and is once again keeping things from me has me more worried than I already was. Time to fill Ryan in on what I know, or what the lunatic Tree Goddess told me, that is.

"Well, I had a little chat with my powerful friends, and it appears there may be more to this than what Shane may have done. Terra said two men would be causing havoc. Well, one she said was not quite fully a man and that Shane would be in the middle of it all somehow. So maybe Shane is being manipulated, set-up even, and maybe it's that weasel Greg and some new baddy he's brought to the team. We both know he's barely a man, more of a vicious snake with no balls, by the way...fucking coward!"

Ryan's eyebrows go up at my less-than-ladylike language but he knows more than anyone how evil and manipulative Greg can be. Greg spent a year torturing me, posing as Dr. McAdams, and now he is running free, holding the same grudge, I am sure, maybe even worse now that daddy dearest is dead. Ryan should have picked up on something though, right? Maybe not. Greg hid himself from me all too well, but I guess I thought that after what we had been through with him, we would know instantly when he was afoot, like we had his power signature down pat. Ryan must be off his game.

"Yes, I'm getting to that; guess your impatience hasn't changed since you've been in the desert." Now, I was adamant about Shane not telling Ryan where I was, so either he knows because, well, he is Ryan, or Shane spilled the beans to his new BFF. I keep all these comments locked away in the vault and let him proceed as he jumps on five north toward the Pacific Beach ocean access before we head to the hospital in La Jolla.

"There were definitely traces of an Earthen power signature present while I swept the car, and there was something odd I found under the demolished driver's seat." He digs around in his pocket and pulls out a shiny object. I take it from him, because, well, I'm an idiot, and it immediately shocks me from my palm to my shoulder, the jolt causing a muscle spasm that brings my shoulder to my ear and the ring to the floor mat.

"What the hell, Ryan?" He looks confused then worried. I guess it doesn't have the same effect on him as it does on me. Damn booby traps rigged for my pleasure, eh? Bring it on, Greggy boy. I send healing waves into my arm and back, enough to relax me, and then coat myself in protection as I reach back down between my feet for the object. It is a golden one I know all too well: Greg's college NCAA championship ring for baseball that his team won his junior year. The thing is massive, heavy and solid in my hand. All of my anger at what Greg did to me is ten-fold now; I know he played a hand in what happened to Shane, maybe in everything that was happening to Shane. I should have never left the ones I love alone right after all that craziness happened. Greg knows who I care about, so why didn't I worry that he would come for them?

I guess part of me hoped he would have gotten a clue when his daddy, who by the way, Exlax, isn't your real father and never was much of one to you anyhow, tossed him to the Demon in exchange for his freedom. You can't fix a lack of common sense though and now I am reminded of that fact the hard way. I am beginning to think Greg is a full-on dumbass with a death wish that may just come true by messing with me again.

Ryan gets us to an easy access along the coast and I jump out of the car and walk to the ocean, my feet bare and determined. My body sings with the intense feelings of the ocean water, waves, sea life, and the carnal, pure presence of Gaia's energy as I pull it within me. I still have Greg's devil baseball ring in my hand and feel the urge to destroy its very existence. I hold it on my open palm and begin to send my power into it, wishing to destroy it, not merely bind it away. But before I can wrap the vines of my power tightly around the circular surface, Ryan's warm, strong hands roll my fingers into a ball, cooling my raging fire instantly.

Silver drifts of power fly into the night air like sparks off a crackling fire. As I look into Ryan's eyes, I see need and sadness fighting each other. Stars glitter above us as the water caresses our legs and moves sensually around us. Ryan's hand on mine, the look in his dark eyes, and our breath in time with the hushing and rushing sounds of the waves; it is like time is standing still and only Ryan and I exist. I should have known this would happen. Ryan and I connected instantly in the dark alley months ago, and that connection won't die just because I run across the state line. His lips part, and I feel mine go dry as I wait in anticipation of what he is going to do or say. He seems to change his mind with his next intake of breath, and the result is less intimate than I had...what? Hoped for? Longed for? What is wrong with me?

"We may need the ring, Lex; it's our only link to Greg right now. Ease your anger. You'll only be wasting your strength on a monster when we need to help a friend." He is right. I hate his fine ass, but he is right. I should be grateful the spell between us was broken; I don't want to hurt Justin or myself again. We return to the car and speed off in darkness toward Shane.

I hate hospitals more than most things, and this one is no different. The smell of bleach, sickness, and death coat my senses, causing me to walk briskly toward the desk. Before I can plaster on my fake smile to the lady standing guard at the desk, Ryan gives me the old stage right hook and pulls me toward the elevator.

"They're waiting for us, honey. I know her room number so let's go see that baby!" Oh, my good goddess, who is this man? If I didn't know better I would think Mr. Serious and Brooding is loosening up and feeling happy, but right when we get in the elevator that buoyancy immediately shuts down and the Ryan I know is back to business.

"We aren't allowed to see him while he's in critical condition, but Sandra snuck in and told me how to do it. We have to be quick about it, and you may want to follow my lead and cover yourself in a disguise." He pauses and gives me a quick up and down. "Maybe a nice nurse outfit." Okay, now he is crossing the line into flirtatious behavior. I want to spit at him that I am very happy with my boyfriend Justin. My strong, muscular Irish-Italian stallion who is honest with me, caring, and who can rock my world just as well as Ryan can. That would be petty right now, wouldn't it?

It takes ten minutes of maneuvering, but here we are in Shane's room. I go to move the curtains aside when I hear Ryan's voice.

"Just brace yourself, Lex, he's unrecognizable from all the swelling." Damn it, this sucks; I am going to kill Greg. I take a deep breath, release my power disguise, and slip around the curtain to Shane's bedside.

"Oh, goddess no! Oh, Shane, fuck. What in the hell did he do to you?" Ryan's elbow nicks me in the side, and I rephrase, even though Shane looks to be completely unconscious anyhow. "Shane, can you hear me? It's Alex; I came as soon as I heard." No response. Ryan moves alongside me, looking down at Shane and shaking his head.

"Shane, it's Ryan. The club is doing well man, so take your time and heal up. We'll be running the show together again, soon." Man, this bromance is something to behold but not as much as the gruesome sight of Shane. The right side of his body is completely covered from his shoulder down in numerous casts, and the left side of his face is so swollen I can't even see his eye. Iodine stains, stitches, and dried blood cover him from head to toe. Pretty much any piece of skin I can see is altered in some way.

There is no time to waste. I pull into the earth and hover my hands over his head. My fingers begin to float less than an inch above, searching out the internal bleeding that Ryan knew was there. His bones, muscles, and tendons scream in agony at what I had always thought was a painless scan that no human without powers could sense. Perhaps the state of his body is making it open to any change in the world around it. I want to fix every part of him right away, but I have to stop the bleeding first. His body is also under attack by multiple infections that I need to help treat, but I don't know how much that would take out of me. Putting an end to the hemorrhage in his head is the most important thing right now; that I know for sure.

"He's thinking about Carmen; I can see it in his mind. He thinks he will never see her again. Damn, I think he may be giving up." Ryan's statements hit me hard, and tears begin to grow, heaving against my eyes. I will not let them spill out, not yet at least. I need to concentrate and save him.

"Can you talk to him, Ryan? Try to give him hope, tell him we're here." Ryan's expression doesn't change before he speaks, so I know the answer before I hear it.

"It doesn't work that way with normal people. I can't reach them the way I spoke to you in Steven's house."

"Can you at least try? I swear his body is so raw that he can feel me

using my power on him, so maybe he'll be susceptible to you as well."
He gives me a slight nod, willing to try anything. Meanwhile, I can tell
I am getting closer to the source of the blood loss. I zero in on two
areas on each side of his head, specifically the lower region of his
brain—shit, that is his temporal lobe. I can't fathom how a car accident
could cause such precise damage to a particular area of his brain. It is
more like something, or someone, purposely injured Shane in the area
responsible for so many important functions of the brain, including
vision, hearing, and memory.

Fucking Greg is going to get his soon, I swear it. I take one hand
away from Shane and absently fidget with the deadly wooden hairpins
tangled in my hair with a promise of some action soon. Ryan is
watching me, and upon eyeing my weapons his eyebrows shoot up. I
think I may have even seen a flicker of pride and piqued interest flash
across his face. Oh, if he thinks I'm going to give him the pleasure of
sparring with me, he is greatly mistaken.

I put my full attention into the lower left and right sides of Shane's
head and feel a cold, dark, gray promise of death seep into me. It is
Greg's power signature all right. My anger only fuels my power. I feel
Ryan move toward me, but I have already begun to rein it in, knowing
I am working on a delicate part of Shane's body. Healing it just right is
essential, and we can only hope that any damage already done is
reversible or at least treatable now or in the future. I know I am a
strong Healer, but this is new territory and a far cry from a broken
finger or an animal's leg. Pushing doubt aside, I continue to pull on
the Earthen energy all around me and will it to flow into Shane. I find
the holes in the blood vessels and work on sealing them, to cease the
gushing blood and normalize his body's processes. It is intense work
since each time I fix one area another one pops up.

After a while Shane's breathing begins to change and his heart rate
starts to stabilize. I just start to feel secure in my ability to fix what the
doctors haven't been able to when a cold shock hits me hard in the
chest and I fly backward toward the wall. Ryan is faster than a bullet,
grabbing me before I hit the wall and accidentally alert the hospital
staff to our presence. I fall into him hard while the cold continues to

creep into me. Ryan yanks the necklace holding my ring off my neck and quickly slides the ring onto my finger. His power slips into me, creating a wall that keeps the icy coldness from spreading and slowly begins to burn it out with his silver glow. The cold power is relentless; it continues to poke and prod at me, searching for an opening in Ryan's protective circle. I realize I am doing a whole lot of nothing, so I start to scan Shane's body, searching it out for the source of this curse that works like a storm of evilness attacking us.

As I scan, I find numerous areas of internal blood loss from his other organs. What an evil fucking spell this is; it feels like nothing I do will truly stop it. When my scan reaches his ankles, I pick up on something radiating from the exterior side of his left one. I move to stand, bringing Ryan with me, and we make our way to his bedside. Shane's vitals are going to get wacky soon and we need to stop an alarm going off.

"I think I found the source of Greg's curse, but I need you to keep these machines from going off, or we're done for." Ryan is still holding my hand, concentrating on fighting off the coldness creeping around us.

"If I stop concentrating on protecting us, the curse will overtake you and I'm not a Healer, Lex. I won't be able to help you if he takes you too, and then what about Shane?"

"We'll have to be quick, that's all. I need to get to the other side of him and see what's on his ankle. Something foreign is there. I need to see what it is. We'll have to break from each other and hope for the best. I only need a minute or two so let's boost ourselves up and make a go of it." Ryan's look of concern only lasts two breaths before I feel a surge of his protection filling me. I pull on the Earthen energy around us and with a last look at Ryan I bolt from him to the other side of the hospital bed.

Ryan goes to work on the machines, making sure the alarms don't go off, forcing us to leave the medical staff with a situation they can't possibly fix. I brace myself as I make it to his lateral left ankle and notice a small black, cresting ocean wave tattoo that was no way Shane's doing. Cold anger rakes against me; apparently being close to the source only intensifies the onslaught, duh.

"Found it!" I focus all my power on the tattoo and proceed to pull out the ink and its wicked energy with it. My green vines wrap around the ink and lift, tug, and yank the vile picture from Shane's skin. Once I have it floating in front of me, my vines smothering it with green light, I ratchet it up a notch by flowing my grandmother's icy blue dandelion seeds into the black wave. I struggle, trying to destroy the wickedness for good, when I remember my father and the golden boost he endowed me with in a childhood dream. As if on cue, a single spark of gold leaves my finger where Ryan's ring remains. When it hits the blackness we watch the evil explode into its own tiny little supernova. Ryan looks at me with interest, something he does quite often, but this time he looks confused, a question playing on his lips. I will fill him in on my father later.

I waste no time as I turn everything I have onto Shane's body, closing up internal wounds, mending and clearing out overflows of blood and infections. I scan all the way up his body and into his brain once again. This healing will still be tedious, but much easier now that Greg's shade of evilness has been removed.

"Lex, I think he's normalizing now. I'm going to release my hold over the machines and let them function normally before things look so normal that that sets them off as well."

"Good point; I think he's stable enough now to keep the alarms off. I have a feeling we're going to have to leave soon anyhow, since I'm sure rounds will be starting any minute now." I smile down at Shane, finally feeling that his recovery is likely. "His body is looking good, but I still need to work more on his head. I can stabilize him and then come back after the next rounds are done. I need to talk to Sandra anyhow, and a shower would be nice." Thinking of a shower makes me think of the stress-induced sex with Justin in the shower that still makes me tingle. Ryan's head spins toward me, seemingly triggered by my arousal. He may not be in my brain, but he can sure sense my moods. I guess there is no blocking it all out completely. From the look on his face I can tell he knows my memory isn't of him. He avoids my eyes and goes about gathering our stuff. For some reason, I feel appalled that I am thinking of Justin, not only around

Ryan but also with Shane having just been hanging on to life. What is it about intense situations that seems to get me fired up on all cylinders? Ryan interrupts my thoughts and I realize his ring is still on my right ring finger, the chain hanging from it and twisting back and forth around itself in its near free-fall state.

"I can drop you off at Sandra's and then pick you up when you're ready." Why is he being so helpful? What does he want from me? Well, I guess Shane is his friend as well, so why wouldn't he want to help? Guilt trickles into me at my selfishness. I mean, he knows we don't have a future, so I am sure he has been moving on as well. The least I can do is thank him.

"Thank you for your help with that creepy bastard's curse. I've heard about Healers creating tattoos to keep someone healthy, but never to use for such damage. Greg is a fucking menace and is right at the top of my shit list. My mom is going to have to deal." I leave Shane with a protective boost of energy around his body and mind, and we make our way out of the hospital. I will need to learn the non-evil method of Greg's trick so I can be more efficient in my healing. There is no use kidding myself that this is a one-time thing, not with all the craziness that lies both behind and ahead of me.

When we are both in the car, I feel the broken necklace tickling my leg, which brings me back to the matter of his ring. I use my power to apply a slight heat to one end of the broken chain, melding it back together, before putting put it back in its place around my neck.

"I'm happy you're still wearing it, at least in some fashion. I'm surprised you didn't leave it when you bolted out of town."

I laugh out loud at his statement. "Oh, I tried, believe me. Your little ring of magic came right back to me. Don't act like you don't know that would happen." But Ryan seems genuinely surprised, happy even. Great, what does he know that I don't?

We ride the rest of the way in silence. Only the music playing in the background and the wind from the lowered windows surrounds us with sounds. Morcheeba relaxes me as Skye's voice reminds me that there's never an easy way. Her vocals empower me and bring me peace as we head over the hills and down into the jewel that is La Jolla.

I am too tired to talk anyhow, and I feel he isn't saying anything unless I start the conversation, like I owe him an explanation. Once we pull up to Sandra's house I get out and he exits his side, grabbing my bag and handing it to me. He keeps a hold on it once I have a hand on it and pulls me a little closer to him, spiking my internal temperature up a notch.

"Don't run away again, please. I know this isn't the best time, but we need to talk. Can you give me that courtesy before you disappear again?" I guess I can do that.

"Sure, Ryan, I'll see you in a few hours and we can talk." He lets go of the bag and in turn the warmth leaves me. Moments later so does he.

CHAPTER 8

Chaos Magnet

Journal Entry:

I find it best to huddle in a back corner of the room like usual. There is no way I am speaking today. What would be the point? Nobody can help me heal, not if I can't even heal myself. I flinch as a man attempts to walk in front of me to find a seat. Why can't he go around to the other side, the fuckwad? Can't he feel the 'leave me alone' vibes rolling off me? I wish there were only women survivors of sexual abuse in this group, but I can never make that one due to practice.

Men continue to bother me the most, but I can't even change in front of my basketball team anymore, either. I find myself a nice bathroom these days, hidden away from anyone's eyes. Even some of my best teammates wouldn't begin to understand what I am going through. The shame I feel each day collapses upon me, and I can barely breathe sometimes. Even though Steven is gone I continue to look over my shoulder, and sleep does not come easy. It's been a year since I bound Steven away and the story of his suicide leap off the Monument became a false reality I continue to portray today.

Even though I am getting out of high school early, thanks to summer school classes and some dual enrollment at the local community college, I can't get out of the Nestrour house and its memories soon enough. I think my foster mom feels the same way; she keeps talking about selling the house like it's an organic extension of Steven that needs to be removed—or rather hacked off. I wouldn't be surprised if she and Chey move once I am gone; since Greg barely visits anyhow, they don't need all the space.

I shake inside, the chill of the draft-riddled room and thoughts of Steven create the physical response that can take me over an hour to rid myself of. I pull my sweater tighter around me, willing the tremors to stop. The man that walked in front of my personal space looks over at me and tries to give me a supportive smile, but I turn away quickly before the snarl at the back of my throat hits my lips. I can only believe he wants something from me, not that he has actual concern. Nobody could possibly care for me right now. I am disgusting and weak. All the strength and power I felt after I rid my life of Steven and saved Chey has been burned away by torturous memories I cannot free myself of; believe me, I have tried.

My powers, my healing magic, cannot heal my own mental wounds. Any physical injuries I can nearly always repair quickly, but what Steven did to my mind was like having jaws dug into my psyche, like a vicious tick. Anytime I try to remove it the bastard digs deeper. So, instead, I cover my body in loose clothing to conceal any part of me that would draw attention from even the most well-meaning boys at school. I have no interest in entering a relationship. What could I offer? A broken body, heart, and mind? Thinking of kissing someone or having them even touch me shatters my brain into a million pieces. Will I ever move past this? Will I ever forget or forgive myself for letting this happen?

I leave yet another meeting without speaking and without accepting help. The group leader makes eye contact with me as I rise to leave, and when I notice her moving in my direction. I bolt out of the dusty basement room like a feral animal, up the stairs, and into the blazing sunlight of the Colorado winter without a single glance back. She can't save me; nobody can.

The drive home is treacherous, due mainly to the chill I cannot contain. Yes, it is cold, and winter in the desert isn't easy, but this feeling is truly all in my head. I grab a sandwich when I get home and head to my room for the night. I take some of the melatonin my foster mom bought for me, and try to have a dreamless sleep.

I panic when I wake in a flowing gown on warm, soft, mossy ground. The dozen bunnies curled up next to me bolt up, noses twitching, and quickly huddle against their mother. She looks at me, eyes wide and then to the right where I follow her gaze to a path alight with fireflies and sparks of magically floating lights. The soft glows change and flash a variety of colors as they flow around effortlessly in the warm breeze. I rise, and curls escape my loose braid, tickling my neck and cheeks, causing a slight alarm at the touch. Yet I know this place, I have been here before, so my tension eases and I move forward along the path.

Frogs croak on toadstools and crickets chirp from blades of tall grass while I move along the trail, searching for the glowing greenhouse ahead. The thought of seeing the boy again makes me somehow at ease, something I never feel these days, least of all about a boy. The last time I saw him was well before my grandmother passed. I wonder if he will look the same or appear older, as I do, well, as I think I do. I look down at my hands, feeling as if they are sixteen-year-old hands and not the twelve-year-old ones that held his the first time we met. But who is to know, nothing is normal in this magic dream, and that gives me calm and safety because all I have known in the 'normal' world lately is fear and pain. Neither of those dwells here; neither of those feelings lingers now.

I reach the greenhouse and look at my reflection in the glass. My sixteen-year-old self stares back at me with wide eyes, and I see my long braid wrapped around my shoulder. It's a style I never wear. Instead, I'm often using the length and curls of my hair to cover and protect me from eyes all around. My disappearing act is typically complete with the addition of bulky clothes topping off my attempt to disappear into the background, away from prying eyes and hands. The light cotton gown I am now wearing would be my last choice, even at bedtime, yet in this comfortable, magically warm, safe place it feels natural, pleasant even.

A bird trills in the distance, and I break the hold my reflection has over me. Turning quickly, I glance back down the path before realizing that others just like it radiate away from the greenhouse. I circle the glass house, seeing a tall boy coming down another trail. His dark brown eyes are reflecting like polished stones, catching the light off drifts of microcosmic specks, and various enchanting plants and creatures. It is obvious from the distant look on his face that he hasn't noticed me yet. His dark hair is short, messy, and unbridled on his handsome face. He has changed so much, but of course he has, so have I. How will I react when he comes near me? If I shy from him won't he know something is wrong with me? That I'm damaged?

The concern in my mind causes me to break my frozen stance and shuffle my feet against small rocks, which in turn causes them to ricochet off the glass of the greenhouse and gain his attention. A smile forms on his lips, and his body turns my way without hesitation. The adorable boy is clearly transitioning to manhood and my heart flutters as he walks toward me, my physical reaction startling me. Is it excitement, a natural reaction to his appearance right here, right now? It is such a foreign feeling, being one caused by hope and happiness rather than by fear. Here is someone I can trust, someone I can relax around. It has always been that way. He gives me a small wave and then closes the distance between us, stopping about three feet away before giving me a quizzical look.

"What's wrong? Are you sick? You don't look well. I mean, you appear fair, but not well." He stumbles ever so slightly over his words, but it is more endearing than anything.

"I...I guess I'm not well. Memories are like poison I cannot get rid of even though I am rid of him. It's not working, healing myself, mending my mind and freeing it. It's as if he's still here, still holding power over me. Maybe he is. Maybe he's not really gone at all." My hands are trembling by my sides and the boy brushes them gently, stilling them immediately.

"Let me help you. You are human after all, most of you at least. Please let me take your hands." I nod to him, keeping my eyes on his as he takes my hands into his. The strength and warmth of them makes me melt just a bit, allowing my mind to relax and fight off fears and past demons. My eyes travel up his arms, seeing tree branches and flowers painted upon his skin.

Words begin to drift into my mind like a mantra, accompanied by my awareness of low tones of tribal-like drumbeats.

"It wasn't your fault; you didn't ask for any of this; you deserve to be loved, to be free to trust, to have friends—to be happy." The boy's words mix into a soothing elixir in my mind, drawing out my own thoughts and affirmations in line with his.

"It wasn't my fault; I didn't ask for any of this; I deserve to be loved, to be free to trust, to have friends—to be happy and whole again."

The tones of the words from both of us dance around, intertwining in harmony, allowing me to sense him more deeply than I had before. The boy is wild energy; he smells of rich, wet earth; woods; and a salty ocean breeze. He is like nothing I've felt before, and I wonder if he is an Earthen Protector or a Healer like me, but I doubt it instantly. No, he is something else entirely.

His words slip away from me slowly, followed by the release of my hands. In response, my heart skips a beat again, but this time out of longing and worry that he won't touch them again. As I watch his hands draw away from mine, I begin to feel a burst of confidence and positivity I have been missing for years. It is working; whatever he started inside of me is sticking, despite his absence. It is as if he only cajoled the power I have to heal myself from its hiding place, as if it was there all along.

"It will still take work and time, but you are on the right track now. I wish I could have helped you sooner. I am sorry for whatever happened to you, but I know it doesn't have to be in control of your heart and mind any longer. You are strong; you just need to remember that. Try to stop blaming yourself for what happened. You tricked yourself into thinking you were and are weak, and in turn it became a self-fulfilling prophecy. You were misled into thinking you were too weak to heal yourself." He is right, I suppose, and I find myself nodding as I reply to him.

"That makes sense, hearing it outside of myself. It's hard when you're trapped inside and unable to see someone else's point of view. I don't really have anyone else like you to talk to. They're either dead, in hiding, or people I don't want to find me. I honestly think this may be the most we've ever spoken, but it doesn't feel that way. It feels like we are lifelong friends. I guess in a way we have grown up together, in this dream world at least." The boy cocks his head to the side as if confused, then looks around him and shrugs.

"This is my world. This is my family's greenhouse, deep within our property, but ours nonetheless. Are you telling me you aren't from here? That Avalon isn't your home?"

The name Avalon takes my mind instantly to the stack of records my mother gave me. Avalon is the title of an album by Roxy Music, one of her favorites. She said the albums were my dad's, but I think that one was truly hers. We would sing and dance every time she played it, the memories causing me to sway and hum the tune even now. The boy smiles at the instant whimsy that is taking me over.

As if on cue the song begins to play and the boy takes my hands again, pulling me into a twirl.

89

"I'm so glad to see you happy, and you're right, we haven't spoken much at all. My name is Lestan; my mother said it means true and just. What is your name?" I don't think, not even for a second, but something foreign escapes my lips as if I had been saying it my entire life. Here, here in this place with Lestan, I am not Alexis or Alex. No, here I am stripped down bare to my purest form, to my purest name.

"Eila, my name is Eila."

Before I even open my eyes I know something is definitely off. My dreams have been fitful, ranging from a gruesome movie-like synopsis of what happened to Shane, to being held down passionately by Ryan the next. I had stumbled into bed earlier this morning, barely taking a second to kick off my shoes while trying not to wake Sandra. She told me to wake her whenever I got in, but I doubt she meant three a.m. Pitter was conked out with her I am sure, although I can now feel his little body nestled against my left foot. The warmth coming off him can't shake the icy feeling I have, and now I feel another nudge on my right hip, and Sandra doesn't have any other animals.

Pushing myself upright, I instantly catch the scent of death and lilies. I toss the forty-winks sleeping mask into the air, fully aware of Pitter launching off the bed. My eyes fly open as I spy the Demon Valant, in his perfectly pressed suit, push lazily off the bed where my feet used to be, wearing a smile that spreads clearly across his face.

"So nice to see you again, Alexis. I genuinely enjoyed your dreams, my dear, so realistic and emotional; how I do love the rawness of your fear and lust. Oh, and an A+ for your imagination with all of poor Shane's bone breaking and blood loss. Oh, and were those handcuffs with our powerful Ryan? You naughty girl..." Before he can continue I grab my hairpins from the side table and leap out of the bed, calling to them to form into my twin fighting staffs, Serenity and Chaos.

"I warned you, Demon!" I spit at Valant while crouching into an attack position. "You do not get to decide when to drop in. It's called invasion of privacy, you jackass!"

I lunge at him, swinging my Chaos staff in my right hand upward to connect with his jaw, and then spinning inward to give his left knee a whack before crouching back down and moving away. Oh, that feels good, and I think I shocked the shit out of Valant. He appears wounded at first, but more emotionally then mentally as his jaw plops back into place and he shakes his knee out like he had a mere muscle spasm.

"Now that's more like it; been doing some training, have we? I do like my girls wily, tenacious, and sexy. What a complete package you are. Now let's try that again, my brunette Buffy. I wasn't quite expecting your delicious attack and I do hope we can go a couple more rounds. Life has been so dull and undernourished since you and your boys left." He pats his flat stomach after removing his jacket; the muscles underneath his tight button-up shirt flex as he rolls his shoulders and cracks his neck from side to side.

I am not impressed with Valant's show of strength. However, the pop reference was unexpected, even causing me to smile a bit. Cut it out, Alex, this is a Demon. A rotten stench of a Demon who helped torture me for a year, and now he breaks our contract by popping in before I can even pee or cuddle Pitter. Not to mention I am freaking hungry!

Valant's platinum blond hair is stick straight but thick, brushing the tops of his shoulders and nearly glowing off his navy blue pinstripe suit. Boy, he really does like being dressed up like a human business tycoon, doesn't he. Guess it's best to dress like a snake if you are one. Ugh, enough wasting time sizing him up—he is going down.

I pull energy from all around me, lighting the vines on my staffs to a glowing emerald green in preparation for my next strike at Mr. Peeping Tom. I guess he isn't going to leave even if I ask nicely. Surprisingly, that excites me as I realize I would enjoy kicking the shit out of him for a few more minutes. He motions with his hands for me to come at him again. I feign innocence, standing up out of my attack position, tilting my head to the side and blinking at him as if confused. He grins back at me, showing his sharp teeth, and I charge blindingly fast at him again.

This time I leap up, attempting to give him a crack in the head, but he is quick and he crouches down, grabbing me by the ankles before I can land a strike. Before I have a chance to scream he flips me over and throws me bone-breakingly hard to the floor. I manage to put a protection of power around me before I fall so the force only mildly knocks the wind out of me. That quick thinking saves me from more than a few bruises and scrapes.

I move slowly off the ground, testing to see if Valant will back down if he thinks I am truly wounded. But I forget that I am dealing with a Demon and am reminded soon enough when Valant grabs my hair, yanking me up until I am standing inches from his face, his hot breath blowing on me as he laughs.

"Oh, I do love you, Alexis; how much fun you are to play with. Now, shall we talk or go a few more rounds?" I gasp out my response, struggling with my neck being forced to a ridiculous angle by this monster.

"Ya know, Valant, you caught me on a bad day. I'm in a bit of a pissy mood considering my best friend is in the hospital after your fuck-wad buddy Greg put him there. I didn't get much sleep, as you know, and I am fucking starving. So unless you brought me waffles, or my foster brother's head and sesame-sized balls on a platter, you better prepare yourself, fang-boy, because I am wickedly pissed off this morning." Valant launches me across the room, forcing me to use some of my ability to slow me to a stop, rocking off my heels just before hitting the wall. I bring Serenity and Chaos together and will them to become one.

I hold the staff close to my right side, slightly behind my right leg as I take off at a run, throwing Earthen energy into my speed. Valant crouches and snarls at me, waiting for me to rush into his brick-wall body, but instead I hit the floor with my staff and vault over him. Spreading my hands out on each end of the staff, I hook it just below his chin as I sail over him. We hit the wall hard, his momentum knocking the wind out of me again for a moment as his back collides with my chest. Regardless, I hold on, refusing to let go. Power courses through me and I grasp tight and fast to the staff, allowing the power to build into it, watching the carvings of vines and Vex light up, giving an eerie glow to Valant's face.

"Okay, big guy, do you think you're likely to intrude on me ever again?" My feet are starting to slide slightly as Valant's bulk begins to swell. Oh, shit, he is angry, and I am feeling a little nervous about him hulking-out right now. Valant chokes out his reply and a sliver of dread tingles up my spine.

"You are but a child, Alexis. Now, I have been nice during your little temper tantrum, but don't force me to kill you, my dear; I rather enjoy you." My moment of worry is all he needs. Soon his hands push the staff away from his throat and he spins on a dime, taking me by the throat and raising me into the air.

"Enough, Demon!" The air grows misty, and I cannot see in front of me. Sandra's voice rings in my head, and instead of gratitude I feel only fear for her safety. Despite my building dread she continues, instead of running for the hills like I hope.

"Demon, you are breaking a contract, so shall we nullify it altogether or do you want to review the terms in a civilized manner?" Sandra's voice is stern and raw, and soon Valant's hands leave my throat and I plummet to the floor.

"Sandra, you have to get out of here. He'll trap you." I regain my footing and see her across the room at my bedroom door, her hands in front of her, directed at Valant, who is staring white-eyed and frozen. I have never seen Sandra as awe-inspiring as I do right now. She stands firm and balanced in her short-sleeve sleep shirt and matching shorts. Her blond hair is tussled expertly like she styled it to look that way. Many a poor sap mistook her sexiness, perfectly perky boobs, and cute girl voice for weakness. Sandra is sweet as a button unless you cross her, and right now Valant is in the hot seat.

"Demons rely on their senses and I have taken his sight. Isn't that right, Valant? Not as fun to toss women around when you can't see their fear now, is it? Shall I let you free so we can talk, or is it time to see how much stronger Alex has become in other ways? I'm sure she has some other tricks up her sleeve." Valant's head starts to shake and a smile creeps across his face.

"Oh, Alexis dear, you do have some powerful friends, don't you? Damaged, I see, but powerful. Where is your twin, Miss Sandra? Still sullen toward you?" Sandra slumps a little, but doesn't release the blinding power she holds over Valant. By the look of the flinch he just gave I am pretty certain she can do much worse.

"All right. Don't get your panties in a bunch, ladies; I concede. It's been so boring since I lost all my human contact through Greg. Once I felt he was at it again I came to see you, Alexis. I didn't know I would get to feed off your dreams, but it was a tasty treat." I go to raise my staff at him again, and I can tell he feels the charge in the air. He speaks quickly, hands up in a placating manner.

"I won't do it again, Alexis. Cross my heart and hope to die." I swear he is fluttering his eyelashes with this fakey show of his. So far, my experiences with Demons have been living up to their reputation. They are sinister tricksters and should be avoided at all costs. Trust me, I never intended to mix with their kind. It was my lovely foster brother who became Valant's pen pal, not me.

I know I am glaring at him as my head spins with these thoughts. Will I ever truly be rid of Steven? His power transcends his death even now. Valant's white eyes turn to stare blindly at me. He must sense my small depressing pity party. I need to check my emotions around him; he's like a wild animal, preying on my change in pheromones or something. Still staring toward me, Valant continues.

"I only ask that you take me to see Shane. I can help you put the pieces together of what happened and take the psychological pain away, as well. You know I can. Greg spilled the beans on that little trick with his patients while you were all beaten and bloody. I don't think you will succeed on your own this time. Not if your nightmares reflecting how fearful you are of not being strong enough to heal him completely are true. I think you need a Demon's help, my dear."

Despite my rage at his intrusion, Valant has a point. Healing Shane's body has been a hard task, and I haven't even begun to work on what may have happened to his psyche. I sense that I need Shane coherent to be able to gauge the extent of the damage, but perhaps Valant doesn't.

"Why should I trust you, Demon? Who knows what you're capable of doing to him?" I hold my chin high and hide the hope in my eyes that Shane could be himself again. Valant smiles wickedly and I gulp at his obvious excitement.

"Healing him only helps me, my dear. His pain is my joy, so let me take it from him." He is grinning too much for my taste, but I did make a pact with this thing, so I need to honor my side of the agreement before he unleashes what he is beyond question capable of.

"Fine, Valant, but you are never to be with him alone, and you will tell me everything you see so we can find Greg's slimy ass. Keep your end of the bargain and I won't let you go so long next time without your depression entrée with a side of suffering." Sandra looks at me, and I nod back to her, giving her a nonverbal thumbs-up to allow Valant to regain his eyesight. His eyes clear and he beams at Sandra, bringing his hands together as if he would clap at her greatness. I know I want to.

"Now give us some space; I haven't even had a chance to use the little girl's room this morning, let alone talk to Sandra after being gone for so long. Make yourself scarce and I'll call for you when I'm leaving." Valant and I have an instant link, and as long as I call him to me he can find me anywhere. Knowing he came here on his own is not something that makes me feel warm and fuzzy. Creepy, right?

Valant nods to both of us, entwines his fingers, and looks up at the ceiling as a small, burgundy-colored tornado-like cloud swirls around him, and he is gone. What a drama queen.

Sandra and I hold each other in a fierce hug and move to her room where Pitter is hiding under the bed. Once we persuade him out, Sandra and I sit on the bed and go over what she knows about Shane. Pitter snuggles in her lap, giving me sly looks that could kill. I am not sure whether it was my absence or the Demon I invited into our lives that bothers him more. Every once in a while I tap at my leg, trying to get him to come to me. Besides a once in a while motion of his paw in my direction, he blatantly ignores me. Fine, I will give him his space for now.

"Has your mom found your father yet?" I have been keeping Sandra updated on the progress, or lack of progress, in the search for good ole dad. Most recently sharing all the weird happenings with Dana's Dreamwalk and my realization that my father helped me many times throughout my life.

"No, nothing yet. I think she's close, but that's been the status since I left San Diego." Sandra reaches over and squeezes my hand. Her touch is immediately reassuring.

"Any word from Vex about the Healer? Is he okay?" I don't know what I would do if I didn't have Sandra to talk to about all of the craziness in my life. Having a best friend in this magical chaos is something I've never had before.

"Not a peep since I left him on the brink with Terra. I don't think I'll pick up anything about the Healers without him, either. It's scary, Sandra. There are so many things happening at once and I have no control over any of them."

"Control is only a perception, I think. Chaos is the real captain on this ship. But, perhaps if you have something of your father's, I can help out with that search?" I nod. I am so caught up in my worry for Shane that I haven't thought about asking her about my dad.

"Thanks, Sandra, when Shane is better I'll take you up on it."

Sandra gives me a smile and reaches over to her bedside table to pull out a small box from her drawer. I know Shane has all his fingers and toes intact, so I'm not sure what she might have in there that she needs in order to discern what may have happened in Mexico. I look away while she opens the box, but when I look back I see only a lock of Shane's hair.

"Oh, that's all? Man, I was prepping for some ritualistic body parts shit the way you made it sound when you were heading to the hospital. Hair is nothing." I spoke too soon as she moves the hair aside and I see entire bloodied fingernails and...is that a tooth? Gross.

"These were all part of the clean-up process from when he came in. I didn't do it myself, Alex. Geez, I'm a Seer, not a butcher. Stop being a baby. Look, I'll close it. See?" I peer over, and the lid is indeed shut.

"So last night I did a little digging around after I brought these items home and I found power signatures from a dark source." I nod my head in agreement.

"Yes, I picked up on that as well in the hospital room when I tried to heal him. It is most definitely my foster brother Greg's doing. He even left me a trap of sorts, like a spell, that unraveled when I was repairing the damage. It took Ryan and me working together to destroy the damn thing." Oh boy, her eyes are as big as saucers and a smile tugs at her twitching lips. I brace myself for a large dose of her sexualized sarcasm.

"Ryan, eh? Geez, you don't waste time do you, Alex? Or should I call you Lex?" I smack her in the arm at the blatant reference to the nickname Ryan gave me when we first met. Pitter gives me an annoyed look, and I point at Sandra as if to say she started it. He could care less as he adjusts himself so his hind end is toward me completely, which is pretty much the cat version of giving me the cold shoulder—maybe even the finger.

"Cut it out, Sandra! He picked me up from the airport with his all-knowing-everything ass and I needed a ride, and maybe some muscle for back-up and that's all there is to it." I think. I mean, ya, that's all there was to it.

"Plus, Justin and I have reconnected on an entirely different level this time. He doesn't lie to me either. Ryan acts clueless, which is only continued lying if you ask me!"

Sandra has a wry smile on her face. She is never totally serious when it comes to men. After being burned by one, she isn't too serious about any of her conquests, and what was that jab about her twin brother Valant brought up? I'll have to ask her about that one later. Right now we need to focus on Shane. It is almost visiting hours, which will give me access without all the sneaking around, so I need to get my ass moving.

"Sure thing, Lex. Ten four. Ryan bad. Justin good." The way she says "bad" makes an image of Ryan pop into my head that is full-on sexpot style. I make a move to swat her again, but instead motion at the box for her to get on with it.

"I'm pretty sure Greg is still in Mexico, on a boat of some sort. I followed his power signature off Shane's samples." Ugh, why doesn't she just say parts? It's just as nauseating a picture in my head as 'samples.'

"He hasn't gone far from the source of Shane's trauma, and I can smell the ocean air, hear waves lapping against something big, and the hum of a motor. He's good at covering his tracks, but at least you know he hasn't gone far." I can't decide if Greg is a dumbass—cocky like his so-called father—or he is just trying to be found. If I were Greg's shyster ass, I would be tracking down my true dad, and a lobotomy, but hell, that requires intelligence and a pair of balls.

"Thanks, Sandra. You're the best. I'm going to shower and head back over to the hospital with Ryan. I guess I'll have to call for the Demon and lay down some ground rules before I head over there. Damn deal that gives me nothing in return. Greg is gone, and Valant still gets to stop in for his sadistic peep shows. Oh well, he did heal Greg's patients when he was known as Dr. McAdams, so maybe I should let him help with Shane. What do you think?"

"Demons love deals, but they're tricky by nature. I've never encountered one myself, but my brother did, and let's just say things were different between us after that. Some words of advice: Make sure your deals are simple; Demons can find too many loopholes when deals are convoluted. On the other hand, overly simplified deals leave wiggle room as well." Once again with the make sure it's this but not too much and not too little. It isn't so easy to follow grey area directions when you are in the moment. I need to prep myself for tangling with Valant. Yes, we may need his help but what price will he extract?

I kiss Sandra good-bye, and tell her we will have some time to actually talk when Shane is truly on the mend. She gives me a smile that suggests she knows better. I take a quick shower, text Ryan that I am just about ready, and then call for Valant.

"Okay, Valant. I call upon thee to get your ass here right now."

"Such a foul mouth for such a pretty girl. Do you kiss your mommy with that mouth? Where is mommy dearest, anyhow?" Oh man, he is already starting in on me and I was going to try and play nice. Something must have caught fire in my eyes because he backpedals quickly off his high smart-ass horse.

"Okay, no more jabs. In fact, I'll do one better and let you in on something you have forgotten, or maybe I took it from you by accident while you slept. Hmm, trivial really but here it goes. You had a dream about a Healer last night. It was such a vicious attack that I was drawn to it fiercely, like a moth to a flame, and must have accidently devoured it. I can't be certain, but it felt real, like it was actually happening." Did Valant go on a Dreamwalk through me? Did he see another Healer being destroyed? Was Vex in it?

"Did you see Vex? I mean, a fox, by chance?" Valant gives me the most human "huh?" look I have ever seen. I guess that is a no and I nearly laugh despite the seriousness of, well, of everything.

"Valant, you have to tell me what you saw. I will call for you when I'm with Shane, but you're going to need to make yourself more presentable. And by that I mean get some dentures or something! Do you know how freakishly pointy your teeth are? I mean, how do you not cut your lips off with those?" Valant tilts his head in a "well actually" gesture so I raise my hand, shaking my head to cut him off immediately.

"Never mind, I don't want to know what you're about to say unless it's about the dream." Valant smiles at me with his razor teeth that then shimmer and change right in front of me to perfectly human-looking chompers. I wonder if all Demons look like Valant. He is more like the idea I always had in my head, or how they are portrayed on TV, of vampires, but without all the sexual voodoo shit they tie in with them. I mean, I guess Valant is okay looking for a Demon but, ew.

"Yes, I'm happy to share with you as you in turn will share with me. There was an older man in a field of flowers around a lake. He was showing younger Healers, maybe in their late teens, how to heal a nest of baby field mice that a cat had attacked in the fading light. It was practice at the expense of a hungry kitty if you ask me. Anyway, a hooded figure appeared off in the distance, hovering above the lake. As it approached, the twilight sky began to darken rapidly until it was a storm-like darkness. The cloaked figure seemed to freeze the Healers in place and then took the essence of their power from them before taking their lives." I shiver; this sounds like the same type of attack from my Dreamwalk, and the attempted one on Vex and the boy as well.

"Did anyone say anything, Valant? Did you notice anything about the hooded figure that could help us identify or find him or her?" Valant shakes his head and for a moment even seems concerned.

"Nothing about the figure stood out to me and I couldn't pick up on a thing, even though I tried. I mean, who wouldn't be drawn to that kind of evil?" My eyebrows raise and he grins back at me. "Okay, not your cup of tea I see. Well, at least not all of the time, my little chaos magnet." He gives me a wink and then continues.

"There was a voice echoing all around me. It was indistinct, lacking a male or female connotation. It sounded more like a raging fire or a thunderstorm. It did keep telling them it was for the good of the cause, that what was happening was a saving grace of sorts. Creepy, if you ask me." Creepy is all I think about when I am with Valant so if he thought this Dreamwalk was disturbing then I am kind of glad he took it from me. Damn, I am not going to start believing a Demon pal is a good thing. No way, no how! But I should appease him a bit; staying on his good side is important right now. I have a friend in need.

"Thank you, Valant. This is most helpful. Now, I'm going to hightail it out of here and I'll call you as soon as I get to Shane's room. Try to blend in, will ya?" He shimmers a bit and comes back into focus wearing scrubs, a stethoscope, and a short hair do. I do a double take, nod professionally, and turn away to gather my things.

"You'll do. Now get out of here so I can get to where we both want and need to be." When I turn back around, Valant gives me a once over, as if trying to judge if I might ditch him or not.

"Look, I get it. You can help. If that's what you call it." More like devour. Gross. He gives me a wry smile, looking more like a young, hotshot doc than a Demon, and quips, "It's nice to be needed from time to time, Alexis. I do hope our relationship will be a long and fruitful one." I think he licks his lips, and then is gone. And I thought my life was a circus before! I'll take Nic's flamboyant drama any day over this craziness—wouldn't I? Sometimes I wonder if Valant is right. Perhaps I am a chaos magnet, and maybe part of me likes it, even craves it.

CHAPTER 9

Team Alex

Journal Entry:

After my dream with Lestan, I feel freer, happier, and able to focus at least on getting better. I begin to participate more in school and with my team, slowly taking the time to reconnect with some of my friends in the process. My solemn look and my days spent hiding within myself lessen, and I begin to love life again. Aside from continuing to rehabilitate myself, I can heal other parts of my world again. I spend time with Bear, exploring the land around my foster home, ridding my fears and worries that Steven's ghost is within the woods, hiding in the dirt, trees, and riverbanks. It is slow going at first, but soon injured animals come across my path again, and I am able to heal them. Trees and uprooted bushes revive quickly with my Earthen power. With each act as a Healer and Earthen Protector, the stronger I become.

I think of Lestan often, wondering if he is thinking of me, or if his magical world of Avalon even truly exists. Hard not to think when the boy's name literally means True. I have lots of guy friends at school, but I never feel the same comfort or those tingles of excitement like I did during my healing dream with Lestan. If I didn't know better in my sixteen-year-old heart, I would think I love him.

Who would blame me? He helped bring me back from a life of despair, from a loss of self and, best of all, he allowed me to realize I am strong enough to continue healing myself. I will always have the wounds from what Steven did to me. But instead of staying stuck in them, instead of allowing them to define me, I can move forward with them tucked away, somewhere far away from the person I am and want to be.

Aside from telling me I smell like rotted food spoiled in hell, otherwise known as smelling like a Demon, Ryan is pretty quiet on the ride to the hospital. I know, what a shock! We are about ten minutes out when I drop the bomb that I would be calling for Valant when we get there and how I think he can actually help Shane. I top it off by saying I smell just fine thank you, but take a couple whiffs of myself to be sure.

"It's funny, Lex. You seem to trust a Demon. Oh, and let me remind you, a Demon who helped torture and manipulate you, but who seems to be holding a pretty big damn grudge against me. One minute we're together, surviving a night in a dungeon with a Demon and two psycho Absolute Protectors, and the next minute you're gone." He runs his hand through his dark hair; it has gotten longer since I saw him last; he has some facial shadow as well. He looks tired now that I can take a good look at him in the daylight, and maybe a little bit sad. Part of me is glad he is a little miserable.

"But it's all good, Lex; you believe he can help you. You always want someone around when they can be helpful, but once that's done I guess it's dead air for weeks." Okay, I thought Valant would be a non-Ryan-and-I topic, but I guess not. If he wants to get into this right now then fine. At least we are almost at the hospital so there isn't long for him to wiggle out of the truth.

"You want to talk about manipulation? How about the fact that the whole time during your little dance of seduction you knew that you and I could never be. You know the Council forbids it and you took advantage of my naiveté by keeping that important morsel of information to yourself. Well, good thing Dana filled me in on your little secret before I actually formed *real* feelings for you." I want that last part to hurt him, mainly because it isn't true, but if I am hurt he should be as well. Then again, why do I care if he is hurt by me not caring for him? Justin and I are better than ever. Petty feelings from a crush can only create havoc in our relationship. I do succeed in plucking a nerve though; Ryan does his typical tight squeeze onto the steering wheel in response. His muscles flex and tug on the sleeve of his shirt, causing me to stare a little too long for my own good.

"That's what all this has been about? The Council? Did you not get the clear picture that I don't care about what the Council thinks?" He isn't yelling, but I still feel my entire being press back against my seat by the intensity of his words. Along with the physical reaction, a 'that does ring a bell' notion pops into my head followed by strings of other colorful words and second-guessing thoughts.

Why was I so quick to agree to go with Dana anyhow? Maybe if Ryan wasn't so secretive all the time I would have been more willing to give him even the smallest benefit of a doubt. Maybe even allowed him time to explain before taking off. Not to mention the news of my father being alive triggering the release of a wide range of feelings from happiness to anger and distrust. I mean, he did have us believing he was dead this whole time, and the result was an intense flaring anger directed at Ryan. Ryan, who seems to be just another man in my life keeping truths from me, one being that he would eventually abandon me, just like I thought my dad had done. All this thinking is getting me riled up again; weeks of pushing myself physically and not giving these feelings a verbal outlet are about to overflow in this car right now.

"Well maybe if you spoke up every once in a while and gave it to me straight I wouldn't have jumped to the conclusions that you knew there couldn't be an 'us' in the future and that you'd fall in line with the Council's rules. It's not like I've known you long and in that time you seem to have held back quite a bit from me." Ryan's jaw flexes tightly, but he doesn't interrupt.

"And I'm sure there's some whack-job Council member hopped up on power just twitching to delve out the punishment to those of us who don't follow their rules, right? You should have at least let me know before I started to fall for you, you jackass!" Ryan's face crumples a bit in a look of relief mixed with humor, yet he instantly resumes his stoic look teetering on indignation. When his mouth opens I hold my breath, wondering what he will say after I bared a little bit of my soul, the little bit that is still bonded to Ryan after all we have been through.

"Lex, things have been a little crazy the entire time I've known you, if you don't recall. There wasn't a whole lot of time between keeping us hidden one second to keeping us both alive the next. We were in it together, you know, and I had, have, my own feelings entangled as well. Something you obviously didn't consider when you fell off the face of the earth." He is right. Things had gotten so intense between us in a very short amount of time. He had to save me the first time we met, for goddess' sake. No, no no, I am not getting sucked back into this. We can be friends but that is all, and even then I still don't know what to believe half the time with him. He knows so much, and I know so little. I've always been at a disadvantage, at the mercy of both Dana and Ryan, only telling me things when it is convenient for them. I guess you can throw Terra and Vex into that mix as well, all telling when they want to, but what about when *I* need some answers? Maybe I am not asking enough questions.

The reality is that Ryan has something none of the others have and that is his family connection to the Council. They are a group I need to know about, and Ryan is my best link to that world, that's for sure. Ryan has done a lot for me; the least I can do is open up the possibility of friendship. A big part of me has been missing him, so now let's see if I can keep it platonic. I owe my happiness with Justin a shot. Time to let Ryan off the hook a bit and take him at his word.

"Okay, Ryan, maybe I should have talked to you about what Dana told me before I left, and perhaps my knee-jerk reaction had a lot to do with the daddy issues that took over with mine being alive and all now." That got Ryan's attention. He gives me a rare Ryan look of surprise and I can tell his brain is ticking away.

"I had no idea. That's a lot to deal with." His voice is low and I suspect he knows a great deal more about that drama than I had. Until now, that is.

"Ya, pretty major reason don't you think! Please keep it secret. Even from your parents, please. My mom doesn't want the Council involved at all, at least not yet." Ryan is definitely surprised by this news. It's nice to know he doesn't always know everything. Point for Alex.

"I wish you'd told me, Lex. I could have helped. I mean, I still can." I nod, but Shane is the priority right now. With so many things going on I have to concentrate on one thing at a time or I am going to go crazy. I haven't even mentioned the Healer issue to Ryan yet. He's gonna flip his lid. Well, at least I won't be the only one.

"Look, I'll promise not to fall off the face of the earth, but the secrets have to stop if we're going to be friends." Ryan's eyes shoot to me, first with a hint of hope and then suspicion. I sit there wondering what he might say next, the silence becoming more and more uncomfortable and the vibrations of his power beginning to fill the car with his intensity. I think I am going to burst, until he finally speaks, releasing me from my held breath.

"Friends? It's Justin again, isn't it? I guess your daddy issues didn't keep you from being with him—only from me, I suppose. Well, I'm not one to push, but I do know this: You can block your mind from me all you want but your body language cannot be hidden." Gulp. My thighs press together tighter and I breathe in shallow gasps. I feel the heat of my face flushing and turn away so he won't notice. I guess it is a little late for that! How dare he insinuate such a thing, and out loud even! Well, at least he is talking, which is what I wanted, right? Damn, how does he make everything sexy? I bet he could make a few old timers keel over just with some crocheting, given the chance.

Ryan stares straight ahead as he turns into the parking lot, but even his driving is a turn on. I lick my lips and grasp my knees a little too tightly—something else, think of something else, damn it! Oh yes, I do have a question.

"So, is there a punishment, something the Council will do to Protectors who try to stay together?" Yep, just an innocent question; I mean I'm allowed to be curious without it necessarily being about me, right?

"Nothing I couldn't handle, Lex." Son of a bitch. Ryan parks the car, turning to me before getting out.

"I've been meaning to tell you that you look good, Lex, really good, much stronger. I'm guessing Dana had you working hard out in the desert. Let me know if you want to continue your training while you're here. I think there are some other things I can teach your body to do." And with that he slides out of the car leaving me to sit there stunned and completely turned on. Fucking Ryan.

The remaining time it takes to get to Shane's room is in silence, I fuming about how easily he can spin me into a tizzy with his sex-oozingness, and he being all Zen-like.

I take a deep breath and close my eyes as we enter the elevator and rise to Shane's floor. I visualize my body glowing with emerald-green vines fully charged by Gaia and poised to do my bidding. Full control over my body, over the power flowing within it and over this very moment rings through me as clear as a bell. I am not at the mercy of Valant, Ryan, Greg, or Steven. No, I am stronger than my past when I immerse myself in the present. Shane will be okay, and there is no way I am leaving this hospital until he is. I'll impersonate the damn doctor if I have to, to gain access to him all day and night. No matter what, I will get it done.

When I open my eyes, I see Ryan staring at me. His look is one of trust and support. We have each other's back from this moment on; nothing about the car ride or the weeks of silence will get in our way. We are Earthen Protectors, and we have a purpose and a job to do.

Shane looks so much better. So much so that I nearly weep when I see him. Color is touching his cheeks and the grimace of pain that was pasted on his face has disappeared. Once the nurse fills us in on his positive and miraculous progress and excuses herself to give us some privacy I waste no time summoning Valant. I am not going to risk waiting till Shane has no hope of coming back from this fully intact.

"Oh, what a naughty boy; pumped himself full of cocaine. I can still taste the rush and excitement within him even after his multiple transfusions. Maybe if he hadn't been so out of control, he could have avoided this." I make a step toward Valant, chin held high, my eyes shooting daggers into his. He is dressed in scrubs now, fitting in well with the hospital staff, but my knee is about to fit well with his groin.

"Uh uh, Alexis dear, would you like to take a glimpse at what could be if we don't play nice?" Before I can answer he waves his hand at me, his fingers twinkling like they are playing piano in the air, and I am suddenly in the room at a different time. Murmuring voices draw my attention and I turn around and see Shane's neurologist speaking to Carmen. What I hear next rocks my very soul and vibrates my body with its deep sadness and agony. Carmen's screams hit my ears, along with sobs and then her voice breaking into painful wails of "no, no, no" over and over again. She drops to her knees, her head falling against the cushioned seat as her body refuses to comprehend, let alone stand. Her fists bang over and over into the seat cushion; the chair creaking underneath the physical manifestation of her misery.

My heart begins to break, and my eyes follow suit as tears beg to be released. I cannot control the coldness creeping over me with the realization that Shane has gone; his mind forever removed could not mend enough to come back to us and then his body followed suit. Shane's bed is behind the doctor and I move toward him. Blaring alarms and signals keep time with Carmen's wails of anguish, heartbreak, and blind rage. I make a move to touch Shane, but someone grabs my arm, piercing me with fingernails and drawing blood. Before I glance up I see Carmen's contorted face mirrored in my tears as they plummet toward the sterile hospital floor.

"Don't you dare touch him, Alex; don't you ever touch him again. This is all your fault. You've brought this on us; you've brought this on us all." Carmen is blind with grief and my heart aches for her.

I take a breath, readying myself to calm her but the vision fades away and I stand once again with Valant and Ryan. Carmen's screams are replaced by Ryan's intense tones warning Valant to end the wicked daydream at once. Valant is looking warily at Ryan, the one person I have seen him react to that way before. Once in the wine cellar with Greg and now here where I just experienced what it would be like to lose Shane.

Having someone around who a Demon fears is either extremely lucky for me or perhaps extremely dangerous. Valant wipes pretend dust from his shoulders, trying to appear unfazed by the build up of Ryan's power before speaking matter-of-factly.

"No harm done. I just wanted to make sure you knew what this could all lead to if we don't all get along like best buds. Now let me take a look and see what I can do for the lad." Valant and I walk closer to Shane, the Demon flanking my left while Ryan moves to the opposite side of the hospital bed. I look at the monitor, seeing that he remains stable, at least physically. I am not sure what will happen next. How do Demons feed off trauma and anguish anyhow? Should I look away? Get him a straw? Gross.

Valant moves closer to Shane's head, the area of interest for him as he sets about trying to remove the damage inflicted upon him by Greg. I keep Valant in sight as I scan Shane's body to check on the internal bleeding I had repaired, and for any lingering evilness of Greg's curse. I check his ankle once more, making sure the tattooed source of the curse is still gone. All is well, and his body scan comes back amazingly well. I catch sight of Valant placing his hands on both sides of Shane's head, so I move my scan upwards and find that the darkness is still hovering in his brain.

"Okay. Alexis, I will take over from here. He may react a bit so you and your GI Joe may need to hold him down for me." Ryan moves toward the door and uses his power to lock it temporarily. We post up opposite each other, our hands on Shane as we brace ourselves.

"First I'll numb his larynx a bit so he can't scream. Very handy I might add, though I typically enjoy hearing it." He sees the shake of my head and shrugs his shoulders.

"Some people are just no fun. Okay, silenced and ready for some of Valant's magic. Sit back and enjoy some real power."

Ryan and I stare as Valant closes his eyes and twinkling grey creeps from his hands into Shane's head. Nothing seems to be happening at first and then Shane seizes up and Ryan and I are forced to hold him down.

"Oh, he's damaged all right. Looks like Greg was the one who met him at the bar and sold him some majorly bad stuff, hoping to shatter his brain. Oh, that boy is so smart with the biochemistry, isn't he? Boy, his father would be proud. Not the real one of course, he is such a boring goody two shoes, well, apart from playing doctor with Steven's wife of course. But Steven would be amused, maybe even impressed."

"Focus, Valant! Pull that shit from him and fix him like you've been boasting you can." Shane relaxes for a moment, and I make the mistake of moving a stray hair from my eyes. His fist flies up, managing to graze my cheek before Ryan snatches it and uses his whole body to hold him down.

"Oops, watch yourself Alex, he thinks he's fighting off Greg right now. Oh, this is interesting. He wants to die; Greg placed in his mind that your Carmen found him and broke it off with him. Oh, such a treacherous and delicious lie. I'll take that from you, big guy." Fucking Greg is going to get it! First he poisons Shane with bad drugs and then places poisonous lies in his mind so he doesn't care if he lives or dies. It must be why he took off so carelessly in the car. Shane, despite his mistakes, would never drive when he was intoxicated.

"It's all coming together now. Greg used his power to get Shane to leave the market he was at with him and go to a bar where he dosed him up and had him doing lines in a back room. Then the mind-fucker tricked him into thinking his Latina love caught him and ditched him. Oh, such a cruel and elegant trick. Shane, feeling nothing for his life—or much of anything, really—got in the car and took off at dangerous speeds. Greg followed right behind him and nudged his car off the road right in time for it to hit massive boulders, fly over them, and flip onto the hood. The boy is lucky to be alive."

I don't think him being alive still is an accident at all. Greg purposely did this to Shane so I could find him in this state. He left the ring for me, and the cursed tattoo of evilness. All of it was done on purpose, all of it to torture me even more than he already has.

"Valant, is there anything you can get on Greg, where he is, was? What's the name of the bar they went to? Did they talk to anyone at the bar who seemed to know him?" Valant appears to be smiling, and his body is trembling a little bit too excitedly for my taste.

"Oh yes, that's much better now that the nasty chemical imbalance has been removed, and his brain is back in balance. I have removed the vision of Carmen breaking his little boy heart, and his self-worth is coming back. Now, before I take the whole unpleasantness out of him, let's take a deeper look at where they were and any seedy characters we may be able to beat the truth out of." We? Oh boy, I will deal with that later.

"Yes, remove all of this and just leave a hit and run accident. Shane doesn't need the guilt of the drug use or any trace of it in his system. You never know what that may trigger in someone who used to be a bit of an addict. Ryan and I will get it erased from his hospital record as well. No need for this to haunt him personally or professionally." Ryan was able to ease off Shane and give a large exhale. I can tell he has been as worried about Shane as I have. I get the feeling Ryan doesn't have many close friends. All that secret life stuff does get in the way. Valant looks up from Shane and smiles my way. His eyes are grayed out, making him look even more terrifying as his sharp teeth twinkle at me.

"Okay, yes, the bar is called Rico's—shady-ass place—and Greg has befriended a few people in there, one being Rico's son, Luis. Oh, he's a character all right; definitely the one Greg got the cocaine from. I can tell they have known each other for a while, maybe even years. I think Greg was getting some good deals from the Mexican pharmacology for some of his past work. Anyhow, it's a good place to start. Shall I remove it all then?"

I nod quickly, eager to get Shane back to normal and to find Greg as quickly as possible. Carmen has asked me to watch the club one night but after that I will be off. I guess I will need to ask Ryan to go with me. Valant is another story, but I will cross that bridge later. He would only get in the way, and I need to take care of Greg my way. No Demon's playtoy future for him, that's for sure. Greg is too conniving, and I don't doubt he would find some way to weasel out of Valant's clutches like he did before. Besides, Valant's near reverie for Greg's evil display at Shane's expense is enough for me to keep them apart.

Valant continues to work on Shane and I scan his head again to check on the progress. The dark energy has lifted and things seem to be back in order. His body is relaxed and his breathing even. I feel my own relief and subsequent exhaustion creep into my body. My phone vibrates in my pocket and I glance at Ryan before grabbing it. He smiles at me, looking relieved as well, and tilts his head to the side signaling me to answer it. Justin's number flashes across the screen and I hit the ignore button, feeling a stab of guilt that I try to push away, knowing that this is not the time to talk—not that it has anything to do with Ryan being mere feet away from me.

Right on the tail of Justin's call is a text from Carmen. She has already been to the Feelyne office and Rapture and is on her way here. Noises come from the other side of the door at the same time I read her message and I move quickly to Valant's side.

"Wrap it up doc; we have company!" I stand a little too close to him, not realizing until I brush against him slightly and we both jump away from each other. Hey, I'm the only one who should be disgusted, geez.

"Finishing up now, naughty nurse, and there we go. Some of my best work yet I would say! I'll be waiting to hear from you again soon, Alexis. We have your lovely brother to catch next." He puts his hand in front of him, his palm facing down like we are going to have a 'go team' hand pile up, and his eager face looks from Ryan to me before he sighs and gives up.

"Ah, such a serious bunch. You know what you've been missing, oh, besides the bumping of your uglies? Me! Everyone should have a resident Demon expert on any good team, right gang? Well, I'm full and ready for a nap. Later!" In his dramatic fashion, he swirls into his small, dark red tornado and disappears. I swear he is drunk off his drama-filled feeding. Who am I kidding? He is always like that.

My eyes meet Ryan's and we smile at one another. The voices stop outside the door, and I know our visiting time is over. Carmen will be here soon and...Shane's hand in mine stops me in mid-thought while my head tips toward his.

"Thank you, Alex, Ryan, thank you." His voice is a whisper and he is asleep again before I can respond. Instead, I squeeze his hand and kiss his cheek. Hopefully he will think this all a dream; if not we can address that later.

Ryan subtly unlocks the door, and we stand by Shane as the doctor and nurse enter. Carmen comes soon after and I leave her to hear the awesome news about his recovery. As Ryan and I make our exit, we hear Carmen's cry of joy as Shane grabs her hand. She whispers that she loves him. My heart swells and I enter the elevator with a smile on my face. But that soon turns into a sneer as I feel Greg's championship ring in my bag while I search for some gum.

"All I need is a boost of energy from the surf; I'll do some work at the office and then I'll help out at Rapture tonight. But after that it's down to Rosarito and not for the Cerveza and tequila. Nope, the manhunt for that little pissant will be on." I turn to Ryan, a questioning look in my eyes, but I already know his answer.

"Whatever needs doing we'll be doing together, Lex, you don't even need to ask." We smile at each other, old times creeping back in, and just as I felt when we first met, I know Ryan and all his badassness belongs in my life.

CHAPTER 10

Rapture

Journal Entry:

I wasn't particularly surprised when my foster mother announced that we were tearing down the house. Oh, she used some rationale about the foundation crumbling beneath us, and having to move the whole thing altogether. I knew that deep inside she wanted to bring this place and all of its Steven-ness to the ground. And I, I would be happy to provide the matches and the gasoline. Instead, I spent that last semester my senior year of high school helping her plan out the rebuild. It was going to be beautiful: soft, warm, and homey. I could understand why she didn't want to move from the gorgeous plot of land we had, surrounded by not only our acreage but also the protected environments close to the National Monument.

Aside from the multitude of light and bathroom fixtures I waded through with her, I also had to meet some of the contractors and land management people. Believe me, I could sense their desire to build more and more, to rip up parts of our undeveloped land for more homes near us, maybe even shopping centers and a golf course. I know the Lorax would have a fit down here, but since he isn't real, and I am, I decided to take his place.

One day, nearing the end of the plotting out of the new house placement and before things really got moving, we came from our nearby rental to check on things. In our absence, some land procurers were out marking off areas outside our property line. I sent out my senses and felt their greed and trickery. I made a note of the dates and times they spoke of returning. I knew they were counting on us not being around. Their plan was to clear some areas outside of our land 'accidentally' and then pay a fine. At that point it would be too late, and they would claim that without the trees and plants there, the land was still sustainable to allow for new builds of all sorts. What's a small fine to these guys? Nothing. The worst of all was that they planned to encroach on our land and blame it on my foster mom, stating that she wanted a guesthouse area out there and they were just clearing it for us. What a bunch of dickheads.

I went to tell my foster mom, but she was super busy running around with last-minute house items and getting ready to leave for a business trip. She had started speaking publically about suicide after Steven 'took his life.' Sometimes I wondered if by her believing he had done it, I had saved her life as well. She is a survivor, and she knows how to reach others in need.

So it is up to Bear and me. The night before they are supposed to come in with their diggers and tree cutters, we camp out deep in our land, Chey safe in our rental with my foster mom's aunt who is watching us while my foster mom is away.

In the morning, the rumbling mechanical monsters make their trek up and I motion Bear to stay with me. Arms waving and voice strong, I yell at the beer-bellied man behind the gears of the cutter, shouting at him to stop at once. His look is one that tells me he doesn't get paid enough to deal with crazy teenagers, but he stops anyhow. Once he tells me where the man in charge is, I leave Bear to stand there growling at the man, keeping his hand from turning the key again.

Bill is the boss man, and he is in his suit keeping his hands clean in his souped-up pick-up truck. He is startled to see me and the oh-shit look in his eyes is telling. Busted! A bulldozer roars nearby, and I whistle for Bear before yelling to Bill.

"Turn your engines off now; you do not have permission or the right to be here. This is our land and you're trespassing." I pull Greg's old BB gun from behind my back and allow it to hang by my knees. The Earthen energy around me is intense, as if it can tell something awful may happen, that the earth's soil, roots, and body may be ripped apart at any moment. But I will not let that happen, not today, not ever, for I am the Lorax today–maybe more like Gandalf from The Lord of the Rings–telling these iron monsters that they shall not pass.

I keep my eyes on Bill while I walk toward the bulldozer. I stand in front of its massive body and dig deep into the earth, willing Gaia's help as she sends her power into me. I allow it to seep from me into the engine and lines of the machine, warping and slowly eroding them, reveling in the silence as the engine dies. As if on cue, a hawk swoops down from the circling sky, landing right above me, head darting around, beady eyes staring down at Bill. Bill's truck door opens and he climbs out, scratching his head at the bulldozer and looking suspiciously at me.

"I'd like to see your papers, Bill; you know, the ones that allow you to trespass on protected land, or our land for that matter. I have a feeling you don't have those though, Bill, now do you?" The hawk cries out and Bill jumps, not having seen the massive bird at first. The hawk stretches its wings and calls out again in the chill of the morning; echoing calls are heard elsewhere, as if an army of troops stand at the ready to take on this attack. Bear growls next to me, and Bill is perspiring despite the coolness at this time of day. I can tell his brain is trying to make sense of what is going on. I even toy around with the idea of tinkering with him a little myself, but he seems to be reaching the best conclusion all on his own. Plus, I am pretty sure he is hardcore superstitious, and shit is just not going his way for a reason this morning and he isn't about to risk seeing what may happen next.

"You know what, little lady, I just thought to myself that we were in the wrong spot. Major error on my office's part, I'm sure. We'll be going, of course. Sorry for the confusion." He looks worriedly at the bulldozer, wondering if I am going to call the land management people and whether I have the proof I need with his machine dead in its tracks. I believe this will be the end of it now, as he knows I am on to him, so I allow my power to seep back in and repair the damage. No need to keep the ugly destroyer here any longer.

Within minutes they are all gone, and only the tracks leave a trace of the near destruction of the land. The hawk gives me one last cry before taking off to the sky. A family of deer walks by in his wake, unafraid of Bear and me and grateful for our intervention, the fawns innocently bobbling as they try to keep up with the pace.

I feel powerful once more, a badass soldier in a secret war, not to be trifled with now or ever.

Waiting for news is torture—news from Vex about the Healers, from my mom about my dad's location and from Sandra as she tries to get a firmer location on Greg. The edge-of-my-seat, pins-and-needles feeling makes me grind my teeth, creating a symphony of noises in my head as my pulsing eardrums keep the bass beat. Each one of these intense happenings is driving me mad with the sheer lack of control of when or what will happen. Why do I have this sickening feeling that it may all crash down on me at once? I wish there were three of me.

I am itching to tell Vex and Terra about the Dreamwalk Valant stole from me—ah crap, they will freak about Valant—but don't they have to know already? Jeez, it's hard enough agreeing to work with a Demon. Now it's like I feel I have to hide that I'm hanging out with that 'bad friend' we all had and were forbidden to bring home. Knowing those two, they have already heard about this incident, but maybe not specifically the words that Valant heard, that it was "for the good of the cause." Boy, this person has some crazed agenda if killing innocent Healers is considered good. Ah, so many things to worry about and my hands are fucking tied at the moment.

Oh, and to top it all off, who in the hell taught Dana how to text? I'm getting about one text an hour asking me when I am getting back to the desert. I know she doesn't live in the world I do. Dana is in the Protectors' world, and she cannot understand how I can live in both or why I am still hanging on to 'normal' life and people. After what happened to Shane I am sort of seeing her logic, but then the last text she sent was a sick attempt to get me back there so I could see Justin as well. Yuck, who taught her about Internet porn anyhow?

At least being at the club is distracting enough for now, although my teeth continue to grind and push a chill through me over and over. The loud, pulsing music and dressed-to-the-nines crew in Rapture tonight manage to make me smile. I didn't get an opportunity to watch the opening fully unfold over the last few weeks, or even assist in working out the kinks. I think that Carmen, Sandra, and the boys did a fine job. It's been less than a month yet for some reason being here feels so alien. All of the things I had developed with Shane: the music thrilling through me, the lights playing all around me, all things I have loved and lost myself to are just not giving me the same spark right now. My mind is too heavy with worry, my muscles triggering to fight rather than dance. However, fighting is a dance of sorts and my picking up on it is most likely attributed to the movements and sequences I've been performing for fun all these years. No, training isn't the same as club dancing I know, but it has been fun and challenging. Seeing some of the characters here, I can tell things may get out of hand at some point, so I am glad I know how to subdue someone, either gently or in a quick takedown.

The club is doing well though, and women and men appear to be dancing without fear of unwanted groping and advances. I see plenty of wanted ones, so that is A-OK, even though I have to turn away every so often—yeesh. Yes, Ryan has this place under control. Troublemakers pop up now and again I am sure, but I bet they are quickly and easily squelched. He makes the boundaries perfectly clear here at Rapture. Act like a disrespectful idiot and get your ass kicked out.

Calvin Harris fades out as I do a sweep of the dance floor, hearing Kygo's "Firestone" take its place. My body responds as it has a hard time ignoring the smoothness of the song and the lyrics. My mind tingles, signaling that the badass mental Peeping Tom is nearby. I pick up my pace through the throngs of people and after walking up a few steps to the next level that leads to the bar, I see Ryan standing on the far side of the dance floor. His eyes immediately connect with mine and the dream I had of us at the club in the desert fills my head and causes my thighs to press together. My back arches as I try to keep my arousal at bay. Oh, I am in trouble being around this man again, especially now that I am listening to his side of the story instead of storming off in a rage.

My body sings with the electronic tones and tribal bass beats, but I feel disconnected with this life. As if that Alex disappeared a little in Greg's basement, sinking into the floor along with my blood as it dripped away, sinking sickly into the wooden floor.

I make my way to the bar, looking at my phone for the hundredth time for any inkling of an update on everything that is hanging on the precipice. I laugh a little at myself thinking of Vex texting me, and it is much-needed comic relief to all this seriousness. I order my double vodka and soda and drain it. Sandra saddles up next to me, ordering her own, and is greeted in a flash by a buff, handsome bartender brandishing her drink and giving her a sly smile and a wink. She takes it and allows her fingers to touch his hand briefly and somehow extremely seductively before taking the glass away.

"I'll give him his tip later." Her declaration nearly has me spitting the last remnants of my drink into her face.

"Looks to me like your 'tips' are getting you some serious VIP status at the bar." Sandra is a bombshell in her hip-hugging red dress and fuck-me high-heel shoes. I find myself staring at the metal heels and thinking how fucking cool it would be to have Dana's influence on a pair of those. I make a mental note and order another drink.

Sandra is a sharp and sexy businesswoman who never needs to cross the line to get the VIP treatment, yet she always has the boys eating out of the palm of her hand. She has a draw, and I suspect her Seer status has something to do with it as her mysticism oozes from her being. I've missed her and being around her makes me feel more at ease and at home in my own skin, despite all my inner changes.

"Any word or vision on Greg? Did the information on the bar and the skeevy drug dealer buddy Luis help out at all?" I don't want to wear her out with all the vision work. I'm unclear on how it works, and really why it works, but if it's anything like my Earthen power, it's easy to be quickly drained. Sandra shakes her head and takes a long sip of her drink. I am starting to think that maybe she could drink right along with me all night.

"I'm going back to the hospital tonight and make Carmen take a break; I want to work on Shane a bit more. Keep your phone close, but my concern now is that Valant has drained everything from him and I may not have much to work with. I may need to use my other skills to get my hands on the samples they took and kill two birds with one stone. We need those samples to disappear anyhow, don't we?"

She is right on that one. Ryan and I took care of changing the nurses' and doctors' memories of the existence of drugs in his system, but didn't get to the samples. I had planned on morphing my appearance a bit to get them later, but I bet Sandra has some good tricks up her sleeve.

"Always with the blood in this racket, isn't it? Well, have another with me before you go. I'm on high alert as it is, and that last one barely eased a single muscle."

"Sure, but you have a tiger coming your way at six o'clock so we better make it quick. Oh, and maybe you should give Justin a call, eh? Been avoiding him a bit since you've been back to Ryanland?" Grrr. I do need to get back to him after the two missed calls and a text asking me where I am. Even without her heads up, I already knew Ryan was coming; I can feel his power signature purring into my spinal cord. Sandra orders two more doubles with a silly-ass grin on her face. She loves my personal life drama much more than I do.

"Hey Lex, Sandra. Lex, do you mind checking on one of the female patrons in the bathroom? I think her abusive douche ex-boyfriend is messing with her again, but I haven't located him yet. We bounced him out weeks ago. He's been sending her some threatening text messages tonight and I sensed him a little while ago but lost the trace of him on the dance floor."

My skin prickles with rage as I think about some jackass who tosses his girlfriend around being here in the club. I reach out to grab my glass, intending on taking it down, when I feel Ryan's eyes on me intensely. I follow them to my chest, and before I smack him for looking at my breasts, I realize he is looking at the dolphin pendant I changed his ring into. I open my mouth to say, "what of it, it's mine isn't it," but instead I nearly smack myself in the forehead. I grab my purse, fishing around for the ring Ryan had given to me.

"Sandra, I almost forgot. Here's Greg's ring that he left on purpose in Shane's car. Geez I'm an idiot; I totally forgot to give it to you after Valant intruded on us this morning." Ryan's eyebrow rises and he looks from Sandra to me with a smirk on his face; I give him my best 'really?' look. He shrugs and laughs it off. His sexual innuendo breaks off the inner beating I was giving myself for forgetting to give Sandra the ring. What a fucking whirlwind this has all been, but no matter what, I need to keep my head on or I will lose precious time.

"Be careful; it was booby-trapped for me, but who knows what it may do to you. Why don't you go back in the office and check it out while Ryan and I are here; that should be the safest. I'll have Ryan post up outside."

Sandra walks away, but Ryan lingers for a moment. Oh great, what is he going to say now?

"You going to be okay handling this guy without me?" Thinking of the sniveling abuser in my club has bile rising in my throat. Coolness hits my chest and I realize it is Ryan's ring. Wait...what the fuck? It has turned back into his ring—the sun, the moon and stars chasing each other endlessly. I glance at Ryan with a mix of annoyance and curiosity.

He tilts his head while looking at the ring, seeming just as confused as I am, but he is also much happier with its original state being restored. I blow out my breath and flip a curl from my face.

"Let's ease down a little before you make quick work of this guy," Ryan says. "Maybe you can take a different approach, maybe more like working on him and changing his mindset. He could have been abused when he was young; the circle of violence just needs to be broken and he needs to learn what it means to be a real man." Damn, his words are like caramel dripping off his tongue. He is indeed a real man and for the first time in weeks I find that place in the back of my mind and heart that misses and longs for him. The part that wishes none of what I had believed from Dana was true. But the task at hand is not about us, it is about another broken couple, and in this duo the dude needs an ass kicking.

"Why would you come to me with this and not expect me to want to pummel him?" I am seething a bit, my emotions fluxing from desire for Ryan to the urge to use my training on someone.

"Because, Lex, you're strong, and I know you can disassociate these two people from your past. Use your skills for some real world stuff when you can. We're not only meant to fight the Absolute Protectors. These violent, unhappy people are part of how their evil side tries to defeat us. Let's beat them and balance things out by bringing this guy to our side rather than destroying him altogether, which may cause him to lash out even more on her." Ryan has me there; I remember my mom's less-than-stellar boyfriends coming after her if anyone, including me, even tried to stand up for her.

"Besides, Lex, you need to focus on her as well; she's broken, remember? And I know you know what that feels like. We need her healthy and solid. Her positive, strong energy makes us stronger and the earth stronger." Ah, got me again.

"Fine," I grumble, fondling the bracelet around my wrist. I had warped Serenity and Chaos into a wooden bangle instead of their normal state as hairpins. My curls, untethered, wind down my back and flow around my shoulders.

While Sandra and Ryan go toward the office, I see Ryan's team spread out like wraiths. It is a well-oiled machine and the man at the helm is no joke. I head to the bathroom, not only to keep my nerves occupied rather than pacing outside the office waiting for news on Greg, but also to make a difference in this girl's life. I use my senses to find someone in her mental state and right away zero in on her in a back stall. I knock and identify myself as one of the owners who wants to check in on her. Ryan said her name was Ana and that she would be comfortable once she knew I was his friend.

"Ana? Ryan sent me; he knows your situation and just wants to make sure the guy is leaving you alone. Can you come out or can I come in?"

The last stall door peeks open and a petite blond girl with a short bob and a black dress befitting Audrey Hepburn stares at me with tear-soaked eyes and red cheeks. I smile at her and make a motion for her to come out, but instead she motions me in. The stalls are large enough, so I come to her without hesitation.

"It's nice to meet you, Ana, and I am truly sorry about your ex. Is he here tonight or bothering you in some other way?" She is shaking, which is even more noticeable when she passes her phone to me.

"I'm not sure if Max is really here or if he's just taunting me, but I can't relax thinking he is out there or that he'll do something to me when I leave." This jerk is going to get it, I swear; this little girl shaking like a leaf is about to make me send a blast of power at him no matter where he is. His messages cycle between begging her to give him another chance to threatening her and anybody she was or ever will be with.

"He keeps telling me that everything will be better when I take him back and that he promises not to hurt me again. His dad used to beat his mom right in front of him, and I watched his dad hit him at least ten times last Christmas. It was Max's idea to invite his father over—a gesture of good will, even though his parents have been separated for years. Max hoped he'd be civil, but he was wrong. He's my first real boyfriend. Nobody ever made me feel loved before. I felt safe, sexy, funny, and needed, but then everything changed—he changed. Now I just feel scared." Tears tumble down her face. I hand her some tissue and touch her shoulder lightly. She tenses, her muscles jumping with unease. Ya, this guy has done a number on her and boy, can I relate. She continues through her sniffles and I let her go on, allowing her time to tell her story.

"Do you think Max will ever get better? Even if he isn't with me all I can think about are the other women and that he may never have a family...or what if he does? Oh, what if he has children?" Well, the good thing is Ana knows what the deal is and isn't ready to just give in to Max easily. She isn't telling me she needs him back or that she even misses him; nope, she's worried about him as a person and any other people he may hurt. Those are good signs, rare but good. Time for me to make sure I seal that deal, because whatever the issue is with Max, Ana doesn't need to be his punching bag while he gets help. Even if that help is from me; that is, if I can help with this type of thing. I have helped heal recent mental scars and remove immediate memories, but Max has been turning into this man for years, maybe nearly his entire life.

"Ana, you're beautiful and obviously smart and level headed. If it's a healthy relationship he should make you feel good about yourself, and seeing you right now and reading his texts I can tell that isn't the case." She is nodding her head in agreement but what she says next breaks my heart.

"You know what the worst part is? I want to hit him back. I save spiders, damn it, and now he makes me so sad and angry that I feel I may hit him right back. And then I think about the little boy watching all that violence. Having to stand up to his dad and defend his mom only to get tossed aside. Now, here I am, wanting to hit him. Am I turning into him? He gets into these rages and can't come down, especially when he drinks. He attacked my best friend—a guy—once and now he's telling me he'll get me tonight; I just can't relax."

I understand the fear she is living in; Steven threatened me, my dog, my foster sister, even my friends and coaches all the time. This guy is going down! To hell with this bringing him to our side shit—he doesn't deserve it. But first and foremost Ana needs my attention.

"Ana, look at me." Something old and nearly forgotten comes to me; words rush out like when I was in Avalon with Lestan, back when he jump-started me from my own psychological prison.

"Ana, this isn't your fault. You didn't ask for any of this. You deserve to be loved, to be free to trust, to have friends—to be happy." I send my Earthen power into her as I speak the words, a mantra I told myself over and over for the first few years after Steven was bound away. I don't know how I would have made it in college or ever had a boyfriend if I hadn't worked on myself and believed in these words. I focus on her hippocampus where we all store negative feelings. A woman's is much larger, of course. What a shock as we can't seem to let things go and any new thing triggers the rest of 'em! Ana is so young, twenty-two at most. She doesn't need those negative thoughts, feelings, and urges. She doesn't need to become violent herself. No, she can leave that dirty work to us. Ana will have clear building blocks to her future, without the urge to hurt this man back; I can give her that. The rest is up to her and hopefully the magic of the mantra will help Ana to heal, as I had.

I repeat the mantra again as she looks into my eyes; they light up as the words sink in and the urge to go toe to toe with Max eases out of its hiding spot. I will not allow the cycle to continue. No, she will not become the aggressor in her relationships. Ana begins to smile a bit, and her tears fade. The tiny quaking aspen tree stands a little taller, and she speaks the words back to me.

"This isn't my fault. I didn't ask for any of this. I deserve to be loved, to be free to trust, to have friends—to be happy." I nod to her, and she takes my hand. A little girl breaks free from her, and she is nearly bouncing on her toes. Yes, this is a shallow wound and she is a strong girl, stronger than she had known, but now, now she does.

I delete the messages from Max after texting him to meet me at the lower bar in ten minutes. I hand her phone back to her and then wave my office make-up bag and motion for her to get out of this stall, freshen up, and get back out there with her friends.

While the new and improved version of Ana works on removing the mascara stains off her cheeks, she sways to the music thumping against the walls. I send Ryan a text letting him know where Max will be, if he does indeed turn up. I will meet the boy wonder there, being the most inconspicuous spot, as our security staff usher Ana and her friends to a safe VIP location. I get the 10-4 from Ryan, but he will have eyes on me and be right around the corner. Sandra is doing her thing in the office, and he is still holding his post outside the door. I think her Seer skills give him the heeby-jeebies.

Ana had given me Max's description and it doesn't take long to pick up on his tightly wound essence. He is about my height, thin but defined. It doesn't take a lot of muscle to hurt a person, but the fact that he was both traumatized as a child, and strong, makes him even more dangerous.

What is my plan here? Am I really going to toss his ass out and make a scene, or try to work on him? Is it safe? I know I thought about doing the same thing with Carson when he was deep into his addiction but I worried I would change him too much. Even if I try to tease out Max's violent thoughts toward Ana, he will just find another target. I don't know how deep the trauma from his past goes; I could change him completely. Maybe I can put an idea in his head, one to get help and then he can see my good ole doctor Reynolds. I know she knows another specialist besides fake McAdams, and perhaps they can work on removing his trauma safely. Shouldn't I leave it up to the experts? I mean, I am a Healer and a Protector...uh oh, light bulb: Valant! Oh, he is going to love this. I turn on my heels and go back to the last stall in the bathroom.

"Alright Valant, feeding time. Oh and be discreet, will ya, kind of in the woman's bathroom." In an instant, Valant is in the too-close-for-comfort stall with me, and I let out a guffaw at his voluptuous appearance. If I didn't know better, I would say he is emulating Sandra, but instead I think he truly is the Demon's female version of himself to a T. He runs his hand down his side, cocks a hip at me, and flips his hair.

"What's up, girlfriend? Are we going to have some fun tonight or what?" All I can do is shudder at the thought of Valant and I dancing and boozing it up together like BFFs. He gives me some kissy noises and then flashes a bright freaky smile topped off with his sharp glittering teeth and his tongue moving seductively over them. Ew.

"Look, Miss Thing, I have a tasty morsel for you but leave him sane, will ya, and no stealing him away to your little house of hell; that's not part of the deal." I fill Valant in on Max, and he brushes me off like he has dealt with worse while being Greg's sidekick. Do I feel a little jealousy for a second? Oh no. I'm not starting to like having Valant around, am I?

We flank Max at the bar, and it only takes one touch for Valant to enrapture Max. They move off to a quiet section outside, and I watch them from the window-paned wall. I guess Valant and I aren't very different after all. He is actually a better healer than I am when it comes to the deeply embedded psychological stuff. This train of thought has me wondering more about his dimension. Or is it another world like ours? How was Valant created if it wasn't by the hands of our gods and goddesses who left us with their creation: their child Gaia and her power deep within her being? Maybe some day I'll have a nice little chat with Valant.

My pocket buzzes and I see Justin's name flash across the screen. I slip outside to take his call on the quieter patio where Valant sits with Max not more than fifty feet away. It looks as if Max is crying, and I wonder if Valant picks up on my wish to harm him slightly and is making him grieve and feel sorry for his sins. Does it scare me that I feel no concern for him? I mean, I cared enough to ask Valant for help, didn't I?

"Hi, Justin. Sorry, I've been tied up with Shane and the club. How are you? I miss you." Warm arms wrap around me, and I jump as Justin's lips kiss my neck.

"Surprise." Oh, what a surprise it is. I guess if I had taken his calls or even listened to his voicemail I might have known he was coming back to San Diego. I feel slightly on edge when I should be ecstatic. With that thought, I turn around and embrace him. I kiss him deeply and hold him close. Just as I am starting to pull away, Ryan's silver gift to me turns ice cold, burning my skin and making me jump backward. I turn toward the windows and see Ryan standing just inside. His eyes meet mine for a heartbeat, and when I can take no more, I turn away.

"Justin, what a surprise! When did you get in?" He takes my hands and moves me to sit at a table closer to Valant. Oh goddess, please don't have Valant come over here. Who knows what he would say.

"I just got in about an hour ago, showered, and came here before I head to the hospital. Do you think I'll be able to see him?" Before I can answer, Sandra comes rushing out the doors, nearly skidding to a halt when she spots Justin. Her eyes are wide and wild, knowing in them a secret location I have been waiting for all day. I quickly turn back to Justin and ready my face to reflect a mix of friendship, duty, and a rare dash of guilt. In truth, I am not sure any man will ever come before the responsibilities I know I have as an Earthen Protector, but I can't deny the delicious taste of potential revenge that wraps its way around my core.

"Justin, I'm so sorry, the Mexican police have asked Ryan and me to come down with some of the American police to see about the guy they think is responsible for what happened to Shane. I told them we wanted to help in any way that we can, and Sandra was just on the phone with them getting details. I think they need us to come now." Justin's face drops momentarily, but I know he sees the eagerness in my eyes. He also knows what Shane means to me, and being a stand-up guy, he quickly places a look of understanding on his face and takes me into his arms.

"Of course, Alex, I wouldn't expect anything less. I'll go see Shane and wait for word. I'm sure Carmen and his family will rest easier knowing you're helping apprehend the jackass who did this." Ryan comes outside to join us, and Justin parts from me to shake his hand.

"Take care of my girl now." Ryan gives him a nod and turns to me.

"I'm ready when you are. Sandra and the guys will handle things for the rest of the night and if all goes well, we'll be back to help out tomorrow." I see Justin flinch a tad at the overnight statement. I don't think he suspects anything between Ryan and me, but maybe I am just kidding myself.

I give Justin one last hug and kiss and follow Sandra and Ryan into the office. In the small space, Sandra relays the details of where we would find Greg. We would have to get a boat, and Ryan chimes in that he has all that taken care of. In fact, we are leaving San Diego by boat. Is there no end to what this guy has at his fingertips?

Sandra is pretty shaken-up as she tells us what she saw, the most defining moment being when Greg looked at her in the vision and snarled, "Come and get me, my sister!"

CHAPTER 11

Into the Storm

Journal Entry:

When I met Carson, I knew then and there that I could finally be intimate with a guy. Why? Because nearly every night I'd dream about being with him in that fashion. It got embarrassing when I saw him at the lab, knowing what my mind was allowing him to do to me. A year earlier, I never would have felt it possible. I now not only had feelings for a guy, but they involved wanting to be physical as well.

Last night Carson and I made love, and now I am back at home, bouncing off the walls, giddy, trying to get to bed. Carmen must think I am insane and is possibly second-guessing her decision to allow me to move in. I talk Carmen's ear off for about an hour before Bear snuggles up his sixty-pound body on my bed and I fall quickly to sleep. The final thoughts playing around in my mind are of my body next to Carson's. My ability to love and feel safe in his arms breaks apart the fury and anger of my past. Sounds disappear from my room, my body began to feel a lightness, and then I am gone.

I know where I am before my eyes even crack open. The fairy light and the mossy earth beneath me are all I need to know I am back in Avalon. I rise to my feet quickly, eager to see Lestan. We used to see each other in my dreams a lot more than we do now. Actually, when I think about it, the more I dreamed of Carson, the less I thought of or saw Lestan. Perhaps Avalon was a childhood dreamland, and I am growing out of it as I finally move into womanhood.

As I make my way toward the path, my squirrel, bunny, and bird friends keep tripping me up and flapping around in my face. The more I wave them away, the more my uneasiness increases. Soon the greenhouse comes into view, and I can tell right away that something has happened here, something bad.

I take my time walking around the glass house. Lestan loves this greenhouse. Growing and tending the plants was something he and his mom used to do together. She died when he was young, so we were both sort of orphaned. He by death and the arm's length at which his dad left him, and me by a deceased father and a mother who was who-knows-where.

The greenhouse is glowing less than usual, and every few feet there are cracks in odd places. What happened, and am I safe here? Pushing my worry aside, and drawing some Earthen power into my being, I make my way toward the door, which is barely hanging on its hinges. Once I wedge myself through the doorway, the sight is devastating. The once-gorgeous orchids, trays of unique mosses, vines with blooms glowing and bursting with light are all barely hanging on, if not destroyed altogether. Dirt, rocks, roots, and bits of gloriously colored petals are strewn all over the greenhouse floor. I crouch down to assess the damage further when a huge black cat comes through the door. I freeze. The creature eyes me immediately but plays aloof and walks on the outskirts of the greenhouse, stalking around, sniffing, patting, and flicking his tail along the way. I keep my eyes on him, turning in a slow circle in my crouch, my breathing silent and my nerves on edge.

"I dare say his father does have a temper, doesn't he?" What the fuck was that? The chilling, sarcastic voice echoes around me and in my head. Crap, is Vex here? Dang, I didn't do anything else, I swear!

"Who said that?" I hear a thunk and spin 180 degrees, spotting the cat instantly atop one of the only tables that is still intact. He is absent-mindedly licking his paw, his body half the size of a panther and nothing near the size of the domestic cats I have ever known.

"Only two of us here that I can see, unless I'm just a voice in your head and not truly here at all." The cat continues to lick himself, but I have the sneaking feeling that he is the one speaking to me, crazy as that sounds. Though why do I still think it is crazy to be around talking animals and magical places? Terra and Vex have already christened that whole market.

I rise slowly and make my way toward him, power in my fingertips, the green leaves trickling off my fingers.

"Whose father has the temper? Lestan's?" The cat stops licking his paw and looks at me briefly before eyeing my glowing fingers. His eyes return to mine and his voice is once again in my head.

"You are not from here, but you can wield our Avalon power all the same. Who are you, girl?

"My name is Eila and no, I'm not from here. So this place does exist? This isn't all in my head? And you didn't answer my question. Who did all of this? Where is Lestan?"

"Well, Eila, Lestan's father—the king, our king—is the one who tore this place apart. Lestan's favorite and most cherished space brought to ruins. The woods echoed with his fury at Lestan's failure." Failure? What did Lestan do, or rather what did he not do? The cat's voice answers my question even though he doesn't say it aloud.

"It had something to do with you, Eila. Yes, your name was the one tossed around in the fury. Lestan did not do what he was told when it came to you. All I heard was his father yelling 'here, Eila was supposed to stay here!'"

Whoa, what in the world is going on? Rather, what in this world is going on?

"Lestan helped me heal; he spent time with me, telling me stories about his mom and teaching me about these plants. He never asked me to stay and never asked to come with me. Honestly, I thought Avalon existed only in my head. A world created as a way for me to escape all the pain and fear of my world." The cat stands and stretches, his claws raking into the wood and causing it to groan under his sharp nails and weight. His eyes dig into mine, flecks of gold swimming inside the pools of his eyes and glowing like the sun. As he makes his way toward me I freeze, yet nothing in my power senses danger, only wariness. When he rubs up against me I am in shock, my mouth opening and closing like a fish out of water.

"Oh, we're real, Eila, just as your dimension on your earth is real. You're a dimensional traveler and one that our Sir King permitted to enter. No, no one is allowed here besides our own. You're different somehow, and he wanted you to stay."

"But why? Why didn't he just ask me? There are many times in my life I would have been happy to stay."

"That I do not know; perhaps Lestan can tell you more. Though I don't foresee when he'll be permitted to leave his home again. Coming here may be too painful *for him anyhow. Look around you." He is right. His place, our place, is in ruins. And then an idea comes to me: I can heal the plants here, can't I? I am not certain since I have never healed anything in Avalon. Or have I? I did heal myself, with Lestan's help that is. My eyes glint and I look at the cat.*

"Oh, I've seen that look before, girl. That look is one of gloriously terrible ideas, it is." *Yes, perhaps it is a terrible idea. Lestan's dad did destroy it, after all. He may not be delighted to see it back in one piece. Of course, with what he has done to Lestan, I could care less about what His Highness thinks.*

"May I ask your name, Cat? You're much more than a cat though, aren't you? I can tell most definitely that you're more powerful than a mere pussycat like those in my world. How about you help me fix this place, Lestan's place? You obviously care for him in some way or you wouldn't waste your time telling me his sad tale."

"Perhaps you're right, Eila. Perhaps I do care about Master Lestan. He did allow me in his Greenhouse; it was where I helped keep the pests at bay and away from his plants; kind of a pact of sorts. And when the pests were bigger— and trust me there are some interesting creatures in this land that can take down a place such as this with one strike—well, I became bigger as well." *The cat stretches, leaps from the table, and in mid-flight he changes. Not into a larger cat, no, he turns into a massive elk, horns as wide as the walls are tall. A gorgeous sight he is, though I worry about the glass being shattered if he turns the wrong way too quickly.*

"Oh, don't worry about me being clumsy, Eila, for I can change in a blink of an eye. Lestan calls me the best guard in all the land." *And on his last syllable his eyes spark gold and he changes into a massive winged bird with claws as sharp as knives and eyes glinting and as beady as any of the Earth-dwelling raptors I study.*

"Of course, Lestan is the only one who knows about me. That is except you, of course, and you won't tell a soul here, will you? No, you're bound to Lestan, and now we shall be bound as well with our secret. I cannot say what the king will do once he sees what we have done, but perhaps if he knows you helped, things may not be so bad for Lestan."

Now that is an odd statement, and a chill runs up my spine. Why would it matter if the king knows about me being here? And why would his knowledge of what I will do to help Lestan appease him? Before I can ask the questions swarming in my head like hornets, the bird changes into an enormous gorilla and casually lifts massive pieces of a destroyed table. Once he has all the parts somewhat close together, his eyes swim with gold again and the table is mended in an instant. Shock hits me first and then a smile spreads across my face.

"My name is Thatcher, Friend Eila, and I am a shape-shifter and fixer of inanimate objects. Course, I'm a destroyer as well, and being both has exiled me from my people. Even my own parents watched me leave without a word. One makes a few mistakes and, well, here I am." Well, I guess I'm not the only hybrid with magical abilities that has been abandoned, sort of kismet for Thatcher and I. I reach my hand out to him and he changes in an instant into a smaller, hamster-like animal and stands up in my hand, whiskers twitching in time with his fluttering heartbeat.

"Nice to meet you, Thatcher. As you're Lestan's friend you're mine as well. I accept you for the unique and incredible creature you are. You may count me as family till yours get their heads out of their asses. Now, shall we get to work?" Thatcher looks up at me.

"Lestan took me in and gave me a home, and so I will help you fix his beloved house of glass, the place special to him for his mother and you. He shall know it has been done and that his Eila helped."

Well shit. Let's get to it!

Thatcher leaps off my hand and turns back into a raptor. He makes his way toward another table and lifts heavy flowerpot pieces, shaking the dirt from them, and laying them together. In an instant they are back together again. It is time to do my part and I move toward the shredded and broken bits of plant and flower, willing them to reform.

We find a wheeled cart and rope, Thatcher turns into an elk, I latch the cart to Thatcher, and we move delicious dirt in from the outside. The plants nearly moan with happiness as we cover them in rich soil and water them with stream water. I smile as we make our way through the madness. Two abandoned hybrids, cleaning and mending the destruction.

Leaving the San Diego Bay, Ryan is at the helm as we boat toward Baja Mexico. Greg has been playing back and forth between Rosarito, some seedy streets in Tijuana, and by boat amongst the mainly uninhabited and mysterious Coronado Islands. He must be cloaking himself whenever he nears them. Most people aren't allowed to come near the islands very often, and a Navy outpost dwells there, as well as lighthouses geared to spot visitors in the vast ocean. Sandra said he hasn't been on land much lately, so we make our way in the darkness of night toward the Islands. My main concern is to conceal ourselves in Gaia's power, but I also need to conserve my energy. Ryan is relatively quiet most of the trip, and I can't help but hear Mumford and Son's "Believe" in my head, wishing him to say something.

Things hadn't gone so smoothly when we left the club. While we walked to his SUV he gave me a sort of cheap shot, and I sort of snapped. 'Snapped,' as in giving him a little taste of the training I got from Dana over the last month.

When we neared Ryan's car in the back alley, he quickly and aggressively spun around. A charge in the air instantly put me on high alert as I felt him use his powers to cloak us in secrecy. The feelings, brought up by the memory of the night Greg took me in a similar alley, had my brain roaring and my muscles itching for a fight.

"Why is Justin around when I'm not, and when you're with me you're usually keeping Justin at arm's length?" My face formed immediately into a look of innocence and confusion. Not my best choice, being the voice of all things should be honest and all.

"Don't look at me like that! You haven't been answering his calls or texts. Don't think I don't notice. That is except for tonight, of course. It looks like your mouth is just fine smothering his when I'm only a short distance away!" My mouth made a move to talk, but he was on me in a second. He gripped my shoulders, pushing me up against the SUV while his silver power created cold fire in his eyes. Kissing Justin in front of him hadn't been the smartest of ideas, but I am in a relationship, damn it—one with loads of honesty.

Well, at least one of us is.

I should have been understanding and soothed Ryan. Yet the force of his hands restraining me, and the reminder of Greg's actions only weeks ago, had my muscles posed to strike. I mean, we were both amped-up at the hope of finding Greg, so I made a 'great' choice and lashed out instead.

"I've already explained myself, Ryan! I figured we had no future, and I've known and trusted Justin long before you. Well really, if you think about it, I've never really trusted you! He was there when I needed him and for what I needed him for."

I had definitely pissed Ryan off now. He began gripping me tighter and leaning toward my face. Okay, that was enough, big guy.

I pushed him with not only my stronger physique, but also with the power of Gaia within me. It sent him stumbling back with a look of shock on his face that was immediately followed by a sneer as he came storming back toward me. My back to the SUV I crouched, waiting for him and eager to let off some steam.

He feigned a high lunge at me and when I swung my fist at his face, he crouched and swept my legs in a tight, low spin. I fell to the side, but caught myself in a plank so I was able to push up with my hands and flip away from him. As I landed I grabbed Serenity and Chaos off my wrist and willed them to take shape as my two fighting staffs. Green vines sparked down their length, and I felt a snarl escape my lips.

"Think I can't take you, Ryan? A lot has changed in the last few weeks. I don't need you to fight my battles and I sure as hell don't need you putting your hands on me!" Well, maybe not this way—shit, was this turning me on? I would never be able to do this with Justin.

Ryan smiled and spoke into the night.

"Come on darling, let's see what else you've got." I ran at him, spun in the air and came crashing down, striking him in succession with a rapid one, two rhythm on his arms as he blocked my assault. Ryan came out of his defensive stance so I ducked and smacked both knees in succession with Serenity striking first, followed by Chaos. He groaned and dropped to his knees. I straightened, satisfied that I hit my mark and had given Ryan a piece of what I had been working on in the desert. I shouldn't have let my guard down and gotten so cocky.

In an instant, Ryan leapt at me from his crouched position and wrapped his arms around my waist, taking me down toward the dingy alley ground. Before we landed, he swiftly slid his right arm up along my back till he held tight to me while cradling my head. His left took the force as we fell, his hand, palm down, slammed on the brakes but I didn't feel him falter. Ryan was fully on top of me, and as soon we were both safely lowered to the ground, he pinned my arms over my head. The bulk of his body made it easy for him to hold the rest of my body still. He was breathing hard, inches from my face, and I met him eye to eye, feeling the heat of the gaze roaring between us.

Despite my state of mind and the fact that we were fighting each other, I couldn't stop my body from having a mind of its own as it pressed up against his. I kept my lips tight, biting down on the bottom one, caring less if I drew blood, while I hampered the moan that built up. It took some self-control, but I released it silently in my mind. There was no true way to completely hide it from Ryan though and his biceps flexed in response. I swear I even saw his solid arms quiver. After he exhaled deeply, a smile spread across his face, and he looked down at me in the sexiest way possible. What a smug asshole.

"Impressive, Lex. I have no doubts now about you holding your own against Greg this time. But you can't yet take me, not unwillingly that is." His eyes swept down my body, and I flushed at the burning sensation of passion as they roved over me. The ring I wore on my chain glowed silver nearly on his command, and his eyes made their way back up to meet mine.

"When this Greg business is over we need to talk about your dad and how I'm going to help you find him. We work well together and, believe it or not, I care about what happens to you. But I will tell you this. If you're fully devoted to being with Justin, if you think you love him, then why is your body saying something else all together?" With his last words, his lips hovered less than an inch from mine, and I felt the urge to meet them with my own. Instead of giving me a chance to give in to my fever, Ryan lifted off me, leaving me chilled and completely fucking turned on.

Man, I couldn't even try to kick his ass without wanting to tear off his clothes.

Ryan stood, giving me his hand, cool as ever of course. He then rounded his SUV and slid into the driver's seat after opening my door. I smoothed down my top and skirt and looked around, knowing no one would have been able to see or hear us anyhow. Nevertheless I couldn't help feeling exposed and a little remorseful. At that point I was getting sick of guys altogether! Maybe Dana was right, I may need to clean house or keep things very distant and professional between Ryan and me. No way was I going to spar with him again, well, at least not for a while.

Reliving what had transpired, while we make our way toward Mexico on Ryan's friend's boat, I realize I am not the only one impacted by our little tryst, and I need him to be focused. I don't think the big guy would allow anyone to get him off track when on a mission, but our relationship has been exceptional at best. Only Sandra and Dana know where we are headed. Dana had wanted me to wait and allow her to join us but time is of the essence and I can't afford to postpone my reunion with Greg any longer.

All this time in silence is winding me as tight as a guitar string. I haven't even been able to talk to him about the Healers yet, and I am going to need him on the front lines with that one as well.

I finally get the nerve to rise from my seat and am walking to Ryan at the helm when he suddenly cuts the engines. He holds his hand out, motioning me to stop. My irritation at him subsides when I realize he must have found something.

"Okay, Lex, we're nearing the Coronado Islands; time to shadow ourselves from the lighthouse guards and military presence." I already have a subtle protection over us—mainly our sound—as a way to preserve my strength. Yet on command I move to the side of the boat and reach my hands into Gaia's ocean, pulling her power into me, manipulating it into camouflage. Ryan can feel the subtle difference and nods in my direction as he completes his level of disguise. His is more trained and geared for battle.

Ryan and I both move to the rear of the boat. We begin readying the Zodiac; with any luck we will be able to take Greg by surprise. We lower our snorkel and scuba gear into the Zodiac as well, never forgetting to have a plan B. Ryan lowers me into the boat first and then climbs in. He takes the oars and we maneuver silently around the southernmost island. Cloud cover has started to roll in, making it difficult to see. I use only the faintest power to clear our pathway, still utilizing the natural cover to our advantage.

A fifty-foot vessel comes into view and Ryan's paddling ceases. The boat is large enough to hold sleeping quarters below deck. We hug the rugged and nearly barren South Coronado coastline, a few meters away from the boat. Sea lions sleep on the rocky shore, and in the distance the lighthouse beam shines across the water. We secure the Zodiac to shore. With masks on, we slip into the water and swim toward the vessel in silence.

As we near I can sense Greg aboard the boat. He sleeps, fitfully of course, as he appears to have been hopped up on his personal chemical mix of amphetamines for days. I wonder if he has slept much at all. Great, not only is he dangerous enough as is, but now this unstable state will have him more of a raging psychopath. I open my mind to Ryan's so he can hear my thoughts.

We reach the boat like wraiths in the night, no noise escaping. Ryan motions for me to wait while he climbs the ladder first. He slips his gear off, laying it on the boat ledge, and starts up and over the side. I briefly see his lips set in a grim line; I know he is fiercely prepared to take Greg down, no matter what.

An explosion tears out of the sky and Ryan goes flying off the ship, nearly landing on the craggy shore. Instead, he is plopped perfectly into the Zodiac. Suddenly, I can't see past the boat's edge as dark clouds with burgundy flecks crackling like lightening encircle the boat. My senses tell me Ryan is alive, but then I am cut off from him entirely. I hurry aboard in a crouch, feeling the boat moving quickly away from the shore, away from Ryan. I walk slowly toward the helm, readying my power to take Greg down, but freeze at the sight in front of me. Valant, in his male form again, holds the wheel. A door below slams open as Greg scrambles above deck.

I look from Greg to Valant, thinking of the best plan. There is no way Valant doesn't know I am here, but Greg, he may think only Valant has tracked him down. That possibility is one I need to use to my advantage. I slip toward Valant, staying low and hoping—goddess I hope—he can't sense exactly where I am. I cover myself even further in Gaia's power, this time trying to mimic some of Valant's power signature so Greg believes it is just the two of them there. With a little luck, I might be able to keep my exact location from Valant as well. I slip silently by the Demon, hiding at the front of the boat. I know Valant will try to trick Greg into being his again, but I cannot let that happen.

Greg's voice comes out shrill. He is high and exhausted at the same time. Being on that edge of psychosis will make him very unpredictable. I'll see how this plays out first. I still cannot sense Ryan, the darkness of the clouds wrapped around us like a cyclone keeping my sight of what is beyond at bay.

"Valant! How did you find me, Demon? Are you working with my bitch sister? Should've known you'd trick her into utilizing your services, just as you did to me. *Where is she?*" Valant's laugh in response is sinister, to say the least. My skin crawls and a shiver goes through me. I keep my mind open to Ryan, but I don't hear a thing from him despite my inner dialog letting him know what is happening.

"Ah, Greggy dear, not looking well I see. Shall I allow you a longer nap before we deal with this trivial matter? I can be patient." Apparently Greg cannot be patient; as I peer around the corner, cloaked in disguise, I see his eyes darken. His powerful dark-gray swirl consumes him, and a shimmering darkness flies at Valant like a lightning bolt.

"Valant, if you think I'm making any more deals with you or going anywhere willingly with you then you've wasted a long trip from your hell." The darkness hits Valant, covering him in a dark swirl of madness. I lose sight of Valant and momentarily wonder if Greg has the power to hurt him severely, but I actually doubt he is strong enough, especially in the state he is in.

Laughs erupt from the grayness and then it explodes away from Valant, disappearing in a blink of an eye. The boat comes to a stop and Valant takes a seat, crossing his legs and putting his hands behind his head. He looks relaxed, bored even. I half expect him to strike up a stogey and blow the smoke in Greg's trembling, pissed-off face.

"Now, now, Greg, that's no way to greet an old friend. Let's make a deal, shall we? I've already gotten rid of one adversary for you tonight. And Alex, well, I'm sure she's here somewhere, hiding in wait for her dear brother. Are you there, Alex? Time to come out, little kitty."

Damn it. I had hoped to remain a ghost on this ship, able to steal Greg away from Valant. I am not sure how I will be able to do any of that since for some reason Valant seems hell bent on dealing with Greg.

"Where is she, Demon? This night is for her and me, not you!" Dark-gray spirals curl up his leg as he prepares to take on Valant again.

"No, Greg! The moment you tricked me was the moment you signed yourself over to me. We demons love tricks, as you know, but if we are to be tricked, well that is the greatest dishonor, and I'm here to collect. There is no escape for you. Don't you remember our agreement? Not the one with your father but our agreement when I came to work alongside you? If you betray me, in any way, shape, or form, you become mine!" Oh shit, contracts with Demons. This isn't good. How am I supposed to get Greg from him now? Greg is shaking his head madly, like a tantrumming child.

"No, no, that's not what happened. I didn't trick you at all. It was my sister I tricked. She's the one stupid enough to believe me. It was never about you; I actually helped you. You got a deal out of her instead." The whining in his voice escalates ever so slightly with each word from his lips.

Valant rises, his height seeming to increase even greater than the size I am used to. His razor-like teeth glimmer, even in the dark clouds circling us.

"Enough, you weak little human, lying to make a deal that involves me is equal to manipulating me. You cost me a body. Alex is barely a suitable replacement, the way she starves me day after day. No, Greg, you will be mine as well. That is your punishment for your breach of contract. Now play nice and come willingly before I change my mind and devour parts of you instead. And trust me, they won't be parts you want to lose." Damn it, how am I going to get Greg now? This is a Demon contract issue, and I am not willing to give Valant anything else for Greg. Fuck, I am in the same situation as I was last year, but without anything to negotiate.

Shit, Greg is not going to go down without a fight, and I am going to be right smack dab in the middle of their pissing contest. Locked on this boat, in the middle of the ocean, without my backup.

The swirling mass around Greg grows darker and tighter, bulking his frame, his muscle, and stretching his height. Instead of striking from a distance, this time he runs full force at Valant. Their frames slam together like two speeding semi-trucks. The boat rocks and dips dangerously. I have to stop them or at least two of us are going to die. I am certain Valant would swirl himself right out of here without batting an eye, whereas I wouldn't be so lucky. Terra's warning echoes in my mind and as Valant and Greg rage against each other I realize I am watching her prediction.

When they break apart, Greg's face is bloodied but otherwise he seems unharmed. His wild eyes dart back and forth, looking for Valant who has momentarily disappeared. Before I can make a move toward Greg, hoping to get him under my control before Valant does, the Demon appears directly behind Greg. Valant picks him up by his neck and shakes him in the air above him like a rag doll. Okay, enough of this.

"Valant, drop him!" Oops, wrong wording. Valant shrugs and makes a move to drop Greg over the side of the boat—freaking literal-ass demon.

"Not over the side, you jackass; on the deck, damn it."

"Boring as ever, Miss Conner. Fine, as you wish, but he is mine. You cannot kill him or take him; you have agreed to work with me, my dear. Not against me."

I can't help but roll my eyes at Valant. That second in my lack of composure costs me as Greg is upon me in a heartbeat. He leaps at me, throwing us to the floor, positioned so both of his hands can wrap easily around my throat, squeezing it like a vice. The pressure nearly knocks me unconscious in a second, but my power pushes against his hands, creating a small airway for me to breathe.

Creeping my hands out from underneath him, I summon my wooden bracelet to change into Serenity and Chaos. I force the titanium metal out of each of them and position the metal to pierce devilishly into his back. Greg cries out in pain and confusion, releasing my neck as he springs away from me. I roll to my knees and leap to my feet, staff ready and poised to take him down.

"Oh, what fun! Thank you, Alex, for this entertainment. Do go on. I sure would like to take him a little beaten and bloodied first. It's been a dull and exhausting last few hours trying to track your movements. Worked out nicely, though. Now the whole family is back together, oh, except Daddy, that is." Nice, Valant. I swear he said that on purpose to piss off Greg even more.

Well, it worked.

Greg straightens, rolling his shoulders back and shaking off the wound that he no doubt healed already. A knife comes from behind his back, the same one he made me use to slice open my arm in his basement. He sneers at my recognition of it and dances from side to side, preparing for what is next.

"How did you like my present, Alex? Did your buddy Shane make it home in one piece? Oh, I'm sure he'll never be the same, though, poor pathetic excuse for a man. I did him a favor if you ask me. All sprung over some whore. Like most men, even my father. And she like most women, just like my mother, like you...never knowing when to keep your legs sh..."

I cut his stupid-ass mouth off by screaming like a wild animal and tearing off toward him. I keep my balance despite my speed, so when he swings high at me, I dip low and spin to knock his legs out with my sweeping leg. Greg flies up, avoiding my initial blow but as he lands my tight spin continues and I crack both of his ankles with Serenity and Chaos.

The sound of his bones breaking is followed by the sound of his body falling in front of me on the boat deck. I kick the knife from his hands before pushing off my feet, planning to jump on top of him and pin him down before he can heal and move away from me. Before he can make a move, I am straddling his stomach with my knees to the floor. My power begins to work in a way I never thought possible, as I prevent him from healing himself.

142

With the drugs he has pumping in his system, the pain is probably slightly tolerable. However, when I find myself wickedly pushing his ankles down with my power, re-breaking them as he tries to mend, his tortured cries echo in the sky. I think I hear birds screeching and sea lions taking to the waves in fear as the echoes bounce off the cliffs.

"How does it feel, Greg," I spit out viciously as I stare down into his grey, soulless eyes. "You broke Shane apart, didn't you, you little shit! But you had to use a car to do it, didn't you? Well, watch real power as I break you myself!" I ease off his right ankle, allowing it to heal completely and then I rise, taking Chaos in my right hand and swinging it down again, taking his small anklebones apart with one blow.

A thrill runs though me and I look over at Valant, his hands clasped together in a sick show of glee. My stomach drops and the power pouring from me clears as I realize what I am doing. I am not this person; I am not a torturer, no matter what Greg did to Shane. No, Greg needs to pay but not in a manner that excites a Demon, for goddess's sake.

The boat seems eerily still in the ocean; no movement comes from below, yet Valant's funnel continues around us like a prison. I shake my head and step away from Greg's writhing form to address Valant.

"He must stand trial for his crimes against Shane. Let Ryan take him to the Council. They'll deal with him." I can't believe what I am saying, but what other choice do I have? I can't give him to the real police. I can't trust Valant not to let him loose on the world again, and I know the Council has punishments for his actions that only our world can understand. Yes, it would have to be this way, but how to get him from Valant is the real trick.

"Alex, you don't trust or even know the Council any more than you trust me or this little cockroach here." Valant is in front of me now, stepping on Greg's throat as he completes the last word. Greg's hand fights to remove Valant's shoe from his throat, to no avail.

"Valant, let him go! Let me bind his powers from him so he can be taken in. You've made your point, and you won't have to deal with him again. If we're to work together, we have to be able to negotiate.

Give Greg to me; I'll agree to let you help me strip him of his powers. Isn't that payback enough? Won't it be satisfying knowing he will be magically neutered?" I can see Valant debating this in his head, seeing if it is worth it at all. He releases Greg's neck from underneath his shoe and turns away from me. I use my power to keep Greg still, pressing him down into the boat's flooring. He is frozen, just as I was under his influence, something I guess he taught me. I work on freezing his mind while searching his entire body for his power before I begin squashing it. I can block it, but I won't cross the line and try to take it all together.

"Okay, Alex, we'll work together; now let's get Greg all nice and comfy before we remove him of all that makes him special and powerful." As I bend down to lift Greg up, our eyes meet, and I see what looks like relief. Am I making the right choice? Do I want him to suffer more or less?

"Don't be too relieved, Greg. I'm sure the Council has some pretty sweet punishments waiting for you."

"Oh, I'm not relieved at your decision, sister, I'm relieved at your stupidity." He breaks through my power over him and grabs my hands, pulling and forcing me down while rolling on top of me. His gray power races from his hands, commanding his knife to return.

The knife flies into Greg's hands and he raises it above his head, shouting out into the dark night. "For my father!" The knife comes streaking down toward my stomach, and I am terrified as I watch it in slow motion, paralyzed by his power. Will Valant save me? Would he care if I die? I am sure he can get Greg back one way or another. He is a Demon, after all. Do they even have feelings? A soul?

A hand comes into view, grabbing the knife easily by the tip before it can reach me. Greg, still holding fast to it, is flipped backward. Valant turns from me and storms toward Greg; the funnel cloud begins to turn black, and deep red lightening dances around us as the roaring sound of the ocean causes my chest to tremor.

"You dare take my newest contract from me, boy? Have you learned not a single lesson?" Oh shit, Valant is really pissed off now, and his ire is causing some serious shit to happen with the cyclone around the

144

boat. I wonder if he knows what is going on or whether he is too caught up in Greg to care. He is basically creating a tornado around us. The boat begins to dangerously dip and roll in the water, our own private storm is brewing up death, and more than Greg will pay the price.

Standing, I grab the railing; could I get through the darkness and into the water? What might be waiting on the other side? A rocky island shore? Empty ocean? Sharks? I don't know and my powerful senses are useless in this Demon storm. Valant and Greg are trading blows, oblivious to the storm around them and to our lives that are in the balance. Rage consumes them both and I fear that Greg's mind is in such bad shape that he might not care if he dies tonight, not if Valant and I can go with him.

"Valant! Valant! You need to stop the storm now!" My voice cries out, but is lost amongst the crashing sounds of the waves and the thundering nightmare around us. Could I make it to them safely and intervene? First I want to see if I can get through Valant's storm and off this boat. I cover my arm in protection and move to touch the swirling madness. I immediately feel a shock that runs up my arm and down my spinal cord, collapsing me haphazardly to the deck floor.

Okay. I guess not. Well, time to attempt to break up their rumble and not get tossed into the sickly shocking clouds of fun. I keep my hand on the railing and fight against the forceful winds to reach the dark figures at the back of the boat. I am only about twenty feet away yet it seems to take an eternity to make any headway toward them. I keep calling out to Valant but get no answers as they savagely hurl dark power and limbs at each other, Greg's gray nothingness colliding with Valant's velvety red power as the world around us seems to signal our destruction.

Ten feet away, eight, and then I see in a flash Greg's knife in his hand as it comes down on Valant, stabbing him right in the chest where a human's heart would be. Burgundy liquid bursts from his wound and Valant reaches out to grab it, turning it into a cloud-like consistency and pushing it back into his body. Greg appears to be melded to the knife that still protrudes from Valant's chest, his eyes watching in horror as Valant pieces himself back together.

The storm becomes silent for a moment and in the broken funnel I swear I can hear Ryan and perhaps even spot him in the Zodiac in the raging waves. I struggle to get to the funnel opening, but just before I can slip out, it closes back even tighter. The storm grows stronger than ever and I am shoved to the floor by the force of the boat nearly capsizing. All I can do now is brace myself. My cries to Valant go unheard and I dread what may happen to us once the storm rids itself of the boat and I am thrown into its ferocity.

A massive thud echoes in my head at the same time a figure slams down, feet-first, upon the boat deck. The vessel appears to groan and sink under the force, yet springs back in sync with the figure's lengthening stance. It is a woman— gray dress flying in all directions— caught in the storm's winds. Valant and Greg turn toward her and I get a glimpse of the woman's blond hair, pulled back in a long ponytail.

My mother.

"You *dare* put my daughter in danger, Demon? Be gone! Now!" Her voice echoes in the darkness, roaring over Valant's storm and causing its immediate silence. Valant, wide-eyed and confused, immediately disappears. Greg is held down by the force of my mother's power alone, his quaking noticeable despite her hold on him. She moves to stand over him, her face looking down at him in disgust. I scramble to my feet and slowly make my way to her side.

Blue power crackles and surges off her in spurts. I had only seen it briefly before, but this, this is what she can really do. She sent a Demon away on her own. Something I thought they could only do themselves. Judging by that appalled look on Valant's face, that was just as alarming to him.

"Use this, Alexis; tie him up tight. They'll block his magic as well without either of us having to exert any effort." I take the flexible metallic rope and begin to tie Greg's hands together behind his back. The rope is sharp and I see blood dripping from his wrists as I pull tighter and create solid knots to keep him from escaping. Once that is done I stand and my mother embraces me fiercely.

"Thank the goddess you told Dana where you were going. I was on my way to you all anyhow and got to you as fast as I could. Are you hurt?" I shake my head; my self-healing completed already. She has my head in her hands like I was still her tiny child, and I savor the moment.

"Where in the hell is Ryan? Isn't he supposed to be with you?" As if on cue, Ryan climbs aboard and comes toward us, and my mother turns her fury on him.

"You! What were you thinking, letting her go this alone? Were you thinking at all?" My mother releases me, and a hiss of power quivers around us like a rattlesnake poised to strike. I touch her arm lightly and her ferocity wanes only slightly.

"Mom, it wasn't his fault. Valant caught us unaware and Ryan was kicked out of the bat-shit-crazy storm Valant conjured up. My power couldn't even sense him, so I doubt he was able to break in, even if he regained consciousness." At first I think I am easing her mind, but then a switch flicks and she is in Ryan's face in an instant. My mom's hands flex by her sides and blue lightening power plays around her fingers, as if begging her to unleash its fury.

"So let me get this straight. You are some renowned Protector, trained by the Council since birth. Supposedly unbeatable and un-trickable, yet you manage to not only get shut out of a Demon storm but also knocked out? Were you even paying attention? How on earth did he get the jump on you?" Her right hand starts to rise and she holds it near his face. Even though he doesn't flinch, I can see his eyes cast down. Is he ashamed?

She goes on. "I can see someone getting the jump on Alex; her training is minimal. But you? You have no excuse. Where was your head?" Oh shit, I think I know where. I knew this business between us was an issue, and now we have both paid for it dearly. But it all could have been worse. So much worse.

"Mom, I..."

"No, Alex, she's right." He doesn't use his nickname for me. He doesn't use 'Lex.' I suppose if he did she would really know something was up. Not that Dana hasn't told her already, but I see no need to bring light to it all now. I turn to Ryan and give him a supportive smile.

"I should have been prepared for anything and I wasn't. It won't happen again." He straightens up like a soldier while he looks my mom in the eye. It isn't a look of defiance he gives her. No, it is one of admittance and commitment at the same time; a promise that it would never happen again. My mom seemed appeased for the moment, but she does not back down, although the intensity of her power lessens.

"You must always stay focused, Ryan. Never let emotions get in the way of a mission." She turns to face me, the look in her eyes one of knowing and caution. Oh, she knows about us all right. If Ryan and I can't focus and work together, I fear he may disappear for good.

I give her a smile and a nod, all of us understanding the unspoken words between the lines.

CHAPTER 12

The Rising Sun

Journal Entry:

It has been a month since I helped Thatcher fix Lestan's greenhouse. A beautiful sight it was for us when we were done; we even helped ourselves to a few Avalon fruits as we lay in the moss, Thatcher a giant white tiger and I covered in dirt, leaves, and satisfaction. I smile at the memory, wishing I could see Lestan's face when he saw his greenhouse back to its glory. The thoughts wake me and I roll over in my bed, expecting to see Bear's big furry black face, but instead I am greeted by a stunningly elegant orchid on my pillow with a note from Lestan.

> Dear Eila: You are my most cherished friend. I love you as you love me and someday, someday soon, we will be together forever.
> All My Love,
> Lestan

Well, this is new...how did he get here and what does this mean? A text tone interrupts my thoughts and I reach over to see a message from Carson. My heart flutters and then thumps as I remember Lestan's orchid and note. There is no way Lestan and I can be together, is there? I brush off the thought, place the orchid in a bud vase, and get ready for my day with the guy I love, with Carson. Lestan is only a dream, someone I can never have or truly be with.

149

After getting a suite at a hotel, Mom and I sit in silence while we eat, a thousand questions playing on my tongue as always when I finally have her in front of me.

"Have you found Dad?"

"I have a starting place, but we'll talk about that tomorrow." She rises, having barely touched her food, and kisses me on the top of my head.

"Get some sleep, Alexis. We'll talk more in the morning." I almost tell her it is morning; the sun will be up in about an hour. The crazy hours continue no matter what my profession. Earthen Protector, party planner, club owner...there's a pattern to my madness. My mom's hand touches the doorknob to her room within the suite and the air around us changes, revealing Valant.

"I come in peace, with news, and as protection." I can't help but laugh out loud. Mom shoots me an unamused look, turning calmly and taking on the appearance of coolness, though I can tell she has already powered up for a fight.

"Be quick, Demon. I'm not as easily trusting as my dear Alexis, but I'll grant you a second or two." Ya, my mom is badass.

When I look at Valant, my feelings of reverie are equally reflected in his face. Motherfucker, he's crushing on my mom! Valant's eyes meet mine and the look disappears and a fakey pleasant smile takes its place. But I saw it. Oh ya, you whipped-ass Demon. I'm on to you. Time to give him some lip, and maybe a crack or two in the jaw.

"Haven't you done enough, Valant? Let's just call it even and promise to never see each other again." His eyes shoot back to my mom. Is she looking at her fingernails? What a pure show of boredom toward Valant. She is ignoring him like a pro.

"I do apologize for my anger, Alex. How I do hate treachery."

"Funny coming from a treacherous Demon. You could have gotten me killed, Ryan killed. But I'm sure you know that."

"I swear on my future spawn, I did not intend to harm you, or your GI Joe, one bit. They may paint us as evil, uncaring monsters, but we do have feelings." My mom looks at him square in his face and finally speaks.

"Ya, okay great, we don't need a big 'let's share our feelings' therapy session. We're all tired so get on with it, Demon." Valant seems to take that as all being well and forgiven, and proceeds to spill it.

"Alexis, Vex needs to contact you so best get to sleep." My eyes shoot open even wider and I seethe with anger at another intrusion into my private life.

"Don't look at me like that. I don't know how the little varmint got through to me, and trust me he was all tooth and claw about it, so save the dramatics. Whatever the case, I am passing it on to you as a favor and a show of faith."

"I'll deal with this later, Valant. What else do you want? I doubt you're looking to have my mom send you back to the shithole you keeping dying to escape from." Valant turns to my mom and gives her a low bow.

"Stacy, my dear, I offer my protection to you as you return Greg to the Council, as well as ensuring that your daughter and her friend stay out of Greg's mouth and memory." Mom had agreed with my idea to let the Council deal with Greg, so quickly in fact, that it made me suspicious. I know she's been out of contact with me for super secret reasons. Maybe she's been working for the Council this whole time.

What we haven't worked out is what will be said to the Council and what I will do. I am not even sure that I should go anywhere near the Council. My plan had been for Ryan to take Greg, but Mom is definitely joining that party. I would think the Council has rules prohibiting the use of disguises on their property, and I am also sure they have ways to detect when someone has altered their appearance. Plus, it's probably not the best way to stage my first Council visit if I want to stay off the radar or their naughty list. I could just go in as my mom's daughter, like I was just there to check things out. It's not like they know I'm the Protector they sent Ryan to find, right?

Having Valant around to make sure I am kept out of the storytelling sets me at ease on that front. I don't want to be brought into this whole debacle yet. Maybe I should let them take him without me. I am sure my mom will say the same thing. Right now she is saying a good deal to Valant.

"Do I look like I need help from you, Demon? What can you do for me that I can't do myself?" Her hands are on her hips and her ponytail disheveled. I can tell she is as tired as I am; maybe more so after kicking Valant's ass back to never-never land.

"Can you honestly say that you can keep Greg in check and your daughter safe?" Valant responded. "Tell me you aren't worried about the Council getting their hands on her. As of now, her existence is known, but not her capacity. They don't know how powerful she really is, nor that she is whom everyone is searching for. Plus, you have to sleep some time, darling. I, on the other hand, do not." Another Demon tidbit I didn't know, but it makes sense when I think about all the movies and myths about monsters, especially the undead vampire version. Instead of blood, Valant feeds on fears, anger, all of our emotions—close enough I suppose.

Even though my mom appears cool, I know she isn't the only one whose angst about the Council knowing all about me is back to full throttle. Damn it. Giving Greg to them for his crimes seemed like a good idea at the time, well, better than strangling him with my bare hands or giving him to Valant, but I guess I didn't think it all the way through. Valant, however, can create a story in Greg's mind that doesn't involve Shane or me, as well as reinforce that his powers stay stripped down to make the trip safer. Now those are useful tricks. Locking down Greg's force being one that would take a lot more of my mom and Ryan's energy to even come close to duplicating. Even though my mom doesn't show it, I know she is calculating the risks in her head. Valant is offering us something we all need and she knows it.

"Do what you wish, Demon, but keep your distance. I want to be with you when you work on Greg, so do not visit him alone. Understood?" Valant stands straight and confident. Beaming at Mom, reveling in her presence.

"Valant. Please call me Valant."

"Goodbye, Demon." Mom turns her back on him and steps into her room, closing the door behind her. Valant turns to me with a smile and a shrug before he disappears in his tiny, one-demon cyclone. Can my life be any weirder? Does this mean Greg might forget all about me? That he won't harbor this hatred and desire to rip out my throat anymore? Oh darn.

Washed up and in bed my eyes droop and sleep begins to take me over. It doesn't take long before a feeling of not being alone overcomes me and I shoot upright in bed. Vex is making his way toward me, his movements slow and twitchy. I can tell from the get go that he still isn't back to himself. Worry ripples through me as I wonder if he will ever heal completely or, goddess, might he get worse again? What had happened to Shane is still fresh in my mind and I am well aware of what these magics, these Earthen powers, are capable of—restoration and destruction.

"I'm fine, it's you that needs worrying over. Can you keep out of trouble for more than one day?"

"Hey, I had to go after Greg. Stupid Valant had to get his panties in a bunch over some Demon honor code crap. He acts like he has it all together, but I tell ya I think he has a few..."

Vex is looking at me with a very interesting annoyed-fox look.

"Look, let's save your Demon BFF stories for later. He's already on my shit list for intruding on our Dreamwalk connection." Ya, you and me both, Vex.

"I'm here to tell you that you cannot go to the Council with your mother and Greg. We can't risk them getting a hold of you, no matter how cloaked you think you can be."

"I agree, Vex. In fact, I was just thinking about that as well. Even with my plan to sneak in, I'd worry that they'd realize who I am, and I'm not ready for that just yet." Vex gives me a foxy nod and I can tell he has more to tell me.

"We've also found out that the boy who was injured with me was in fact the Healers' Leader, Galena, masquerading as my guide. The Council gave the Healers intel that Galena was being hunted, so they thought having her escape disguised as the boy we all saw, and in plain sight, would be the safest route. Whoever is behind this either saw through the disguise that tricked even Terra and me, or is only concerned with taking out all Healers first, confident that they will get to the Leader eventually."

Damn, I helped heal not only Vex, but also the Leader of the Healers. This is getting seriously intense. Vex takes a deep breath; the memory of what he is about to tell me obviously wears on him.

"The only way we got out of there alive was because the attacker stopped when we died."

"You *what?*" I tremble with worry, picturing his lifeless body.

"Yes, sickly power infected us enough to drain both of us of life; we died there, but Terra and I are bonded and she kept me alive in her being. When we were first attacked I magically meshed Galena's spirit to mine, so when you and Terra worked together, you brought us both back." Physical reminders of the torturous fight for his life nip at my body and mind and I flinch.

"I thought I might never see or speak to you again, and it turns out that was the case, but are you saying Terra and I basically brought you and Galena back from death? Holy shit."

"Yes, and I am forever in your debt."

"Vex, you're my friend; we don't have debt." I want to avoid a blubbering Alex moment so I shift the subject back to the Council and Greg.

"I have pretty much kicked myself in the ass about turning Greg over to the Council, so I have no problems staying away. I know you don't want to hear about Valant, but while he was being a pain-in-the-ass invader of my dreams, he witnessed a darkly cloaked figure taking power from and killing young Healers. He couldn't see a face but he heard the murderer say that it was for the best, like a "for the good of the cause" type of thing. That sounds like the same assassin from our Dreamwalk. Was that who you saw as well?"

Vex nods and his whiskers take on a mind of their own, twitching in agitation, or is it fear? I pretend not to notice. Vex isn't going to think he is weak in my eyes, that's for sure.

"So this has to be some sort of conspiracy since Valant heard the attacker talking about a cause. Sounds like a group of Absolute Protectors taking it to the extreme once again." Vex nods again and his whiskers continue to twitch in frustration at pretty much everything I'm saying.

"Yes, we're facing some powerful opponents, I fear; the lone presence being the muscle, but who is the Machiavelli? Who is behind it all? Now as for your Demon, he seems connected to your Dreamwalks somehow. Watch your back with him—helpful yes, but also treacherous and selfish."

"He was being a nosey pest in my dreams that night and when it turned into the Dreamwalk of pain he kind of took it from me, by mistake he says. Wait, did you say *my* Demon? Hold on a minute I did NOT sign up for adopt-a-demon!" Vex actually snickers; it is nice to see him relax a bit.

"Galena said only her second-in-command, Kierra, knew about the plan as Healers are concerned. However, she did say that Kierra was the one who consulted with someone they've trusted for a long time within the Council and that's where the information about her being targeted next came from. It's safe to assume that the Council contact either fed the info on purpose, maybe even giving Kierra the idea about getting her out in a disguise, or they're innocent and only doing what they were told. Either way, we need to find out who the Council contact is and who they may be working with or for."

"Okay, so how do we find Galena's number two? Isn't that what you want me to do?" I've never been trained much on tracking someone down, but I know Ryan and Dana have. Vex's headshake stops my train of thought and I feel my body run cold.

"Kierra was killed a couple of hours ago. They got to her before we had a chance to ask the name of her Council contact. That's why I needed to speak with you as soon as possible, and stop you going to the Council. We'll be in danger if our major players are all in the dragon's den at one time."

"But is my mom safe? What about Greg? What if the person behind this gets his or her hands on him and sets him free? Or worse yet, gets him to join their plot that's hell bent on the destruction of the Healers?"

"I think we're all pretty certain that your mom has some involvement with the Council. No other group comes to mind that she could have been working secretly with for so long, maybe even since you were taken from her. I think she can hold her own and I doubt she'll leave Greg in the hands of anyone she doesn't fully trust."

"Ya, but look what happened to Galena and Kierra. They trusted someone in the Council and one of them is dead while the other barely survived." I choke on my last word, remembering how I thought Vex might die.

"I understand; that's why it may be best if Dana, or better yet, Ryan, go with her. I doubt Dana will want to get near the Council. She's got quite a few "warrants" with them you might say." That made me laugh and boy did I need it.

"One last thing. Terra, Galena, and I have agreed to keep our attack and survival secret from everyone, so don't speak of this to anyone. Not even to Ryan or your mom. That is one piece of the puzzle we need to hold tight to our chests at all times. Whoever is responsible may let their guard down a bit more if they think Galena and I died without a single witness to tell the tale and blow the whistle. That's been the case so far; we've heard no rumors of the deaths. It's as if they targeted people who no one has yet realized are gone." Well, it's a good thing I never got to talk to Ryan about any of my Dreamwalks, and I've only spoken to Dana about the first one. Sandra is the one person who knows everything and I trust her with my life.

"Dana most likely told my mom about our first one, but not at all about the attack on you and Galena. Shane's tango with Greg caused those details to be left out of any of our recent conversations." Damn, I can't believe he is in the next suite. It would be so easy to...no, I am not a killer and he isn't worth it.

"Ryan doesn't know much yet but I know we'll need him, so I'll fill him in on the parts I can. But, Sandra, she knows everything." He looks up at me sharply. "Oops, sorry. I didn't know you wanted to keep it all a secret and she's the one person I know I can go to for anything. It's hard not having had anyone to talk to for so long and now I have my powerful BFF who I can trust and who can really help us, so sue me." He twitches his whiskers and huffs a little, obviously not too concerned about Sandra, so it is time to change the subject.

"So the Council knows about you? That you and Terra exist? Dana, Sandra, and Ryan know, the last two mainly because of me, but what about others?"

"I appear different to different people and I only truly show my nature to help in unique cases such as yours. However, I could tell there was glee at the attempt at my destruction, as well as Galena's. These murderers need to continue thinking that someone powerful and opposed to them has been removed from the playing field. Once they start to get cocky, they'll get sloppy." The thought of having lost Vex is difficult to even want to fake, but there was no doubt that I would. I lean toward him and he sinks into the bed, relaxing from his all-business, seated posture. My fingers brush his fur, and the usual spark I feel whenever I touch his soft coat is subdued.

"Are you okay, Vex?" His eyes meet mine and he nudges closer to me. I lay back down on my pillow and he curls up close to my neck. I have never been this close to Vex, the foot of the bed is the closest he has ever slept to me and that was long ago. I continue to caress his fur, adding more of my healing abilities to each touch. He sighs and I smile to myself.

"I just need a little recharge more often, nothing to worry too much about. Keep your head in the game and don't spend any energy worrying about me. Your assignment will be to head north. I think we have a location in northern Montana for the lake from our Dreamwalk. We need you to head into Glacier National Park and we should have more of an exact location once you're up there. Dana will go with you; she's a perfect ally for this fight." An icy sensation runs through me. Is that fear? I have been so hopped up and ready for a fight, even getting in a few along the way, but now I just feel scared. What makes me think it will end any differently for me? I am a Healer, after all. Won't this person just take my powers and my life as well?

"Vex, how do I defend against something that has taken so many lives? They even nearly took yours." I continue to touch him absently.

"Most of the attacks on the Healers whose lives have been lost were due to them not being prepared. They were dead only because the killer had the benefit of surprise. We are all banking on the hope that those involved don't know that anyone has knowledge of these attacks, let alone a possible location. Believing we died, and killing off Kierra, has them thinking they're going undetected." Ah, he is a smart, tricky fox. He is sounding sleepier now and I am getting there myself despite the intensity of our conversation.

"We have the lake in Montana nearly pinned down, and now we may have another location from your Valant-stolen Dreamwalk; we need to lean on the Demon to try and pinpoint where that happened. Demons have the ability to extract memories as easily as they can recreate them."

"Oh boy, that sounds like more Alex and Valant time, and perhaps even in-my-head time. Didn't we agree that trusting him with a grain of salt is the wisest option right now? I mean, him messing around in my head, trying to reform a Dreamwalk that he took from me sounds like the exact opposite of that."

"With the hit on the Leader we have to move fast. Valant may have a key we need to solve this before more lives are lost. If we're lucky, we can get some more clues and track down everyone involved."

"What about my mom? I haven't even spoken to her directly about any of this yet, but Dana most likely has. Do you think she can help?"

"When you talk to her tomorrow, see what she knows about the Dreamwalks. I don't think Dana would have kept her out of the loop with something so important, but we need to make sure she knows some of the details. Terra and I believe we can trust her, so ask her to keep an ear out at the Council for anything to do with Healer deaths." Why does my stomach drop a little at the word 'trust' in a sentence about my mom? Being abandoned never gets easier, even with her back in my life now. Vex notices my change in mood and snuggles a bit closer.

"I honestly don't know her anymore, and now that she's focusing so much on looking for my dad and possibly working for the Council, I can't help but think I need to hold back a little."

"Alexis, I know what you're feeling as a daughter, but this is about being an Earthen Protector. Your mom is first that." No matter what my mom has done, whatever she knows or doesn't know, she has been trying to do something right, so I agree with him.

"Alexis, your mom is powerful and smart. She will not let on that she knows anything. Stacy has never fully trusted anyone in a long time. Even though she may work for the Council, she's really working for herself—and for you."

That was how it always felt when I was young, and after I read her admission about tearing her life apart to hide us, I know deep down that it was always about the two of us. So why do I fear she blames me for what happened to my father? No, I am wrong to think she blames me—she has only ever blamed herself. I can't dwell; what I need to do is break the cycle of guilt and loss by bringing my family back together—my Healer dad, my Earthen Protector mother, and me, the hybrid. I have a feeling this pursuit of the Healers will have to come first and only then can I reclaim my family.

Vex is nearly asleep. His meekness frightens me; it is an unnatural characteristic for him.

"Are you really okay, Vex? I mean, will you continue to get better?"

"I'm not sure. Terra says yes, but I think the Leader and I being merged together during both the attack and the healing has left me a part of her and she a part of me. Like I'm more mortal than before." Well, that question is now answered. I have always felt Terra and Vex are magical beings that transcend time and space.

"Let me try again, Vex, and again after I speak with Dana. She can help, I'm sure of it. Maybe sever the bind, remove the mortality from you?"

"Perhaps, but I fear at whose expense. Mine? Galena's? We must tread carefully and if this is my destiny, I will accept it." I hold back my words but I will not hold back my actions as I continue to pursue a way to heal my Vex.

"Sleep now, Vex. Let me do what I can. Perhaps in my world I'll have better luck." His sleepy head nods ever so slightly. I reach from the depths of Gaia, strong and clear here along the Baja Coast. My emerald-green vines wrap around him, sparks of dandelion seeds shimmer and dance along my leaves. I dig deeper and once again find the golden power of my father; it has been buried down deep for so long it is eager to work its will. It has been hidden within the farthest depths of my mind, hidden where the evil of what Steven did to me dwells. Like the warmth of a rising sun, golden sparks flit into Vex while he sleeps. My eyelids feel like boulders, their heaviness impossible to fight, as I too fall off to sleep.

CHAPTER 13

Separate Ways

Journal Entry:

Now that I have met Thatcher in Avalon, not long after taking a crazy trip down to Terra and Vex's land, I wonder if they may be the same? And if not, how many other lands, places, dimensions are there? Can I travel them all, like Thatcher said? Am I like Dr. Who? Where is my cool-ass Tardis? The thought of being able to travel to worlds other than my own has my brain in a tizzy. I begin to write ideas, daydreams, and fantastical theories about what else may be out there for me to find.

Is heaven another world? Can I see my grandmother? My father? Wait, can I find my mom this way? If I can dream or induce my way to other places, why can't I find her? Between studying and spending time with Carson, I will find a way, a way to bring my mom and I back together.

The sun is high in the sky when I wake, beginning its trek west toward sunset. Late nights of danger, magic, and mayhem led to sleeping the day away. Vex has vanished and I can only hope I aided him in some way. When I speak to Dana, I will ask about healing him further, safely so the little rascal can get back to his full, prideful self. I noticed when Ryan rose earlier. For some reason he barely needs any sleep.

Had best check him for batteries since he seems more robot than man at times.

I call Justin after a quick jog and workout on the beach. He answers on the first ring, worried no doubt about all the goings-on in my life.

"Alex, how are you? Did they find him? Did they find who did this to Shane?"

"Yes, they caught him. It's over, thank goodness. Some drunken idiot with no regard for himself, let alone Shane's life, ran him right off the road and left him there to die. He didn't even have the wits about him to seek help. He just drove on, passing out shortly after on his boat. He's in custody now and they're working on getting him back to the US as he's a citizen there, but the crime was here." I hear Justin's sigh of relief but then concern creeps back in.

"But you're done, right? You don't have to stay, do you?"

"No, I'll head back to San Diego tonight. Can we meet at your place when I get back? I really need to see you." Need was the right word, wasn't it? What about 'want'? I do want to see him, be with him, but lately it feels like a carnal need, a need for his body, for him, more than ever before. I've been chalking it up to trying to make up for nearly leaving him for Ryan, and the guilt that comes with it.

But with all the magic in the world, and the similarities in my dreams between Justin's tattoo and Lestan's, I begin to worry that I'm either trying too hard to make up for what I have done, or that once again something else is at play. I brush it aside, as I have been doing for weeks. I am making him Lestan, perhaps missing my childhood friend from Avalon, my first love. Justin is my safe, normal boyfriend. Nothing is amiss aside from my own raging desire for him. Facing my feelings for Ryan—another Protector, like me—and leaving those behind only shows how Justin and I are meant to be, right? And have I even left those feelings behind? Seems easy to think so when I am not around Ryan, but as soon as he is near me, Justin becomes a drifting thought. Once again I may need to think about taking a break from men altogether and do some clean and sober thinking without their influence.

Justin interrupts that decision and I am once again swayed his way.

"Of course, Alex. Does Pitter want to come? You know how he loves the dogs." I laugh out loud. Pitter is a crazy cat. He loves those darn dogs so much that I can't help but wonder if he secretly wishes he were one.

"I can go by your house and grab him for you, so all you have to do is come straight to me."

"Oh, thanks, but he's not home with me yet. I think he prefers Sandra to me. He doesn't much like being left behind more than a few days, so the month away has his little kitty feelings hurt." Justin and I laugh together and it feels natural, not forced, just honest and real.

"He can hold a grudge, that's for sure. Well, I'll stop by and see Shane again tonight and see if Carmen is okay." He is exceptionally thoughtful and sweet. Though a menacing delight in bed. My lower regions tingle and I ache to be with him.

"Let me know how everyone is and I'll get everyone heading back that way shortly. See you tonight." Still no I love you, still the words won't come.

"Okay, sounds good. Travel safely and I'll see you soon." I think he knows saying he loves me only makes me more unable to say it back. I give to him in other ways though, in the only way I can—for now.

With the call ended, I head to my bathroom to take a quick shower. While I am getting dressed a knock sounds upon the door to my bedroom.

"Alexis? May I come in?" It is my mother. Even though I want to speak with her, directed by Vex to make a plan with her, I also dread what is to come. I know some of what is to be unburdened by both of us will leave pieces of us on the floor. It needs to happen, but I fear it all the same.

"Yes, Mom, hold on a minute." Of course I locked the door. I am staying in close proximity to a Demon, a dangerous and sexy Earthen Protector, and my mother who may be stronger than the both of them. So hell ya, I locked it. I'm not stupid.

Dressed, and with a deep breath to stay me, I open the door and welcome her into my room. She closes and locks the door behind her and we both move to sit at the edge of my bed.

"Thank you again for saving us last night, Mom. I'm happy it's your blood in my veins. And, I, I have to tell you something." I swear a cotton ball the size of an apple is lodged in my throat. "Dana and I went into a past memory, a memory of the day Dad was lost to you. The day you thought he'd died and you thought you were responsible." Nothing like an enormous lack of subtlety on my part to start off the conversation with a bang.

"Well, that saves us some time, doesn't it?" She smiles at me. "Perhaps we should never have trusted the then leaders of the Council to do a thorough investigation into your father and Bryan's disappearance. They came to the conclusion that both had died in a very rare explosion caused by a misuse of great and terrible magic. I believed my magic had killed Alexander and Bryan and so my life was forever changed. Nobody else blamed me outright. Well, I know Gillian did and still does, but she kept quiet—I never knew why. Regardless of whatever was said to my face or in whispers behind my back, the four of us were there that day, and I was the key ingredient as the strongest power wielder at the time." More like both of our lives were forever changed. Ever since I saw her past, not a day goes by that I don't wonder how my life would be if it had never happened. Only days to me, but countless years for my mother. I look at her with all the love I have and she continues.

"The guilt was unbearable, and so was the need to protect you. So two birds were taken care of with one stone. I would cease to be the woman who killed her best friend's boyfriend plus the man I love. I would be only a shell of the Earthen Protector. Someone no one would think to look twice at, let alone assume her daughter was of any great significance." Tears trickle down my face as I feel her grief, flashes of her story mingle with the history of ours, and I only wish that day had never happened. And that thought leads me to Bryan, and wishing he had never been my father's friend.

"Mom, what of Bryan? After witnessing that day, it seems to me that Bryan was the one who caused the accident, not you." She looks down and shakes her head.

"I should have known, and maybe part of me always knew he had something to do with it, but I was the main cause. I was the catalyst and he knew it. I should have never agreed, but your father was so certain this would help us make our place in the world and finally have a way to defeat the Absolute Protectors. He was such a force of nature. So hard to ever say no to." Hearing about my father makes me smile. My grandmother always called me a force of nature and I know it's not only my father's description but one for my mother as well.

"Have you heard of Bryan? Is he alive as well? If he meant that to happen, he must have had a plan, a reason." And if his ass is alive, I plan to show it to him.

"After you were taken from me and went to live with your grandmother, I sought to cleanse myself fully once and for all. I took a chance and secretly contacted your father's parents. I needed to make amends, to ask for forgiveness. They agreed to meet me and his mother embraced me openly. His mother said she knew he wasn't dead, that he had come to her in her dreams and told her so. His dad was not so certain, but he knew Bryan's family to be one with grand dreams of power and pretty shy on honesty."

"Bryan looked shifty and up to something from what I saw, but like Dana said, I was a stranger looking in. There was no way for you to know." Mom smiles at me and touches my face. How I have missed her.

"Alexander's family encouraged me to join the Council so I might have access to information that might help us find out what happened to Alexander and Bryan. I joined and was quickly placed in the undercover division. My ability to blend in and stay hidden was regarded as a sought-after talent. Not many know who I truly am; my identity was stripped from me as I was assigned to find those who conspired against the Council." Whoa, my mom is a spy! That is awesome.

"Time went by and I found nothing but dead ends. But one thing was apparent, right in the heart of Bryan's family. His mother did not mourn, not like a mother should. I wasn't certain if that was because she thought him alive, and didn't hide it well, or maybe she was secretly happy he was dead. Perhaps the power-driven parts of the family didn't include her. No matter the reason, I watched her carefully while your father's family sought out a Seer in hopes of finding out what Bryan's mother knew, or what he could see of your father and Bryan." Sandra. I wonder if the Seer knew Sandra's family or if my mother knows about our friendship? If my mom already used a Seer before, maybe Sandra's efforts would be in vain. But things are indeed different now, aren't they? I mean, we know for sure Dad is alive.

"Didn't the Council use a Seer's service from the beginning?"

"The Council would never act on a Seer's vision. They're straightforward and investigate with facts alone. Funny when we're dealing with the fluid nature of Earthen power and magics, but that's the way of the Council." Just as bullheaded as I thought. I would never align myself with the Council, that is for sure. But, I am giving them Greg. Damn it. Can I never make a solid and obviously good decision? Damn my humanity for not letting Valant destroy his ass when I had the chance. Well, my mom and Ryan seem to think it's best as well, so I guess all authorities have their positives and negatives.

"What did the Seer tell you?"

"He could only tell us that he did not see their death. That meant either that he simply couldn't or that they were still alive. Which one, we couldn't be certain. He also told us that Bryan's mother was having strange dreams that she may have sought out. The Seer sent me to seek the help of another, more powerful ally, someone who specialized in understanding and drawing out truths through dreams. It was likely that someone similar helped Bryan's mom as well." Now that would have been handy last year!

"It was in those years I lived many of my more confusing days. Some were dark and empty while others were magnificent and enchanting. I was deep in the world of treachery, as a spy for the Council, going by the name Alana. Yet I also found myself loving another." She does not look up at the last admission. Does she fear I will judge her for loving someone else? I had always hoped she would find someone good, someone caring to allow her back into the light and out of the shadow of my father's death. Not to mention that my shit-storm of a love life can definitely relate!

"Mom, I'm glad you found love. You deserve it."

"Yes, but it was at a price. He was the one man who could help me find your father, and yet the love that grew between us may have kept your father from returning to us longer than was needed. It had been countless years, and I had begun to lose hope again. He was there for me, oh and how we loved each other. But then the dreams began. Dreams that years before this very man I grew to love told me I would have if your father were still alive. It was his specialty, as I said, to bring truth to the dreams. When he saw my hope that your father might be alive, he changed."

"What is his name? Where is he now?" She looks out the window, seeing a past I cannot. Two loves lost, one partially at her hands, and one for the love of the first.

"Tristan is his name. I haven't seen him in a very long time. He didn't take my knowledge of Alexander possibly being alive, and wanting to find him, very well. Tristan scared me, more than once, and I felt I needed to hide myself from him. Once again I became someone else. Stacy was gone, Alana was gone—all the versions of myself I had to keep from you—to keep you safe. All that time I was alone, and then once I found someone, he was soon gone as well. Only Dana and I kept in touch so that I had a link to you in some way. It's been so long since that first dream and now I know he's here...somewhere." Thoughts of my fears living with Steven and then Carson hit me. I know what it is like to have to hide and redefine myself. The anger boils up inside me and turns its eyes to this man Tristan, as well as Bryan.

I am starting to see why I never really saw or heard from her; she was constantly hiding and searching. I am now entangled in doing one of those, searching for answers, joining my mother's quest to find my father and the killer of the Healers. At least one pursuit is over now that Greg is in our custody and soon to be locked away. Now it is time to focus on the other two.

"I'm so sorry, Mom. You deserve to be happy, to have some sort of normalcy in your life. One with love, stability, your own name, and with me...if that's what you want." She reaches over to my downcast face and lifts my chin so her blue eyes shine upon mine. I feel like a little girl again, wanting to hold tight to a mother who always slipped through my hands.

"We have a long road ahead of us, but at least we're together this time. Our company may be small, but we're strong, brave, and deeply connected. We'll work carefully and in secrecy...together." I smile at her and we embrace. With her chin on my shoulder, her voice is a bit muffled but I hear her all the same.

"Your connection to Ryan is strong, but it has already caused trouble once. I think it best that Ryan and I take Greg to the Council and that you meet up with Dana and wait for our return. We'll go to their western headquarters in Flagstaff. Your father is somewhere north of here; my sources have seen him flitting about in the northwest. That's what I know. The dreams where he is moving in and out of our world are finally clearer and I hope to find him soon." It seems Vex was right on target with his strategy to keep me away from the Council. Our planning should go smoothly at this rate. She is right about Ryan and me, but part of me doesn't want to be separated from him for long. Am I selfish for wanting both Ryan and Justin in my life, in some capacity? I can't help that Ryan is so important to me. I can't break or forget that connection, well, maybe momentarily when I am with Justin. Damn, I'm fucked up.

After a deep gulp, I pull away from her as we proceed to hash out our plan.

"Yes, I think that's best as well. Vex visited me last night and told me the same thing. I'm sure you must have heard of him by now, if you haven't visited with him yourself." She nods and looks distant again so I continue talking to smooth the obvious discomfort. I will ask more questions some other time.

"Dana must have told you about the Dreamwalk I had with him, and what we saw happen to the Healer? He also asked me to head north: Montana. I think Dana and I will head there and scope things out."

"Yes, and I've been keeping my ears open within the Council. All I've heard lately has been about the number of Healers who have been turning to the Absolute Protectors' side. Healers mend and repair, so some of them see the atrocities that humans commit and believe they're a sickness upon Earth, just as much as the Absolute Protectors do. There are always rumblings of them switching sides, but I'm not sure if that has anything to do with your Dreamwalk since I've been hearing that story for years. I'll keep an ear out, discreetly of course. Have you had any other dreams? Anything else I need to know about or look for?"

I hate to lie to her right now, but I promised Vex. She isn't the only one in this family who can master secrecy.

I shake my head and decide to move the conversation in a different direction.

"Did Bryan know about me? Do you think being a part of you caused the anomaly and maybe it wasn't Bryan at all?" A look of guilt flashes across her face and I know she thought of that possibility, just as I had.

"I think anything is possible as far as Bryan is concerned, but I don't think you and I had much to do with the majority of what happened. That is, beside him needing me to believe we were there for the reason we'd all agreed on. I'm not sure what Bryan's real plan was, but it wasn't to test my ability to take powers so we could prove its usefulness to the Council." I bit my tongue, still wondering why she would risk something bad happening to them...her...me.

My mother looks toward the window, her eyes looking back in time and I know she wonders the same thing. The memory stalking her every day, and no matter how much of herself she has given, no matter the guilt and pain she has endured, my mother may never think it's enough...not until she finds my father. Her head turns toward me and she kisses me on the forehead before embracing me one last time.

"I love you, Alexis. Get your stuff ready; we need to head out soon." I smile at her and rise as she does.

"Dana will meet you in San Diego; text her where you'll be. Take off secretly and tell no one where you're going. Ryan and I will meet you as soon as this Greg business is taken care of." Oh yay, texting with Dana again. I can't wait.

We are all getting ready to leave, me lingering in my room not wanting to face Greg or Ryan. I am not sure how Ryan will react to our going our separate ways and I am not sure I want to know. After last night, he may feel he needs to separate from me; however there is still so much between us and I know he wants to help me find my father. I hope my mom holds to her word and allows him to come with her when she meets us after dropping off Greg to his sentencing. Damn, the thought of leaving Greg without any of us knowing what he is doing day in and day out gives me a bad taste in my mouth. Maybe Ryan should stay with the Council? No, the idea of Ryan not being with me on the mission to save the Healers has me feeling terribly uncomfortable. Not to mention the fact that my father is out there somewhere and may need help from all of us. It is essential that I let Ryan know about some of what is happening to the Healers before we part ways. I know my mom will be keeping an ear out within the Council, but Ryan has his own sources. As far as I am concerned, the more ears to the ground the better.

I know he is near before I even hear a knock on the hotel room suite door. I open it right as Ryan's knuckles miss their aim, hitting air instead of wood. I opt for some sarcasm this fine day. What's new?

"Not so stealthy, are you? Maybe I should be your replacement at the Council." I hold the door open and bow to allow his grace in. Not without some more jabs of course.

"Some tracker you are. You're as obvious as a stampede of horses." He smirks, and I hope we will have a light conversation, but then his face changes in an instant, letting all-business Ryan slip in.

"Can we speak privately, Lex?" Well, I knew this was coming.

"Sure." I lead the way to my room in the expansive suite and he follows me inside. After closing the door behind him, he turns to see me standing with my arms crossed over my chest.

"I'm sorry about last night. I shouldn't have let my feelings for you get in the way of the mission. I nearly cost us both of our lives—more importantly yours." He crosses the distance between us and my arms release automatically, my body turning to mush on command.

Ryan lifts his hand and brushes his fingers down my left cheek. I respond by leaning into his touch. It feels so right, but also hurts deep down inside. Why does this feel like a goodbye? His hand stops under my chin and he lifts it slightly so I can look into his deep, dark orbs. I feel like searching forever in them. Tingles trickle down my arm as his hand leaves my chin and moves down it slowly before taking my hand in his.

"Ryan, both of us are at fault. I knew we needed to talk about what happened outside the club, but I sat and stewed instead. By the time I got the nerve, we were there already." His eyes lock on mine at first, but then they follow my lips as if they are cobras entrancing him.

"I should have known better. You're new to all of this and I've been doing it for a long time. Nothing has ever distracted me from a mission before. I guess nothing ever mattered this much." My heart flutters in my chest and my darn tears that will not stay locked away began to well up in my eyes. I take a deep breath, trying to calm myself, and on the exhale bite down on my lip to keep it from trembling.

"I'm leaving with your mom and Greg today. Valant says he'll be joining us as well, but he promised to make sure you get home okay. You can take my car; I'll ride with your mom." Damn, I've never seen him take the passenger seat, ever, but it's probably best he has his hands free—better to strangle Greg's neck if he gets out of hand.

I nod and squeeze his hand. I have been gone for nearly a month, leaving on a compulsion led by fear of my feelings for him and the news of my father's suddenly undead status. Now that I am with him again, it feels awful knowing we are separating again so soon.

It isn't only physical attraction with Ryan, although there is no denying that. It is also a kinship of sorts, like he and I are a part of each other. It's hard to explain, even to myself since I've never felt it before. Well, I haven't been around many other people like me, so that's no surprise. I want to speak, but I am afraid I will start to cry. This is painful, and probably why I just left without saying a word last time. Ryan is hard to say good-bye to.

"Once we have Greg well-secured in the hands of people your mom and my parents trust in the Council, we'll meet up with you and Dana. I still want to help you find your dad. I made that promise to you." Oh good, at least he won't stay away from me forever like I feared. I know his position is something he takes great pride in. Having some girl screw that up doesn't seem like a very Ryan-thing to do.

"But, after that,"—shit, I spoke too soon—"I'll leave you alone." Damn it, here come the tears. His left hand rises to wipe them away while his right still holds my hand gently.

"Justin is better for you than I am. You were right to throw that in my face. He's good to you, and I know he loves you." He is right, of course, but the heart doesn't always want to do what's right. Nor can it make up its mind, apparently. Wasn't I just speaking to Justin on the phone not long ago? Now here I am a stinking puddle, blubbering over Ryan. It is obvious, I don't want Ryan out of my life and I will try to keep him in it.

"But, Ryan, don't you think we've learned from this mess? I know I won't let it happen again. You said it yourself; we're a great team. I don't think things are going to be all rosy and sweet once we find my father, do you? And there are also the Healers that we need to help." That gets his attention.

"What Healers? Your dad?"

"No. Well, actually I don't know if he's in danger as well, but since he's a Healer, I guess he could be. I've been having Dreamwalks about Healers being attacked; their powers are stolen and then they're executed. Dana and I have been working on it and I have other sources who told me to gather my "soldier." I don't think they meant only for the Greg pursuit." I look deep into his eyes and step closer. Being around Ryan feels like being in the Death Star's tractor beam—there's no escape.

"I need you, Ryan. I know that for sure now. I guess it took me leaving, and now, faced with losing you for good, I realize that more than ever." I swallow and ease toward his delicious lips. I have been aching to kiss them since our spar in the alley. But, just as our lips are about to meet, he speaks.

"What about Justin? You're happy and safe around him. The only times you've been in danger have been on my watch." I shake my head and let out a "ha" as my head flies backward.

"I've been in plenty of bad situations long before you so let's recap. I went out stalking the source of my nightmares all on my lonesome, and guess what! I was kidnapped. That would never have happened if

I were with you, if I trusted you. Now all I want is to trust you and to be with you." Shit, I am getting myself in deep now. A good deal of me wants to be with him right here, right now. My guilt about Justin seems to be washing away. Damn, Ryan is all-powerful and I am happy to succumb. And, damn it, I am a grown-ass woman and if I want to kiss someone I can freaking kiss someone.

With that fever, I wrap my arms around his neck and press my lips onto his. I think he is a bit surprised seeing as I just laughed hysterically one second and am lip locked with him the next. Obviously being in mortal danger and kicking ass gets me all pent up. Ryan is still as stone at first, but then his warm, muscular arms wrap around my waist and pull me near.

Ryan radiates heat from across the room so imagine the inferno I am swept up in as we passionately kiss each other as if we are seeing each other again for the first time. Or is it that we aren't going to see each other? My tingles down yonder freeze as I fear this is his goodbye to me. I haven't changed his mind a bit, have I? I push him away, yet his strong arms hold me even at the increased distance.

"You're still leaving me, aren't you? After we find my dad?"

"I won't leave until we find your dad, and I'll help to find out what's going on with the Healers. I'll check with some trusted sources when I'm at the Council. Of course, that is until you or your mom tells me to leave. Believe me, I think your mom is close. She knows we'll make mistakes because of what's between us and I think she's right."

"Well, I don't and the story of her losing my father has a lot to do with her fears, that I'm sure of. I think last night needed to happen to remind us to keep business and personal separate. I'm sorry for kissing Justin in front of you. I don't know what I was thinking."

"You were being a girlfriend, as you should be. With a guy who isn't throwing you into harm's way. I can help you for a while; I know I can disengage once I have some time away from you at the Council. It's what's best for both of us."

"But..." Ryan shakes his head and places his finger lightly on my lips.

"This isn't a discussion right now. You said it yourself, your mother wants us apart and I think they're trying to tell us something." My hands go to my hips, their designated this-isn't-over slash I'm-one-pissed-off-woman stance.

"This *discussion* isn't over. I'm planning to clear my head as well, but once Greg is settled, I expect you to hold up your end of the bargain. When you do, we'll see if you're disengaged." The last word hangs from my lips. Yep, these very lips that make their way right back to his again, a mere hair's width away, not fully touching as much as humming with vibrations of need. I imagine him pushing me down on the bed and having his delicious way with me, but that daydream shatters into a million pieces when he steps back from me. Coldness creeps in as a result of his absence and my amped-up libido huffs and puffs.

"You'll be fine once you're back in San Diego, back with Justin. Just as you were in the desert when you thought I couldn't be with you because of the Council." Ouch. Guess I deserve that.

"And now...now I can't be with you because of you? Because you get to make the decision for both of us—is that it? What about what I want? Don't I get a fucking say in this? I didn't think I had one before, but now I know I do! So I would like to practice my freedom of choice and get a say in this when we're back together searching for my dad. Is that okay?"

Ryan nods stoically. He is hell bent on leaving to keep me safe and I love the shit out of him for it.

CHAPTER 14

Records and Flowers

Journal Entry:

Now that Carson is out of my life and school is winding down, I start to think back to what Thatcher said about my traveling skills. I try to envision where my mother is, and travel there in my dreams. I only find the green paths of Avalon or the Tree Goddess's domain. The last time I went uninvited she tossed rotten fruit at me and told me to "get a life" and to "stop pining over your mommy issues." Geez, tough crowd. I never see Lestan or Thatcher, though I look for them once or twice. Avalon doesn't seem as inviting so I never stay long.

I make one last attempt. Wind howls and I hear a whisper of begging and pleading in the distance. It seems like a frozen desert; the blowing sand has an icy, gritty texture. It is cold and bleak except for the succession of words floating and then disappearing into the air.

When I attempt to scan out into the distance I am met with a mental slap of bright red light. I stumble backward and out of the corner of my eye, Vex's furry face comes into view.

Vex hasn't visited since Bear nearly died, and I am so happy to see him that I lift him and squeeze him close to my chest as if he were a teddy bear. He nips at my arms to make me let go. After getting some distance between us he shakes and glares at me through the dark desert night. I laugh a little at his crankiness and stand up, dusting myself off in the process.

175

"Nice to see you, Vex, but what are you doing here? Do you know where here is?" He gives his head one last shake to rid himself of Alex cooties and answers me, sort of.

" I'm not sure how you managed to get here, Eila, but we need to leave NOW!"

"Okay, okay, keep your fuzzy britches on, geez. What's the problem? I mean, it's not paradise, but this is someplace new for me, and I think someone is in trouble."

"Soon to be three people in trouble if we don't leave. You've gotten yourself into a dimension where someone has been sent for evildoings. He's begging for release. I don't think we want to know what landed him here now, do we?" He has a point, but I can't help the draw the voice has on me. Soon the words become clearer and they make me ache for the source of the voice. No one deserves this, do they? A frozen fright flips through me: I know at least one person who does.

"Please, what do I need to do? They need me." Sadness overcomes me and I start walking toward the source of the pleas. That isn't Steven's voice, but I know it all the same, don't I?

"Eila! This is a trap. Those sent to places like this will say and do anything to get out. We can't risk it. Let's go!" He runs up to me and stands right in front of me with his hackles raised. Other than a few nips and a piss-poor attitude, Vex has never been aggressive toward me. Plus, I think he's been around a lot longer than I have so I guess I should listen to him.

"Okay, Vex, I get the picture." He huffs and trots off in the other direction, glancing at me once over his shoulder to make sure I am moving along quick enough. I send my mind outward to thoughts of my house, my room, and my bed and before long I feel a jolt as we travel away from this depressing place. Before I feel my feet on my floor I think I hear a whisper on the desert wind.

"I know how to save us. I've found a way out, my friend."

I was supposed to head directly to Justin's house when I got back in town, but I tell him I want to see Shane and then try to get Pitter from Sandra. It is still early, earlier than I thought I would be home, so he is still working on some things at SDSU anyhow. At least that's what I keep telling myself. No, it has nothing to do with the lingering feelings on my lips where Ryan fiercely kissed me one last time before he went to join my mom and Greg.

It caught me off guard when Ryan's look of a mind-made-up vanished and he took me into his arms and my breath away all at once. His fingertips dug into me possessively and with a need that I reciprocated. His ring, on my right hand at the time, glowed and released an icy heat that added to the passion of that moment. Even though I am still angry with him for his plan to leave me, that final kiss also gives me hope.

It also gives me plenty of guilt while I drive around town finding other things to do to avoid my inevitable encounter with Justin. Maybe I should just tell him the truth; that I am torn between him and Ryan. Damn that sounds like a stupid idea. He would definitely know I have been lying this whole time about what Ryan is to me. But maybe not, if I play it cool and say something just happened with all the drama and stress surrounding Shane's accident. That might be less of a blow, right? Grr, once again, now that I am away from both of them, I think I would be better off alone. Well, first things first and more important: I need to see Shane and then Sandra. Carmen says that Shane is doing awesome and how amazing it is that he is looking so less banged-up and bruised in such a short space of time. "Like magic," she said.

Speaking of magic, Demons are phenomenal travelers. Time and space must become irrelevant because Valant got me home in a flash. Even though I felt myself driving the roads, it was not the same distance and somehow not as nerve-wracking as you would think, either. He was gracious, but I know he just wanted to get back to my mom. Damn is he whipped. I didn't even want to bring up my dad; Valant would probably drop me off in the middle of Tijuana or somewhere. Does everyone have a love triangle thing happening here? Sandra would call hers more of an octagon, but hey, she's having fun.

Even with the small amount of travel time with my Demon co-pilot, I wondered a great deal about whether Dad even wants us to find him.

I mean, after all this time? But then I give myself a mental smack in the forehead, realizing that with all Mom was saying I hadn't told her about the times he helped me. Having just realized all of it myself, I had forgotten that important piece of information. Not to mention that his appearance was so different from the person she knew all those years ago.

After stopping off at the hospital and seeing Shane, I am in a happy place, loving how good he looks and even talking to him for a bit before he nods off again. I head home, smiling with relief that Shane is safe, Greg is busted, and one of my three worries is checked off the list. It feels like eternity since I spent any time at the loft and tonight is no exception. I am here for one thing and one thing only and that is to get something of my father's for Sandra to do a reading on. Everything I have of his is so darn old, things he hasn't even touched since he was a teenager himself, that I wonder if his essence will even be attached to them anymore. Well, it's all I have and perhaps if I were smarter and more on top of things I would have asked my mom for something. Somehow I doubt she would have anything on her in Mexico, nor did I really want to tell her my plan since she may have wanted for me to wait for her. Nope, diving in right now without a safety net is my bag. Always a good plan, right?

When I make my way back out to Ryan's car I have a bag full of several of my father's records. I also repacked my suitcase from Mexico to include some items for cooler nights up north. Montana will be chilly in the late summer nights. After changing into stretchy jeans and a tank top, I pack the car and start the engine. I stare at my loft, feeling I don't belong there either and wondering who I am becoming. Everything has been changing so fast over the last year, but I've come so far and worked so hard on a normal life; not to mention I love my house. My brain runs through the rooms, and when my mind gets to the small patio off my bedroom I suddenly stop putting the car in reverse. Justin's evening primroses are in there and a small gnawing at my awareness tells me I need Sandra to seek for something more than just my dad. I jump out of the car, run upstairs, clip off one of the flowers, and grab one of his shirts before running back to the car. My power hasn't always been on, so best to have a kick-ass teammate in my corner to check on all things right now. Justin has had me in a tizzy lately; my feelings for him were never this intense before our reunion in the desert.

When I get to Sandra's she has some fish taco fixings and I devour them, not having realized how hungry I was; I guess super-fast travel uses up a lot of calories. While we eat I fill Sandra in on what happened in Mexico. If she is shocked by any of it she doesn't let on. While I lay the items I brought with me out on the coffee table in front of her cozy gray couch, she looks cockeyed at the flower and Justin's shirt.

"I have a inkling those aren't all items that belonged to your father."

"You would be correct, Shelock. Something has been off with Justin lately; like an untapped draw whenever I'm around him. And then there are the memories and revisited dreams of Avalon, a place I used to visit in my dreams—and the boy, the boy that I seem to be turning into Justin." Sandra moves her head around a bit, as if she hears something that I don't. Her eyes squint a little and then she looks back at me.

"I've heard that name Avalon before, but mainly in stories as a child. What are your dreams about?"

"They were mainly during my youth, actually starting when I went to live with my grandmother. Avalon's a magical place, one I thought my mind had made up to deal with my mom not being able to care for me, or to escape to when I was under Steven's control. Then when I had them in college, they seemed so real; the boy seemed real. Lestan was his name and he claimed to be the son of the king of Avalon. We'd spend our time in his greenhouse, talking, playing with the animals there, and I think he helped me save myself after Steven was bound away." She looks concerned and grabs my hand.

"You never talk much about the binding and how things were after, except that they were better. I wondered, but I didn't want to ask. I'm sure it was hard for you. No one knew what he'd done to you or what you'd done to him." She is right; I didn't talk about it much.

Just thinking about it always felt too much like dragging it out of the closet and beating the shit out of myself. Talking didn't ever really seem like a good idea, but now that he is dead I feel freer.

"The whole time with Steven was dark for me, but after I finally stood up to him and sent him away, I couldn't stand myself for what I had let him do to me. You know that trusting people, especially men, is hard for me but I lost myself for a while, blamed myself, hid from others and from enjoying life. It was the dream with Lestan that allowed me to heal and forgive myself. He helped show me that I was still within myself, that it wasn't my fault, and that I deserve to be loved."

"He sounds pretty amazing, Lex, but you only saw him in your dreams? Maybe he was your subconscious or spirit guide. The goddess sends us help in mysterious ways and you do love your fantasy and sci-fi. Maybe it was your own mind that came to the rescue?" That is what I told myself for years, but now I am not sure.

"This is where it gets weird; I started having the dreams again, but repeats really. I'm young and so is he, and now I notice his dark hair, his tree-like tattoo, all things that remind me of Justin. And then there are the amped-up feelings I have when I'm around Justin, like I can't get enough of him, and everything else disappears." She smiles at me and flutters her eyelashes.

"Ah, little Alex is in love." Cue her smooching noises and my slap on her leg.

"Perhaps you're right, but when I'm away from him it lessens and I'm locking lips with Ryan." I bite my lip at the admission. I can't help the feelings of guilt even around my trusted friend.

"We're capable of loving more than one person, Alex, but hey, if you really think something may be afoot then we should check it out." Why do I feel like I am forgetting something?

"Oh ya, Thatcher."

"Who-cher?"

"The shape-shifter that lived in Avalon. He said Avalon was real; we even fixed Lestan's greenhouse together after his father became enraged and destroyed it. Something about me set his dad off and I never found out what that was. Shit..."

"What?"

"After Thatcher and I fixed the greenhouse I found a note and a flower on my pillow from Lestan. He thanked me. Now how did *that* happen? Did my subconscious write a letter and sleepwalk my ass to the orchid store? It was just so long ago and I was never able to see him at a later age or time after that. It's so weird, nothing I see now in Avalon is current; they're all replays of dreams, memories—maybe my mind has finally lost it."

"It could have been a test of sorts. Maybe training? Did you do anything in your dream with your powers? Obviously in one you healed yourself, right? Maybe you were being taught by the Tree Goddess or some other Earthen being when no one else could." Huh, I haven't thought of it that way, but I guess she could be right.

"Have you ever heard of dimensional travelers? Thatcher called me one and I swear I went to at least one other place, but that was a long time ago and all I was trying to do was find my mother; it didn't go so well." Sandra looks to be in deep thought; actually I think I've lost her.

"Um, Sandra? Earth to Sandra." She shakes herself free of wherever I had sent her and smiles.

"Some say Seers are like dimensional travelers, that our visions travel through time. But I've only heard of one person who wasn't a Demon be recognized as one, and he's in Quantico now." Ah, her brother. I take a breath to ask more but then she moves my father's records closer to her.

"Your father first, I'm guessing? And then your lover." Her pronunciation of the word sounds more like lahver and we both have a good laugh.

Sandra places her hands on the album I brought and looks down, her eyes closed as her body nearly hums with anticipation. She speaks quietly at first, almost like a whisper to herself and then her face lifts and her eyes lock on mine as she speaks.

"Your father has been trapped but now he appears to be flitting frequently in and out of our reality. He's not alone; there's someone he's with quite a bit...wait...I see something...yes, he's visiting with someone at the Council. This is an older visit though, I'm not sure when but I only know he isn't there right now."

Our surroundings grow hazy and I slip into Sandra's vision. We stand next to each other in an office. Sandra glances over at me, startled.

"Dimensional traveler" I mouth at her with a simultaneous shrug. She shakes her head and gives me a 'oh right' wordless response and we both look toward the sounds of two people speaking.

My dad stands across the room from us, talking to someone seated behind a large, shiny, dark wood desk with their back to us. The person at the desk appears to be milling around in some files within a credenza. My dad's hair is unmistakable, a stark platinum blond, just as he was in the desert and in my dream. Despite his stance that favors his missing leg, he looks strong and stoic as he addresses the faceless body at the desk.

"This will repay my debt, correct? I'll be forgiven for what I did to Bryan and be freed from the hell I've been trapped in?" He bows his head and shakes it slightly in response to the incoherent tones from the person at the desk.

"Yes, I know I'm fortunate, unlike Bryan who lost his life and will not make it out. I owe him a debt for finding a way to communicate with you, and I will repay it to his family once I repent for what happened with the Council."

My dad thinks he did this. There is no way that is what happened, is there?

The person behind the desk answers my father but the voice remains muffled and indistinct even as the seat spins around so he or she is facing us. Of course the face is blurred and I turn to Sandra with a 'what the fuck?' look on my face.

"Can't we adjust the focus on this vision of yours?" Sandra's eyes look strained as she answers me.

"I'm trying, Alex. Something or someone is keeping me from seeing their face. It's like a shield. Whoever this is, they don't want to be eavesdropped on in the slightest." I am sure the Council has a number of defenses against all sorts of magics and powers like Sandra's.

I look closely around the room, trying to get as many details as possible. I am sure there are multiple offices in this place, but maybe something about this one could help my mom identify him.

Desk, chairs, computer, two doors, no window, a fan; damn it, nothing besides what might be in any of the millions and billions of offices in the world. The person gets up and moves to a taller table, and looks to be busying himself (herself?) with a drink, no, a cigar. Scents of clove, mocha, and pepper hit my nose and I nearly sneeze, opting to block it instead and nearly blowing my brains out.

"They can't hear or see us, you know. I think you can sneeze." Sandra hands me a handkerchief and I look at it absently, wondering who carries these things still.

"If we're inside the Council that means my mom is there with someone who knows damn well where my father is and what's happening to him. She told me about sources feeding her intel, but I doubt she knows about this or she would have told me, right? Why is she being left out of the loop? Or is she?" Maybe we are the ones being left in the dark and Mom knows very well what is going on, maybe even helping Dad get released. But why wouldn't she just tell us, and what happened to Bryan?

My dad continues to speak as my worry intensifies. "Yes, I understand. No, I haven't told anyone; I haven't seen either of them in years." More muffled talk responding to my father and in turn he speaks again.

"But, when I've helped the Council track the killer or killers down I can return to them and my debt will be paid?" Well, I guess Mom doesn't know.

The Council member nods and appears to ask my father something.

"Thank you...yes, I have it. Does Bryan's family know?" My dad's head drops again and I can feel his guilt rolling off him in waves. I still cannot believe this is on him. He must have been tricked somehow by Bryan, led to believe he caused it, but it seems as though Bryan helped him, got him out, which is allowing him this chance to return. What if what happened on the rock was all a big mistake and I've been erroneously blaming Bryan this whole time. He was just a kid like my parents. Perhaps all my jacked-up post-Steven shit had me on everyone's-a-dick alert and I jumped the gun. Dana and Mom thought he was up to no good too, but that doesn't mean he meant for all this to happen. Sometimes an asshole is just an asshole.

Dad continues, but I can feel myself pulling away from the vision and I grab on to Sandra as he speaks.

"Will I ever be able to live like myself, look like myself again? Perhaps one of the Council Healers can help me? Being in that place twisted me into someone unrecognizable." Some angry words were thrown his way.

"No, I know how lucky I am. Thank you for helping me negotiate a way out. I'll never forget it." The pull on me is stronger now and the vision is fading away.

"We have to know who he's talking to, Sandra. My mom will need to know. Maybe she can help him." There is still a slight possibility that she does know, but she never mentioned who else might know about my dad. It's not like she's been Miss Communication over the last eighteen years, so why would she start now? Somehow I doubt anyone but my father and the mystery person behind the desk knew what was happening in this room.

"I can't hold on; it's like your dad's presence in this vision disappears and we can't linger when he's gone." That makes sense in our world. Plus, we know he is moving in and out of this dimension and I doubt we want to follow him wherever he is going from here.

Sandra's couch is obvious underneath my legs and the instant I feel myself fully aware in her home I fly out of my seat and begin to pace about.

"Shit, shit, shit—he's working with the Council? Or was, since that was an old vision. Why are both of my parents working for an agency that gives me the creeps?" I shudder, thinking of them sending Ryan to search for a powerful hybrid they had heard tales of—me, that is. Maybe it is the knowledge that they are out to invade my privacy and possibly study me like the research animals I found myself healing and freeing in college that is getting me so riled up. I like my independence and the ability to think for myself.

"Well, whatever he is doing or was doing for them it's enough to help him escape for good." Sandra is trying to keep things positive, and maybe she is right. I smile at her and try to lose my (possibly) misplaced dread.

"True. Damn. Does that mean they negotiate with Demons? I mean, that's who has him trapped, right? It has to be a Demon. I would think that would be a major no-no with the high and mighty Council."

"Well, it sounds like the Council is getting a lot out of the deal as well. Your dad has been helping them track down some baddies, just like you do. Either he isn't done yet or there's a hiccup with him finding you. You haven't exactly been stable lately." What if he is looking for us? Grrr, with everything that's been going on I may be making it hard for him to come to us. Sandra continues as I chew on my lip. "It's good that he's making up for what happened that day; that is, the part he played or thinks he played in what happened to him and Bryan." I shake my head in disbelief at the notion that my dad was the reason he and Bryan were trapped away. As Bryan shifts back to being the puppet master in my eyes, my blood boils again.

"My father didn't do shit to Bryan. If that creep didn't make it long enough to get out of the dimension they were shot off to then it's his own damn fault. Bryan is the one who put them there and no, my father is paying for *Bryan's* mistake. He's been trapped and separated from us for my entire life, will never get his true form back, and will never be able to live as Alexander Conner ever again." Sandra doesn't interrupt or look at me with pity. She nods along and shows her support.

"So now, both of my parents have been living with guilt about an event that I'm sure Bryan was behind. I have no idea how Bryan made my father think he did it, or if this belief is something the Council instilled."

"Why did Bryan do it though, Alex? If it wasn't to prove to the Council that taking powers can be the Earthen Protectors' weapon as well, then why? What did he hope to get out of it? 'Cause all he got was dead."

"Ya, I don't think it worked the way he wanted it to. He was reaching for my mom during the pinnacle of it, reaching like he was trying to take her...take me. But my dad...my dad intervened and was taken instead. At least that's what it looked like to Dana and me."

"Do you think your mom was the target, or you? Why would Bryan want to hurt your mom? Weren't they friends? And I thought she hadn't told anyone she was pregnant, not even your dad?" She is right. So maybe this is all about my mom. I need to ask her, but right now she is inside the lion's den.

I run to my bag and grab my phone. I call her but get no answer, and then I try Ryan, with the same result. I twirl his ring around and around on my right ring finger, wondering if it is my worrying and motion that is causing it to warm or if I am sending him signals all the way to Arizona.

I look at Sandra, giving her my best 'do I call the Demon' look and she tilts her head in a shrug that says, "guess so."

"Here goes nothing. Valant, if you want to show off to my mom, now's the time." I hear a small pop, followed by a hiss and a scurrying of cat's claws on Sandra's tiled floor as Pitter bolts out of the room at Valant's arrival.

"Do you have any idea how hard it was for me to get into the Council to begin with? First your mother wasn't having it and then your darker version of Chuck Norris, and after all of that convincing my power kept sputtering until she helped me. That's right, an Earthen Protector had to help me get in. I'm so embarrassed, so this better be good, Alex!" Why does he make me laugh at the inopportune time? I pull it together and straighten my posture, turning on serious Alex. Valant doesn't know anything about my dad but he is my only link to Mom and Ryan.

"Look, Valant, you need to warn my mom and Ryan. I can't explain it all right now but please relay this message: My dad is working with someone within the Council. He thinks what happened to him and Bryan is his fault so he's making up for it in some way. Mom needs to be careful searching for him, especially if her sources are in the Council. They must be keeping this from her for a reason. We need to figure out why Bryan tried to attack her that day. I think that's the key."

"So, your father really is coming back? I thought that was just part of childish wishful thinking in your dreams that night I came to you. Well, I'm not entirely happy about your mother's boyfriend coming back, but I don't want anything bad happening to her so I'll pass it on. Now let me get back. They're sentencing Greg as we speak and I had to pop out of a bathroom stall, which is uncomfortable enough with those urinal things. How the hell do..."

"Okay, Valant, I don't need your Demon anatomy lesson, please."

Valant snickers at me and gives Sandra a wink. "Got it, Captain. Oh, and Greggy-boy is squirming. The Council doesn't go for attacking humans, and aren't too happy about his work freeing Steven. Course, they don't need to be so harsh with the anti-Demon sentiments, if you ask me." Ya, if you ask me that's a bunch of smoke and mirrors, at least for one person there. If this mystery person has negotiated to get my dad back, there has to be a Demon involved somewhere.

"Don't worry," Valant goes on, "Greg hasn't been able to give up any information on you. They think your mom and Ryan had a Healer wipe the memory of some poor human target of Greg's ire. You're still our powerful little secret. At least I hope so; Ryan's been grilled left and right since we arrived." Concern flits across my face.

"I'm just messing with you. He's as cool as a milk-chocolate cucumber, but you didn't tell me he was your peeping tom. Seems too big to be so spy-like. I mean, even I tossed his ass before even one of his toes hit Greg's boat." I put my hands on my hips and yank a little power into my conscious being from its stored, quiet spots. My synapses are on overload, trying not to worry about Ryan breaking and our secret being revealed, especially right now, right when they are both within the walls of the Council. I doubt they would be happy with my mom not sharing that her daughter is who they have been seeking all this time. I won't doubt him though. I've made that mistake before. I'll face the Council some day, but right now my plate is kind of full.

"Aren't you in a hurry, Valant? Head back, report to Mom, and see if either of them can call me soon. Mom and I need to work this out for Dad. He's been either tricked by Bryan or the Council has got it all wrong on their own."

Valant blows me a kiss, turns into a funnel of maroon glory, and is gone. I sit down and start to laugh hysterically. Sandra moves next to me and puts her arm around me.

"I know this is overwhelming right now, but hopefully this new information will help your mom locate your father safely. She's savvy; being at the Council with this knowledge may be perfect timing. It'll allow her access to find him more easily. Then maybe you can just focus on helping the Healers."

"Yes, I'm sure Dana will be texting me soon to find out where I am. I need to let her know we're going with Vex's hunch and heading to Montana. He'd want us to do that first anyhow." She hugs me fiercely and looks at the objects on the coffee table.

"Since we still have some time, do you want me to poke around with Justin's stuff?" I put my head in my hands and groan at the reminder of yet one more worry. I can't do anything about Dad right now; Mom and Ryan will be on it once Valant reports to them, and I'm waiting here for Dana, so I might as well.

"Why not? Let's see what comes up. I'm sure I've been putting him in my dreams lately. I mean, I would've recognized Lestan if he looked like Justin a long time ago, wouldn't I? But as I said, something is different." She smiles brightly at me.

"Couldn't be love, could it?" What a shit.

"This is serious! Well, maybe not as serious as Healer deaths and a father returning from his exile to hell ...oh, why do I even bother. This boy drama really needs to end."

"Now you're talking. Getting serious with anyone doesn't seem to jive well with your life. Maybe a hiatus is the best course of action." I agree with her, that is, when I'm not around either of them. Regardless, the dreams and obvious changes with Justin are causing my spidey sense to tingle so I eye his shirt and flower and Sandra follows my gaze, reaching for both the items.

Just as her fingertips brush a petal of the evening primrose, a knock sounds at the door. The intensity of the moment has me on high alert and I jump off the couch in an attack posture.

"Easy there, Xena, I ordered sushi for us." Nevertheless, we both tiptoe slowly toward the door.

"Okay, ladies, not growing any younger out here." Dana's voice echoes through the wooden door and Sandra and I look at each other, knowing in our wordless shrugs that our lives are full of things that normal would find surprising. Sandra opens the door and is greeted by the vision that is Dana.

She is dressed in a long grey hiking skirt, boots, and a Bob Marley t-shirt and has her long white hair braided along her shoulder. She has a huge smile on her face and that 'let's kick some ass' look in her eyes.

"Well hello, ladies. You're up to no good, I'm sure. I mean, you can smell the stench of magic in this place. Ooo, is that vodka?" Dana makes a beeline to the bar area and concocts herself a drink, which for her is a long pour of vodka and just plain ole rocks.

"Dana, this is Sandra, my best friend I've told you so much about. We're trying to help locate Dad and I think we've found something interesting." She takes a long draw off the drink and motions for me to go on. I explain the vision Sandra and I had, along with all of my realization about my father's visits when I was young, and look at Dana eagerly.

"Well, what do you think? I called Valant and asked him to warn Mom and Ryan." That is, if Mom doesn't know all this already.

"Yes, yes, very good, Alex. Good thinking on both your parts. If your dad has made a deal with the Council, it may just be part of a treaty with a Demon or alternate dimension holder. He may even be tracking down that person or persons over there and not here at all. That would explain his flitting about. It's not unheard of, at least to those with their eyes open, not up their collective asses like most cases in the Council, but it does appear as though your dad has found someone less inclined to leave his or hers up there." Sandra laughs out loud and makes her way to the bar.

"However, as you said, your dad didn't appear responsible for what happened. So, if Bryan is indeed dead, 'cause no one seems to truly be *dead* dead these days, it may be up to us to clear his name. This will be tricky, however, as my Dreamwalk courtesy of Vex is not exactly 'Council approved' so we won't be able to argue what we 'saw.'" Well shit, I should have known. Dana is an off-the-radar type of gal.

"Well, one, if he's free and his job completed, we'll perform an approved investigation and clear his name. Then we can heal him and we'll be a family." Sandra cringes and I notice her pouring a bit more vodka into our drinks.

"What is it, Sandra?"

"I'm not sure anyone can heal him or that he will for sure be released. I can't shake the feeling of darkness in that office. Being a vision though, I'm not sure if it was coming from the person in the office or perhaps it was coming off your dad, from wherever he's been. Whatever the case, the more I think about it the more I feel like something is off—I just don't know what it is." Sandra was a little overly positive at first, trying to look at all sides. But just as I feared, I think she is right. We still need to find him and he may need our help.

Dana gives an "eh-hem" after downing her drink and slamming it down. I couldn't help envisioning Thor yelling for another.

"Vex and I had a little chat before I headed over and we need to get to Montana as soon as possible. Your dad seems to be safe, but Healers are dying. We need our little company to find out what's going on and stop the killings. Timing is everything and the element of surprise may be our only chance. We need to get to the spot of your first vision of the killings. There may be answers there." Lives versus my father's life; the latter is an uncertain danger, the former immediate. Sandra hands me a drink. After a quick "cheers" she squeezes my shoulder and adds to Dana's words.

"Your dad has made it this long, and apparently under terrible circumstances, so I think you and Dana need to head to the lake in Montana and perhaps I can help from here. Or your mom goes it alone to help him." I don't like that idea. If something is amiss and Mom is alone, she may be in a lot of trouble with whoever is pulling the strings. Of course, being as secret as she says she is within the Council, this person may not even know who she really is to my father. Oh, but I can't risk losing both of them. Not when I just got her back and he is so close.

"I'd like us to stick together once Greg is taken care of—safety in numbers as they say. But you're right, we may not have much time. Word of the attacks on the Healers will start to spread soon and we need to get out in front. We should leave tonight. Valant said Greg is being sentenced now so they should be able to meet us soon, as long as the Council doesn't keep hounding the shit out of Ryan, and Mom has some time to snoop around a bit." Ice clinks and Dana takes a long pour of Belvedere, lifting her glass in the air afterwards.

"Now we're talking. Let's get our asses moving and use your training the way it should be, not for playing Twister with your man candy." I nearly spit my drink out at her as she laughs and looks at Sandra with a knowing grin.

I leave Dana and Sandra to their drinks and gossip and go to my room to call Justin. A rare sight greets me when Pitter's kitty-cat eyes open up in the dark room, reflecting two small moons. He stretches and rolls over, giving me a part yawn, part meow. I slide across the bed to pet him; his purring makes me want to stay here permanently.

"Gotta leave again, little boy. Sandra isn't so shabby, now is she?" He nibbles on my fingers a bit and rolls back over to sleep. Being as I don't want to fully intrude on his highness's sleep I only turn on a side lamp and take a deep breath before calling Justin. I haven't seen his hot-blooded Irish-Italian temper in a while, and I wonder when all my running off will bring that Justin back again.

"Hey there, I'm just leaving campus. Where are you? You hungry?" It is eight o'clock and yes, I am famished but my stomach is tied too tight in knots to eat.

"I'm at Sandra's, but actually I need to tell you something." The other end is quiet and I think for a second that the call has dropped. It can definitely happen in the canyons around SDSU.

"What is it?"

"I actually have to leave again."

"When?"

"Well, now actually." A sigh comes through the phone line. "It's my mom, she needs me and I have to leave tonight."

"So your mom, who you haven't seen since you were twenty-one, suddenly needs you and you have to leave tonight?" This kind of throws me off guard because I didn't think my mom would be the issue at all—leaving yes, but not a shot at my mom.

"I know but I think this is our chance to reconnect. It has to do with my dad, and she needs me." Silence again and I swear I hear his breathing pick up the pace a notch.

191

"Your dad?" The word dad is bitten off in a way that I can practically hear his teeth grind. I decide to ignore it and turn on the Alex charm and sweet-as-cotton-candy voice.

"Yes, Justin; I'm really sorry that I can't see you tonight but I really have to leave. I promise to keep in touch as much as I can. I think service may be spotty where we're going, but I can email, I think."

I can feel the tension on the line and then I hear him say something under his breath but I can't make it out clearly. Something about Dad and killing me. I am sure he thinks this whole thing is crazy. He knows all about my mom abandoning me, so I guess I understand his frustration. On the other hand, he can back off—I am a grown-ass woman and I make my own decisions. However, that version of Alex stays quiet and I smile into the phone and try again to soothe him.

"I'll miss..."

"Is Ryan going with you?" Whoa, where the hell did that come from and did he just cut me off?

"No, I'm going with a friend of my grandmother's actually. Is that okay with you?" Uh-oh, now he's done it. I'm turning from sweet to sour real quick. I take a breath to give him a few more choice words when I hear a deep inhale, a release, and just like that I feel the tension ease.

"Well, I guess this is something you have to do. Let me know that you get there safe. Where is there, by the way?" I hesitate for a moment, once again my radar picking up something in his voice, something sending a warning signal into my brain but also easing and titillating it synchronously. My eyes close and I swear I can smell him and feel his touch on my skin. My body sways and I open my mouth to speak.

A meow wakes me from my trance and my eyes fly open. Pitter has climbed into my lap and is nose to nose with me, making me instantly cross-eyed. He looks at me carefully and, once seemingly satisfied that he has my attention, cuddles into my lap, kneading sharp claws into my leg. I look at him mystified, nearly dropping the phone when Justin's voice hits my eardrums.

"Alex, are you there? Hello?"

"Ya, sorry. Pitter was spazzing out. I'm not a hundred percent sure where we're going. Northern Cali, I believe." Damn, I just straight up lied. Well, who wouldn't? I mean that could have been all typical Pitter, but hell if I am looking a sign in the furry face and discounting it.

"Okay, well be careful and I will see you when you get back." His "will" is a bit too forceful for my taste, but honey covers my tongue and I sign off short and sweet.

After hugging and kissing Pitter, much to his displeasure, I head out to the living room and let Dana know I am ready to go. Outside, I turn to Sandra, give her a big hug, and whisper into her ear.

"Check Justin's things for me, but be careful. I may just be on edge, and he may simply be justifiably annoyed with me, but I'm not taking any chances." She nods into my hug and squeezes me a little tighter.

"Be careful. I'll call you and also send texts and emails if I find anything." I pull away from her and smile.

"I really do have powerful friends, don't I? Watch your back, and Pitter's, too. Love you."

And with that I am gone, away in Ryan's SUV, with the Master of Potions and Weaponry and toting my own battle gear, Serenity and Chaos.

CHAPTER 15

Glacier Lakes

The mountains hold the memories, which trickle to the lakes.
The ice holds the power; beneath it rock will break.

The single-prop plane is not my idea of an excellent way to travel, but driving all the way to Glacier National Park would not get us there as quickly as I fear we need to. A sense of dread and a tightness in my muscles is all I have to go on, but my connection to Gaia helps me know things and tease out things well before others can.

Dana sleeps the whole way, her darn snoring earning me glares from the others. My elbows don't seem to faze her at all as I attempt to jostle and move her into a quieter position. She wakes only during our last minute of taxiing to the gate. She stretches and grins at me with refreshed eyes and a few unpleasant-sounding pops of her back and neck.

"Well, that was a breeze, wasn't it?" She catches the look on my face and the manner in which my fingers still grip the arms rests, and shrugs.

"I told you to take a few nibbles of the muffins I brought, but noooo, all have-to-be-alert-and-in-control Alex preferred to freak out the entire trip instead." I should have taken her advice. Now I feel so strung out and racked with nerves that the hour-and-a-half drive ahead across gravel roads and twisting turns sounds pretty darn awful. Vex told Dana that Polebridge, Montana, is where he wants us to stop and wait for further information while he figures out which one of the glacier lakes nestled between Western glacier and Canada is the one from the first kill site. We will be heading east through Hungry Horse and around the Apgar Mountains. Lake McDonald is there, and even though Vex doesn't feel that is the location we are looking for, the Healers' Leader wants us to do a quick check there as well.

"I'll drive there, little one. At least take a bit of the tea I smuggled in to ease your muscles or you'll be no good to me, no matter how much Earthen energy you can wield."

When we get into the rental car I concede and take a few swigs of a milky substance. My muscles unclench immediately and I sink into the seat while Dana drives us off toward whatever awaits us. It is so bright out. The sun is still up despite the late hour. Being this close to Canada and the Artic Circle, it will be light out till nearly eleven. It is beautiful here; it's somewhere I used to come with my grandmom, so it isn't foreign to me. I was so young then though and would hardly be able to lead the way now, so we have the maps and GPS going.

The car door closing jolts me out of my thoughts and maps fly into the air off my lap. The sun is starting to set and I feel a strange lightness in my head and muscles.

"Feeling better, Sleeping Beauty? All clear at Lake McDonald, as we knew it would be, so let's continue up north, shall we?"

"You went out there alone? And you left me in here alone? What if someone was there?" She merely smiles at me and starts the car.

"Not a single vibration of power being used anywhere near here, Alexis. This is not my first rodeo, you know, plus I need you sharp; the way that tea knocked you down a few notches shows me you needed some alone time." Wow, she has all the nerve in the world.

We continue north, past the entrance to Glacier and the Road to the Sun, and onto the gravely road that is the North Fork. Dust flies all over and my teeth rattle as we hit certain washboard patches in the road. Not many cars are out at this time of night although two truckers pass us and kick up enough dust to slow Dana down momentarily. She is taking our rental Subaru through the ringer though. When we get to Polebridge, the red mercantile sign greets us and we head to the saloon next door. A fun-filled sand volleyball game is taking place between the two buildings and pleasant smells of freshly cooked food waft in the air.

After scarfing down some awesome chili and a piece of strawberry rhubarb pie I turn to Dana and give her an 'okay now what' look.

"I'll be back in a jiffy. Hold down the fort and maybe grab some grub to go. This could be a long night."

After thirty minutes, and five heavy-handed cocktails, Dana returns.

"Bowman Lake it is. Time to head out; do you have your girls ready?" I reach behind my head and touch Serenity and Chaos; they vibrate under my fingertips. They have been itching for action after those teasers with Ryan, Greg, and Valant. Whatever lies ahead for us will be a true test, especially when I am all in to the fight.

"Vex said we have a little hiccup."

"Hiccup? Like what?"

"Galena, the Healers' Leader, left. Apparently she took off as soon as they figured out the lake location and Vex mentioned letting us know ASAP. Tierra and Vex are worried that perhaps it's a trap and maybe she was never the Leader at all." Well, shit.

"Why would she leave and what do they think her plan is?" Dana shakes her head. The whole thing sounds so bizarre. Why go through all of that just to, what? See what Vex and Tierra knew?

"They're worried that the killer is a Healer either working for the Absolute Protectors to wipe out the others on our side or that it's a power-hungry Healer who wants to rule. Either way, it seems odd that the Leader, who's already in power, would be involved. That's why Vex said Galena, or the person posing as Galena, may not be the true Leader or has changed sides." This really isn't good.

"So, she knows we're here? What if we're being set up? I thought the only reason we all felt this would work was due to the element of surprise, and isn't that out the window now?" She smiles slyly at me.

"Apparently Vex and Terra didn't tell Galena who we are, so at least we still have that going for us. I'm hoping we can cloak our power and appear like two normal humans on a camping trip. Hardly anyone knows a thing about you since you've been disassociated from this world, and I'm more wraith than truth." She has a point there. As long as we don't go in guns a-blazing we may still have the upper hand.

"Okay. We keep going then?"

"Yep, onward and upward!" And with that she gives me a slap on my backside and heads out the saloon door.

The drive up to the lake, which is set to a backdrop of towering glacier mountains, is a steep one. The Subaru whines and takes the narrow turns slowly as dust kicks up all around us. I am glad Ryan's SUV wasn't our car of choice as I fear its width would have been terrifying on this road. We are alone at this time of night and the sun begins to make a slow descent as clouds roll in with some promise of rain. They need it here; forest fires are springing up all over, their previous destruction from the eighties still evident.

My body vibrates and my mind reels. Dana has concealed our power with ease, something that always quickly drains me. Here, defensive weapons are just as impressive as offensive ones. What will we find up here? Is this the killer's hiding spot? I know we want to look for clues but something tells me we are in for more than that. As my brain spins I hear my phone chime. There has hardly been any service since about thirty minutes outside of Polebridge, but Sandra has me plugged up to some contraption that I can only guess gives me a boost to a network that still gets me texts and emails.

"It's Mom! She says she finally heard of the Healer killings from her boss, who leads her undercover team. He wants her to get on it and says they may have an identity. She's been told to take out the killer by any means necessary and he's sending her here, so she, Ryan, and Valant are headed our way." This all makes me terribly worried. The Council being involved in anything is sketchy, especially with what happened to Galena and her second-in-command. But if they are up to no good why send my mom? Isn't she good? An assassin apparently, but good all the same, right?

"She says as soon as the picture comes through she'll forward it." Dana stares forward and says nothing.

"Well, at least it's only one person, right? Could be worse!" Yes, optimism, absolutely necessary on a manhunt, that's for sure.

"Something stinks." Dana's reaction has me smelling around my seat and shrugging.

"Not in the car, silly girl. Something about this whole thing smells rotten. We must be on our highest of guards and run point in this takedown. Your mom will be here soon, but hopefully the picture will come first and we can take the murderer down and get out of here before the Council gets its paws on things." She is worse than Moulder with his conspiracies, worse than me!

As we finally near the Bowman campground we pay our camping fee—hey, we have to be legit, right? This is a state park. As we approach the lake, my heart starts to pound and I know in an instant that this is where the first killing Vex and I witnessed took place. I feel my body go cold and feel the rocks underneath me as if I am lying on top of them again. It is darkening outside and raindrops begin to fall around us. No one is about; they're all snuggled in their tents and sleeping back in the protection of the trees and away from the lakeshore.

We exit the car and Dana puts a barrier around the lake area, just as Ryan did in the alley when I kicked his ass. Well, that's how I remember it. I immediately take Serenity and Chaos from my ponytail and they glow in response. I choose my two fighting staffs and move to the shoreline with Dana, the smooth stones underfoot seeping their coldness into the soles of my shoes. My skin trembles and my senses pick up on something cold and powerful. Yep, something is here all right. Something...no...someone.

A cloaked figure, unrecognizable to me in the darkness of its shroud, heads toward us over the lake. Lightening crackles and the wind gains momentum, chilling me instantly. I ready Serenity and Chaos while Dana pulls the biggest fucking gun I have ever seen out of her duffle bag. She is a sight to behold, her hair unraveling in the impending storm and her power rendering her ageless and spectacular.

The eerie voice Valant described to me echoes all around us and shoots a spike of pain through my mind, nearly bringing me to my knees. I am gripping Serenity and Chaos so tight I feel my calluses stretching. I pull Gaia's energy within me as I use my reserves to protect my brain from the onslaught. A chill chatters my teeth and then is gone as my power locks into place, keeping the figure's power away. Gathering my composure, I give Dana a nod that I am okay and take my fighting stance toward the wraith advancing over the water.

A commotion comes from our right as a woman about Dana's age rushes at us from the trees around the side of the lake.

"Wait! It's my son. Don't hurt him; he doesn't know what he's doing. Look at him. Can't you see he isn't well?" Dana points her gun at the woman as I keep my eyes on the killer over the lake.

"Stay where you are, lady; we don't want to have to hurt you. This man has been killing a lot of innocent people and you don't want to be next."

Hearing Dana's words, and knowing that gun, I wonder if Dana intends to stop this woman herself if she doesn't wise up and get the hell out of here. I look over my shoulder and see the lady with her hands in the air, in a placating and pleading gesture, frozen about twenty feet away. Damn, she came up on us fast and under our radar. She is no ordinary human, that's for sure.

"I'm Galena and this is my son, what's left of him at least. He can't be responsible for this; someone has tricked him, set him up. Why would he try to kill me?

His own mother? He could have, but he recognized me and instead saved me by linking me to Vex."

Wow, this is insane. Her son has been taking out his own kind, taking out Healers. Why? I look at Dana and the wheels are obviously turning inside her mind while her finger also itches on the trigger. What if this is a trap, and the Leader and this
monster are working together?

"Let me help him. Somewhere inside him he knows who he really is. Allow me to try and stop him. He isn't himself, I'm sure of it." I look back and forth between Galena and the cloaked figure as it glides toward me. With my right staff raised high, I call out to him.

"Who are you and why are you doing this?" Chills run through my body when tons of ice straining and crushing within my skull triggers my body's response and the voice of death echoes around us.

"I am saving us all." Man, this dude is either off his rocker or he is a puppet in a terrifying game. Something inside me doesn't want to risk never knowing the truth and my decision is made.

"Dana, we can't kill him. No matter how crazy this all sounds, we need to know for sure what's been happening. Let's concentrate on capturing him instead of taking him out." Her mouth sets in a tight line and she yanks back on part of the gun, appearing to change a setting.

When she nods at me in agreement, my phone pings. How it is working at all in this rustic area of Montana I have no idea. It is a text message from my mom, subject "wanted for murder of Healers." When the picture comes through of the man the Council has its eyes on for the Healer murders, my stomach does a flip. Dad? The picture is of my dad. Not the Dad Mom knew, no, this is the man in the desert, the man in my Dreamwalk at the lake. Mom doesn't know this version of Dad. I never told her.

Looking from the picture to the specter over the lake, who is now only about thirty feet away, I can make out a shadow of his face. I cannot believe this is happening. Why is my father killing innocent Healers? Ones even younger than me...children. I can't believe it. There must be some mistake, or someone is posing as him. Sandra's vision hits me like a semi and I recall the task he was sent to do. Can this be it? Is he being tricked, like Galena said, by the Council member in the vision?

"Dana, it's my dad, the twisted version I met when I was younger."

Dana looks over my shoulder at the text and whispers "bloody hell" under her breath. I try repeatedly to send a message to Mom, but my texts keep failing. I make one last-ditch effort then have to put the phone away in the back pocket of my jeans.

I am frozen in this moment, my mind circling, making no sense of who the warped and misled man over the lake is, while he continues to approach us where we stand on the rocky beach. As he gets within twenty feet of us, he drops his hood. The cloak flies open and I see his bald head. There isn't a trace of his platinum blond hair or his missing leg, and his face has become a sadistic version of the man I met when I was a scared and beaten child. There isn't a trace of the young man my mother loved, and now barely a trace of the tall, blond stranger remains either. However, I know in my heart that it is he, and my throat struggles to swallow while my body turns cold once more. I shiver to control my despair. I need to hold it together if I am to save my father while also ending the horror he has been dealing out to those of his kind.

Suddenly his hands arch toward us, and Dana and I both struggle against his will to take our powers. I am brought to one knee, but Dana manages to get him in her sights and shoots the gun at him, coating him in a translucent force field of sorts and boy does he get pissed. The feeling of my power being stolen from me stops and I rise again and begin to take steps toward him. He rages against the invisible fence around him, his horrifying voice roaring like a bear deep in a cave—ferocious and powerful.

"That should hold him for a bit while we sort this drama out." Dana is fidgeting with her gun while she speaks so neither of us sees my father's mother running toward him from our right.

"Alexander, it's Mommy, honey. Please stop and come to me. I can help you!" Alexander pulls into himself, folding his arms into his chest and bowing his head. It looks at first like he is sobbing but then his arms fly out and his head back, and a force hits me so strongly I kneel again to keep from falling over. His mother isn't so lucky as his power tosses her against a large cluster of rocks. Her body slumps to the ground, but I see her breathing so I turn back to my father and begin to light up my staffs, readying myself to attack and subdue him. I hear Dana cursing at her gun behind me and I feel dread creep in, knowing that it may have been a one-time shot.

"Dana, focus on the weapon while I keep him busy," I shout over my shoulder, keeping my eyes on my father the entire time.

My father lowers to the rocking water's edge and strides toward me, his shroud flying behind him. Against the backdrop of enormous mountains and the falling rain he is awe-inspiring, terrifying. Well, I guess it's my turn and I gulp loudly, knowing the power I am about to go up against. I know my goal is only to restrain him, but I still balk at the idea of harming my dad, which is my inevitable first step. Deep inside I know this is just a shell of my dad, but I keep hope burning that I can bring Alexander back to us.

I bend down into a sprinter's starting position, my staffs within my palms like relay batons, and then shoot out toward him. My father quickly tosses his cloak and readies to take me on. His hands form into fists, his fighting stance seasoned, but possibly not prepared for a little Serenity and Chaos action. As he swings at me high with his right, I crouch under his attack with my wrists crossed. Keeping my staffs together, I shoot my arms up toward his face, touching the V formed by my wrists under his chin. I uncross my wrists and staffs forcefully, forcing them downward to smack the inside of both of his arms violently before spinning away. I hear bone break within his right arm and I am satisfied, knowing I have rendered his dominant arm useless. Backing away I ready myself again. He touches his arm and a red glow hovers over it, sparkled with what I know is his gold manifestation of power. The gold barely shimmers in the oozing evil red that has been taking so many lives. I briefly wonder how someone's power changes and why? I just hope I get a chance to help fix him. When the red disappears from his arm, he flexes it and looks back at me. He shrugs, tilts his head mockingly at me, and mouths "Healer" with a sneer on his face.

Damn it! Okay, this is not going to be easy. It's going to require more power than my staffs alone. I pull on the Earthen power and it rushes into me, unbridled in the wild. My staffs glow more intensely but then I feel a whoosh as the wind is knocked out of me. I cough and struggle to breathe and fear builds; I know he is trying to trap me like he did all the others. I call forth my grandmother's energy and use her dandelion magic to poke holes in his hold over me. I instantly know it is working from the confused look on his face.

I use those precious seconds to rush at him again and he charges as well. Right before we collide I drop into a plank on the ground, so he flies over me in a mistimed lunge. I kick up my legs behind me and crack him in the jaw, sending him sailing to the left before flipping over. I do a quick 180 and glimpse him on the ground, but he is up before I can land another blow on him.

My father's eyes lock on to me and I feel him wrap his power around me before I can get close enough to take another crack at him. I am frozen and alone. I scream out to Dana and she tosses the gun and tries to reach me, but when she gets within five feet of me it's like she hits a wall. I take Serenity and Chaos and pound on the invisible force field around me, like the one Dana shot at him. Damn, did he transfer that to us? Whatever my dad is now, he is no longer just a Healer. My powerful staffs bounce off the field like drumsticks off skin; they take the bulk of the shock and light up under my power as I bang away. I try to pull more energy within me, but it's as if the connection has been severed and all I can use is the little reserve I still have deep inside.

Ryan's ring begins to warm on my finger and I hear a loud pop before I see Valant suddenly appear with Ryan and my mom in tow. They rush toward Dana and me, but Dana warns them before they can get too close. I see determination in Ryan's eyes and he moves past her. My father's voice explodes around us and I feel tremors underneath my feet.

"Do not come any closer, Earthen Protector. I have no business with you." Ryan, who has a thing for not following authority of any kind, especially the crazy kind, steps across the barrier and puts his hand in mine.

"If you attack Lex, then you have to go through me as well, you son of a bitch!" My eyes well up as my heart tears. Ryan is once again here for me, but this time the evil we are facing is my own flesh and blood. Ryan's ring must have allowed him to come into my father's trap, but now what? What are we going to do? My dad is a seriously powerful being on a mission and I am not sure how to stop him. I turn to look at my mom and see Dana talking hurriedly to her.

Dana is filling her in, but I think she already knows. My mom's eyes are on the woman slumped on the ground and then she looks back and forth between the Leader and the monster from hell seething on the shores of Bowman Lake. Yes, she knows. It is her love, her Alexander—my father.

CHAPTER 16

A Glimmer of Gold

Don't drag me into the future, for I can't remember my past.
Leave me here in this moment; allow my memories to come rushing back.

Mom is still as stone for a few breaths, but then her knees sink to the ground and tears flow.

"Alexander, it's Stacy. Look at me; you don't want to do this." His cold eyes glance at her and with a flick of his wrist he tosses her across the parking lot behind me. Before my scream dies, Valant is gone in a flash. I hope she is okay, because if my dad lives through this, the guilt is going to kill him. I turn toward him and take a deep breath. Nobody has had luck talking to him, but who am I to give up on a lost cause?

"Dad? Dad, it's me, Look at me. I'm your daughter, Alexis. Remember? You helped me when I was younger. I know you and you know me. You're being tricked by someone. Let me help you." He looks at me blankly and continues coming forward, closing the distance between us and concentrating only on me. Am I another Healer on his hit list or am I just inconveniently in the way? At this point, I don't think he knows who I am, who any of us are. His voice bounces off the mountains in the distance. Ryan squeezes my hand tighter and I can feel power rush into him. He can still pull it within his being where I cannot. I try once again and feel the tingle of Gaia's energy flow into me. Ryan isn't cut off and now we have an upper hand. We don't react, allowing this to play out as my father growls at us through the rain.

"But these Healers will turn bad. This is my mission to get back, to get back somewhere...now I can't remember and Bryan is gone...I don't know where...or why.

I have to, it's the only way I can get back to...to..." He shakes his head, trying to clear his thoughts. "These people are against the Council! He said once I finish this task I can go...I can go home." But my dad wouldn't be going anywhere. I smell a rat and I am narrowing in on the face in the vision with Sandra. Dad appears confused for the moment, his ire taken down a few notches as he searches his mind for answers. I have obviously broken through, for now at least.

I turn to Dana and hear another pop as Valant comes back into view, cradling my unconscious mother in his arms. It's been many years since I have seen her this way and my anger flares. I whisper to Ryan as Dana runs toward Galena who is coming to amongst the rocks.

"I can't explain everything right now, but that man is my dad and I know he's being tricked. Someone has set him up and we need to trap him and get him quickly back to Dana's. Can you get a read on him at all?" Ryan looks to be focusing on my dad, but shakes his head quickly. I'm not surprised he can't hear a thing; my father's mind is mangled. Galena is talking urgently to Dana so I ask Ryan to use his skills and find out what they are saying.

"The Healer Leader is saying that every time your father takes a life he is being more and more removed from himself. She said, 'the Demon realm took my son's image and replaced it with another and now this one is being torn from him as well.' Your dad, he is either becoming someone or something else...he doesn't even know who we are." Man, we are either out of time or maybe, just maybe, he has recalled something of his past and that Alexander is fighting back. Ryan continues as I form my plan.

"Dana is saying that she's heard of this type of thing happening when a Demon wants to live on earth. It gets a human to perform unthinkable acts, forcing them to trade places with them forever. The demon is coming through and your dad is being trapped in the Demon's dimension, or he may..."

"May what, Ryan? This is no time for your patented information withholding."

"Alex, she says he may be dying."

I begin to overheat at the thought of losing my father, again. I look at my dad who is now arguing with himself, but a voice more like a roar is tearing out of him. The Demon, I am guessing, so we need to act quickly.

"I warned you once, Earthen Protector! Leave now or I will destroy you!" My dad is losing the quarrel with the Demon. He is a mere twenty feet away and is starting to take an interest in coming back toward us. I know what has to be done and I don't have much time. I place both of my hands on Ryan's arms and look into his eyes.

"Ryan, I think you need to leave me here and protect everyone else. This is something I need to do alone. He needs to see me."

"What? Are you crazy? I'm not leaving you alone to face what's left of your dad."

"If you don't leave he'll kill you. I can't let that happen and you need to let me try and save us this time. I may have a chance, but not with you. Please. Trust me." Ryan moves his eyes from mine to my father's. He seethes with worry and anger.

"Okay, Alex, but I'm not going far. If your mom or Galena need healing Dana can take care of it, but I'm staying here for you. Please keep your mind open to me so I can tell what's happening. Promise me, Alex."

"I promise. Now go. There isn't much time." I am not even sure if there is any time left, but I have to try. "See if you and Dana can figure out any other way to knock my dad out if this doesn't work. I can't kill him, Ryan. I just can't." He nods with understanding, places his right hand on my cheek while his left grips my hand and fills his ring with an intense boost of his power. He leans in and whispers into my ear.

"Be careful, Lex. He may not be in there anymore. Know that I can't let you die. I won't." His voice and his promise unleash a shiver of dread and awe. My soldier and my protector will give me this chance, but my father won't be so lucky. Ryan's lips kiss my cheek and he slides away from me.

I turn to face my father. I have had a slow but constant intake of Gaia's energy during the brief lull in action. Now it is time to see if I can bring my father back from the brink and cast off his Demon.

"Dad, Dad, it's me, Alex. Stacy was pregnant with me the day you were taken from her. Do you know none of that was your fault, Dad? We all think Bryan was behind it the whole time, so you see you have nothing to pay for, no penance is owed. Come back to us; come back to Mom and to me. We can be a family." My dad's face contorts and it seems as if bones are shifting as he warps into something inhuman and then back again. I need to try a little extra boost to get to him. Time to drop the trapped act.

I point my hands to the ground and draw in a huge burst of Earthen power, allowing my emerald green vines to become visible and twine around my arms and waist and spill from my body. Grandmom's dandelion seeds float amongst sparkles of emerald-green motes and flowing leaves. I use my power to lift rocks and squeeze them out of existence right in front of my father. Dad is transfixed by the display and I can see a question is playing in his mind.

"But, how? You are a Healer. How can you wield Earthen power in such a way?" He begins to stumble toward me, losing focus on his footing as he's being drawn toward me.

"Because, Dad, I am half-Healer and half–Earthen Protector and I have been given the ability to wield both powers—yours and Mom's."

"Lies," a sinister voice shouts from my father's mouth. "Kill her now, take her power; you will be repaid handsomely for this one. Oh yes, he has been searching for her this whole time. He will be so pleased when he finds out we took her. Right under his nose the whole time, too." Dad ends his insane tirade with a wicked laugh and fear slides along my side. It is now or never.

The rain starts to come down in sheets and I can barely make out the rest of my team in the distance. Dad is less than ten feet away now and I know deep inside that Ryan won't let him get much closer. I plead in my head for more time. Just a little more time.

"Dad. Dad. Look at me, please." Dropping to my knees, I reach my hands to the sky. I dig deep and seek out my hidden golden power, the very spark my father gave me so long ago. I draw it into myself from my very soul and imagine wrapping it in my vines and allowing them to escape my body. Vines extend from my hands and then a gorgeous tendril flows out of my heart and hovers a few feet away from my father's face. It springs open and a burst of gold like a tiny sun comes forth.

My dad's hand reaches for the spark, but then his body jerks away and a guttural "no!" escapes from him. The Demon is afraid; my father's own power has been squashed by this creature and it is the one thing he fears.

I rise from the ground and my vines grow out of the earth and trail behind me as I make my way toward what is left of my father. I will more of his gifted power into my being; golden tiny suns burst forth from my chest and ride my vines as I send them at him, surrounding him; the Demon cannot escape. The vines dance around and attach to my father, soaking into his skin and I see a red steam rise from his skin and I hear sounds of sizzling and wicked snarling.

My fingers wrap tightly around Serenity and Chaos as I pull them out of my back pockets to ready myself for one last-ditch effort by the Demon. Carvings of vines, waves, and Vex shine with bright gold power on my staffs, and just as I prepare to attack, he breaks free of my vines and makes a rush at me. His face is crazed and screams of desperation and terror follow in his wake. He lunges at me and I slide underneath his grasping arms and between his legs before immediately jumping to my feet behind him. Chaos hits first at his kidneys and then I bring Serenity down on his head, knowing not to hit hard enough to kill, but definitely strong enough to knock him out. The hits send two massive bursts of my father's golden suns into the body that was once his and immediately I am thrown back by an explosive red wave of power. Rage rushes through me followed by an echo of the Demon's death and finality.

I lift myself up slowly and limp over to my father's slumped body. My power is drained and when I try to pull Gaia into me I fail. I put all I had into this long shot and it worked to rid him of the Demon, but I don't have anything left to heal my father, let alone myself. When I reach his body, I roll him over gently and thankfully he is breathing, but unconscious. His warped face, no longer contorted and grotesque, still forces the tears from my eyes when I get a close look at all the damage that has been done already. I cradle him in my arms and send out a painful call into the distance.

"Help! Please help us!" Figures bound toward us through the rain and I feel Ryan's strong arms lifting me from the ground, but I refuse to release my grip on my father. I have him back now, and there is no way I am letting go.

CHAPTER 17

Truth

And in the end I winked an eye
I disappeared and rode my lie.
Find me fast—or find me not
Either way you'll find me gone.

Once Galena heals my dad and I well enough to travel, we head back to the airport in Kalispell to discuss the chain of events and untangle what happened. Dad is in and out of consciousness. Valant will take him, by unique Valant Express, along with Galena, Dana, and my mom to Why once we reach the airport. Dana is driving Galena and Dad in one car, while Ryan, Mom, Valant, and I are in Ryan's, trying to make sense of everything. Once I retell what I experienced in Sandra's vision, trying to find something that will lead us to the person responsible for what happened to my father, I remember the cigar and the specific scents of cloves, mocha, and pepper. Mom freezes.

"What? What is it, Mom?"

"The man that sent me out here to take care of the Healers' killer— my boss. You just described his cigar scent to the T and he always boosts about how rare his are." She looks Valant's way and they pop out of existence without a word; oh, and right out of a moving car I might add. In only a matter of minutes they return. Her boss has disappeared without a trace, all signs of him erased except his ashtray containing the remnants of a cigar. Who is this man she has been working for this whole time? Who is he really? He is someone who would work to break a Demon free and let my father lose his life, sending my mother after him in some sick and twisted game. Mom said he was one of just a few people in the Council who know who she really is, so this is definitely personal.

Right now the focus has to be on Dad and trying to heal him close enough to the man he would have been if this had never happened. Both Galena and Dana have said that the repair to his physical appearance will be much easier than what has been done to him mentally. I pleaded to go with them, but they told me they would send for me soon and to go home. I have done more than enough for now, they said, so let them work.

Now that Ryan and I are back in San Diego, my mind drifts over everything while my head rests against the window of Ryan's SUV. I try to plan my next steps, where to start looking for my mom's boss, and the graphic ways I am going to deal with him, but I can't hold onto those thoughts for long. My body is wired from the ordeal but my mind is wiped.

As we near my house, The Weekend's "The Hills" comes in deep and throbbing over the Bose stereo system, the sexy tones causing my body to vibrate. Once we pull into Sandra's driveway I can't take much more and Ryan and I collapse into each other. I straddle him in the driver's seat and dive my mouth onto his. Ryan's hands grip me tightly and he moans into my mouth.

"Fuck, Lex, you scared the shit out me. Don't fucking do that to me again." My mouth ravages his again and one of his hands shoots up my shirt, grabbing my breast while the other one grips my hips, making my grinding against his erection even more intense. In a blink my shirt is over my head and his lips find my breasts.

My hands are in his hair and my breath and heartbeat are out of control. I want this man so badly and all that has happened in the last forty-eight hours only feeds this need. For a moment I let my mind go and release into my desires, working my hand down to his zipper. The thumping in my chest continues and suddenly I am scared of the feeling. My head is swimming and I feel lightheaded.

"Lex? Alex? Are you okay?" All motion stops and my head slumps against his chest.

"Too much excitement for the day I guess." I barely get the words out in between gasps. Ryan reaches to open the door and we escape into the cool, early morning air, me wrapped around him in the fading darkness. My head hangs over his shoulder and my heartbeat starts to return to normal. The gasps continue for a heartbeat but the ocean air fills my lungs and Gaia's power heals me.

"I'm sorry, Ryan, I don't know what happened." I lift my head from his shoulder and look into his gorgeous dark eyes.

"You have nothing to apologize for, Lex. It's been a whirlwind for you these last few days. Let's get you to bed."

Ryan carries me to the door and Sandra opens it before he can even get my key from my purse. She helps get me settled in my room and heads back to bed after giving me a huge hug. Ryan sits next to me and moves a few stray curls behind my ear.

"Ryan, you're the one for me, I know it. Can you stay here tonight? Please?"

"I'm going to make sure everything is safe around Sandra's house; I'll be right back. I won't be gone long, so get some rest." He kisses me deeply and my eyes close before he even leaves the room.

I hear a rustling and wake, thinking he has returned, when Sandra's guest room window blows open and Justin appears, hair flying, his tree limb tattoo traveling wildly along his arms. His eyes are dark black, haunted, and not the eyes of the man I have known for over a year.

"You are mine, Eila! My only. Why? Why did you do this? Did you not think I would find out about you and Ryan? Now I have to take you. There is no other way. My father will kill you before allowing me to lose you."

Justin rips me out of bed before I can finish my next breath and tears Ryan's ring from my finger. I swear I can hear each splash of my blood as it drips down my hand to land upon the floor. Justin continues to grip my bloody hand tight while raising his other hand to his mouth and piercing his ring finger with his teeth. He draws blood before grasping our bleeding hands together.

"Now you will always be with me. I love you, Eila. I'm sorry but we have to leave now."

"Lestan?" I manage to whisper. His power is smothering and I can't move, let alone use an ounce of my power. I am sapped and alone. I make a move to scream for Sandra and Ryan but he covers my mouth with his hand.

"Please don't, Eila. I don't want to have to hurt them, but if they try to stop me, I will." With one hand over my mouth, and the other dripping in blood along with mine and pressed hard against my back, we start to make our way toward the window.

A pressure fills my ears as if we are going into a Dreamwalk and I try to kick and hit him away, but then I hear a pop and my mind registers and under Justin's hand, I smile.

Valant.

In a movement quicker than my eyes can follow, Valant grips Justin by the throat and slams him up against a wall.

Justin gasps for breath and his wild black eyes clear; he looks at me, truly confused and scared.

"Alex? What's happening?" Before he can say more, and just as I start to scream for Valant to stop, the Demon snaps his neck and Justin's lifeless body falls to the ground.

I scramble along the floor to him, but his body turns to leaves, fairy light, and flower petals that begin to rise along a magical breeze and I rise with them, watching as they blow out of Sandra's window.

A howl of anger fills my mind, followed by overwhelming feelings of pain and despair. I grab the sides of my head and drop to the floor knowing the King's torment and anguish are consuming me.

"My son!" is all I hear before my sight dims and I fall into darkness.

Thank you for reading my second book
Truth: The Alex Conner Chronicles Book Two

Enjoy a sneak peek at
Only: The Alex Conner Chronicles Book Three
And don't forget to check out my website and follow me on
Facebook, Instagram, Talnts & Twitter.

www.ParkerSinclair.net
www.facebook.com/ParkerSinclairbooks?ref=bookmarks
Instagram: @ParkerSinclairAuthor
Talnts: @ParkerSinclair
Twitter: Parker_Sinclair

CHAPTER 1

Loss

The writhing twists of mortal things do sicken me.
Small grey abominations, I shall teach you of salvation.
And through my eyes and by my will be free.
For fools and mules will kick and spit
And then from their knees cry holy writ,
And grasp at ghosts that cannot be.
But who are you to me?
I'll tell you girl and listen well,
For the king has come a reckoning.
And by my word you mustn't tell
Or death will come a beckoning.
~S.A. Chamovitz, 2015

"You are the power; you belong to me," whispers through the winds in my mind, winds I've felt and loved before—winds from Avalon. Sweat drenches me as I toss and turn, feeling tangled sheets one moment and freshly dewed mossy ground the next.

"Do something!" Ryan's voice calls out in a rage and I feel his ring heavy, cold, and lifeless around my left ring finger.

"I'm working here, boy, maybe you should get some air." I can barely make out Dana's voice, but I know that she is closer than the distant echoes make her sound. I feel her power flowing over me in waves and something warm touches my lips as she encourages me to drink.

My body is wracked with seizures as the first drop travels down my throat. I can hear Valant from a far corner of the room, grumbling and growling impatiently.

Where am I?

"You must let me try. This is in her mind, so let me near her, you fools!" I sense Valant's agitated pacing as he rants, trying to get near me. Ryan is livid. I hear it in his voice and feel his stress even though I must be somewhere else, somewhere far from them.

"You've done enough, *Demon*, maybe if you hadn't killed him he could help us, or at least be forced to."

What? Killed? Who died? Who is Ryan talking about? And then I am hit with unrelenting pain and a swift reminder... Justin, my Lestan, and I weep, falling away into darkness again.

When I wake, my head is pounding and my clothes stick sickly to me in various places. Sandra is asleep in a chair beside my bed. Her folded arms are filled with objects: Justin's shirt, his evening primroses crushed and wilted, along with various other items I am sure are his. How long have I been out and, more importantly, will it happen again?

I sit up and lightly touch her arm. Objects fly off her lap in all directions and she looks around wildly, obviously not thinking the zombie in the bed is finally awake. I smile and give her a little figure wave before croaking out my greeting.

"Hey girlie, you know a Bloody Mary sounds mighty fine about now."

"Oh, Alex, are you okay? We've been so worried."

"How long have I been out?" Please don't say long, please.

"It's been three days. Everyone finally left to regroup; Ryan went to the Council for help, Dana is trying to reach Vex and Terra, and Valant kept getting cock-blocked so he stormed off." Three days? Well,

I guess it could be worse, but seventy-two hours of my life have been wiped and I want answers.

"I've been trying to see what was happening to you, using some of Justin's things, but I can't see a thing—not even a picture, feeling, or sound. I promise I tried before as well. When you left for Montana, I tried right away and nothing came up. I'm so sorry, Alex, I should have known."

I grab her hand. "This isn't your fault. He tricked us all and I also think he was being forced to do something, like he wasn't in control of himself." The vision of Justin falling to the floor constricts my throat and my eyes sting with sadness.

"Sandra, is there any hope that he's alive? I mean, I know what I saw, but things aren't always as they seem in our world." She smiles sadly at me and then her face freezes. Her voice changes to a dark, gravely tone and her beautiful eyes completely white out. She looks incredibly eerie. Her mouth moves quickly and I barely make out her words. Before I can tell her to speak up, she launches toward me, whispering into my ear.

Fairy fingertips tickle my toes.
Lights of the pale moonlight haunt my dreams.
Where has the boy gone, the boy who is more then he seems?
Only the King knows and he is after me.

Oh shit, this is what I fear. I am being tortured for what happened and the king of Avalon, Lestan's father, is coming for me; or rather, I am being brought to him. Sandra withdraws and her eyes clear. She glances around with a lost look in her eyes before seeing me and sighing with relief.

"Oh Alex, I thought you were gone. I was so scared."

"Well, from what's happened over the last three days, along with what I just saw and heard, I'm pretty freaked out as well. We may not have much time so let's see whether we can get some control of the situation. I can get Valant back the quickest so let's start there. Valant, help..." A boom rings out and my bed shakes, glass shatters from the windows, and we are flung into complete darkness. Coldness creeps into my chest and up to my throat where I feel a tightening while screams run inside my head. This is not Valant's doing, that I know for sure. My thoughts turn dark and I know, deep down, that no one can help me, no one can reach me. I'm alone. Payment for the sin is due and now Lestan's father is coming for me.

Inside my mind I tear words from my being and desperately send them to Ryan. I try to reach Valant as well, hoping one of them might be able to hear me, but fearing Ryan is so very far away.

AVALON! He's taking me to Avalon. Please find me!

Stay tuned for
ONLY: THE ALEX CONNER CHRONICLES BOOK THREE
Coming 2016